Aralen Dreams

CHARLES THOMPSON

for the Volunteers

Chapter 1 – The Third World for the First Time

I stepped off the plane with the vague goal of becoming a better man.

And little else. I had no idea where I'd sleep that night. I didn't know anyone. I didn't even speak the language.

Fortunately, as soon as I entered the terminal, a woman approached me. She wore khaki cargo pants and a white button-down. Chestnut hair framed her deep brown eyes and sharp nose.

"I'm Christine Katz, your training director. Welcome to Panama."

Passengers continued to spill out from the plane and the terminal filled with commotion. I looked around to make sure she was talking to me. "Is it that obvious I'm the one you're looking for?"

She shrugged. "Pretty much. I've been doing this for a while now. You guys always seem to have a dazzled look about you." Her eyes sparkled with mischief. "Besides, there's a picture in your file."

"I'm John Dillon, but I guess you know that. It's nice to meet you."

She took my outstretched hand and gave me a firm, brisk handshake. "You too, but let's get moving. You're the last to arrive and the rest of your group is waiting for us. It's almost midnight; I think they're getting impatient."

"Sorry. My connecting flight got delayed."

"Don't worry about it. Someone had to be last, and they'll get used to waiting. You will too. Life tends to move a little slower down here."

Christine, however, was anything but slow. She whizzed through the airport like a hummingbird, flitting here and there, dodging weary travelers and their wheeled belongings. I struggled to keep up with her as she skipped the line at immigration, flashed her identification to the official, whisked me through customs, and led me outside.

Just beyond the airport's doors, a policeman stood in the middle of the street and blew a shrill whistle, over and over again. He tried to keep traffic moving, but his efforts went largely ignored. A taxi lurched to a halt in front of me, and the driver that followed had to slam his brakes to avoid a certain crash. They started yelling at one another in rapid Spanish while the taxi driver tried to wave me into his cab. The policeman, meanwhile, began to blow his whistle even louder. Christine looked back to make sure I was still following her.

"Try to keep up, will you? There will be plenty of time for sight-seeing later."

"How can it be this hot out here?" I asked, wiping my brow with my forearm. "It's the middle of the night for God's sake."

"Like I said, welcome to Panama." She stopped in front of five white Land Cruisers idling at the curb. A gallery of glassy-eyed colleagues stared out at us through the vehicles' windows. Christine jerked open the door of the lead car and motioned for me to climb in.

The Land Cruisers pulled away from the curb, escaped the chaos at the airport, and rolled along a dark road. It was a quiet ride. Eerily quiet. But the others had to share my nervous excitement. I leaned forward and tapped the driver on his shoulder.

"*Me llamo* John," I said. "*Como se llama?*"

"Carlos. *Mucho gusto.*"

"You like my Spanish, Carlos?"

"It's very impressive."

"Good, 'cause that's all I know."

Christine laughed. It got a laugh out of the guy sitting next to me too. He nudged me with his elbow. "It's wicked da'k out here, huh?"

"It *is* wicked dark out here," I agreed. "You from Boston by any chance?"

"How'd you know?" The blue glow from the dashboard lit up his toothy smile.

"Lucky guess. I'm John."

"I'm Kyle. It's good to meet ya. And don't let the accent fool you; I'm a man of the world. After all, I've been to New Orleans. *And* Cancun." He winked. "Stick with me. I'll take care of you."

"It's a deal." We shook hands and he made sincere eye contact. I liked him right away. "You speak any Spanish?"

Kyle sat forward in his seat and squinted into the distance. "Hey Carlos, what's that?" He pointed to a small clearing exposed by powerful floodlights. As we passed alongside it, I could see a crumbling stone tower, sad and alone.

"That's *Panama Viejo*," Carlos answered. "That's where the Spanish built the first Panama City."

"The first Panama City?"

"Yes. The pirate Morgan came here with his men. They stole everything and burned the city."

"You mean *Captain* Mawgan?" Kyle asked. "The guy on the rum bottle? That's awesome!"

"Yes, I suppose. Because of him, the Spanish had to rebuild Panama on the other side of the bay."

"How far away is that?"

"Not far." Carlos drove around a curve in the road and Panama City – the real Panama City – rose from the darkness. A modern skyline, with thousands of brightly lit windows, spanned the horizon.

"Whoa! I wasn't expecting that. It looks like . . . I don't know. . . Miami?"

"It's nice, no?" Carlos smiled proudly.

Glass office buildings and condominium towers loomed over our heads while we weaved through the busy streets. Glittering casinos, awash in flashing colored lights, clamored for tourists' attention and dollars. One casino even had a live show, complete with dancers and a full salsa band, set up over the sidealk. Panama City lived. Captain Morgan should have stayed longer.

Carlos pulled up to the entrance of an under-ground garage where a pair of helmeted guards, armed with heavy machine guns, waited at the gate. "What's up with that?" Kyle asked. "Did you tell them I was coming?"

"Don't worry about them," Christine answered. "They come with the bank that owns this building. We just rent the top floor." Carlos showed his I.D. and the humorless guards waved our small caravan through the gate.

Once Carlos parked and our twelve-person group gathered around the vehicles, Christine ushered us across the garage, through a pair of elevators, and into a conference room.

Floor-to-ceiling windows offered an impressive view of the bay. Moonlight broke through gauzy clouds and cast its glow upon fishing boats bobbing in the water. Off in the distance, lights twinkled on massive container ships waiting their turn to enter the Panama Canal. The hair on my arms stood on end. *Panama. You are in Panama.* The very name crackled with romance and magic.

A squat woman in her fifties stood at the far end of the room. She had short, red hair and a weather-beaten face. She smiled broadly with clenched teeth, as though the expression didn't come naturally.

"Welcome to Peace Corps," she said. "My name is Grace Landau and I'm the Country Director here. I know it's late and you've been traveling all day, but I wanted to take this chance to quickly introduce myself. Also, I want to give you an idea of what you can expect over the coming weeks.

"You are Peace Corps Panama's newest group, Group 44, and we're glad to have you. Nonetheless, before you go through training, you need to understand that you have made a serious decision. You should already know that, but it bears repeating.

"Once we send you out to your communities, if you get injured, or sick, you will likely have to travel for hours to obtain medical care. Also, Panama is generally a safe country, but like anywhere, we have our fair share of crime. Volunteers get robbed or mugged from time to time. And, although rare, Volunteers have been sexually assaulted or even killed. If any of you have reservations about this commitment, you should say something sooner rather than later. We'd rather eat the price of a plane ticket than waste the time and cost of training you."

I followed her pale blue eyes as she surveyed her audience. A few faces expressed doubt or bewilderment, but no one said a word. Grace looked satisfied.

"Good. Tonight you'll stay in a hotel here in the city, but first thing tomorrow, Christine will take you to a site in the interior where you'll spend a week for orientation."

Grace then bid us goodnight and Carlos drove us through a less polished part of the city. Concrete tenements, covered in mold and grime, crowded both sides of the narrow streets where laundry hung from nearly every window, like flags of surrender from the poor. A middle-aged woman leaned out one window, desperate to escape her airless apartment, if only for a moment. She had a baby in one arm and fanned herself with the other. Her weary face watched the Land Cruisers drive by towards something that had to be better, if only because it was different.

What was her story? Did she clean toilets all day in one of the shiny casinos? Did her husband break his back as a construction laborer to maintain their little piece of squalor? I knew nothing of her land, and I loved it.

I watched a street vendor sell a late-night snack from his push cart, an old woman trudge home under the weight of her shopping bags, and a trio of rambunctious teenagers bound down the sidewalk, laughing and shouting. I rolled down the window and took a deep breath of the unfamiliar air. A new, exciting world welcomed me home.

It was nearly one in the morning when we finally checked-in at the Hotel Mocambo. "Does this hotel have a ba'?" Kyle asked.

"There is a bar, but it closed hours ago," Carlos told us.

The lobby sagged with collective disappointment.

"That's ok." Kyle said. "I'll go see if I can't sweet talk the woman at the front desk into selling us a few cases of bee'ah."

We spent the rest of the night crowded into Kyle's room, drinking beers and talking too loud. There were seven women and five guys, and everyone except me was straight out of college. Kyle suddenly climbed on top of a writing desk in the corner.

"I wanna say a few words," he announced. People stopped their various conversations and looked up to hear what he had to say. "I know we're all just gettin' to know each other, and everything is new and strange, but it seems to me we got real good people here." He raised his bottle high and toasted, "To group fawty-fuckin'-faw!"

Chapter 2 – Malaria Condoms

I woke up in a rickety bunk bed in a mildewed dorm in a decrepit training center with no hot water, and I wondered what the hell I was doing there. Back in the States, just two years out of college, I lived in an apartment on Central Park West with a tassel-clad doorman. I worked at a plush Wall Street job with a comfy leather chair. Sleek Town Cars took me to sparkly places with one-word names like *Fuel*, or *Taj*, or *Baron* where men in dark suits unhooked velvet ropes, and waiters handed me black cloth napkins so I wouldn't get white lint on my fancy pants.

My friends thought it was pretty cool. My mom was proud. And I had no interest in any of it. I wanted something different. Something more . . . significant. I wanted adventures in unfamiliar places with eccentric characters.

I also wanted breakfast, so I made my way to the dining room where a large woman in a light grey apron greeted me. *"Buenos días!"* she called out enthusiastically from her position behind a serving table. She used a pair of tongs to pluck a fried yellow hockey puck out of a stainless steel bin, and she waved it back and forth under my nose. *"Tortilla?"* she asked. Before I could answer, she dropped it on a plastic plate, covered it with a slice of processed American cheese, and stuck it in my hand.

"Try not to look so excited," someone said.

I looked up from my plate to find a young woman smiling at me. A half-eaten *tortilla* puck sat on the dish in front of her. I recognized her from my training group, but we hadn't yet met. She'd gone straight to bed when the rest of us drank beers in Kyle's hotel room, and she kept to herself during the first day of training. "It's really not that bad," she added. "But it's not that good either." She scrunched up her nose and laughed.

"Thanks for the warning. Do you mind if I sit down?"

"Not at all."

"I'm John."

"I'm Elena." We shook hands. She had big, attentive green eyes and an unpracticed smile. Maybe breakfast wouldn't be so bad after all.

"Where are you from?" I asked.

"No one's ever heard of it."

"Try me."

"Feather Falls."

"You're right. I've never heard of it."

"Told you. It's in California, northeast of Sacramento."

"Small town, huh? What do you do for fun there?"

"Fun? In Feather Falls? Nothing, really. Just go to church with the rest of the Mormon kids. I'm glad to be one of the few to get out. It is pretty though."

"It sounds nice," I said. But I really thought, *Shit, she's a bible-thumping teetotaler!* A pagan like me didn't stand a chance with a woman like that. As I resigned myself to admiring Elena only from afar, she rose and handed her plate back to the lady with the apron.

"I hope you don't think I'm rude," she said, "but I'm gonna try to get some yoga in before training starts. Do you mind?"

"No, of course not. I'll see you later."

"Ok. Thanks. Enjoy your breakfast. It was nice to meet you, John."

Later that day, we received a medical lecture from the Peace Corps doctor, an intense Belgian named Bernard. He spent a while frightening us with video clips about Volunteers from around the world who had contracted AIDS or been raped, or both, during their Peace Corps service. He spent another hour scaring us about Yellow Fever and Dengue and the horrible venereal diseases that lurked in Panama's heart of darkness. He finished strong with a lecture about malaria.

"This is Aralen," he said, holding up a large, fluorescent pink pill between his thumb and forefinger. "It is your malaria prophylaxis."

Kyle snickered.

"Not prophylactic," Bernard continued, "but if you need any of those, we have plenty. In fact, I encourage you to use them.

"What I said, however, is 'prophylaxis;' though I suppose the pill is sort of like a malaria condom. You must take one every week. We are very serious about this. If you do not take it, and we find out, you will be administratively separated."

"Administrative separation" sounded too ridiculous to be real. I'd learn soon enough that the Peace Corps had an endless array of authoritative, contrived phrases to describe such simple ideas as getting your ass fired and sent home. Meanwhile, "administrative separation" conjured images of being dropped on a deserted island without so much as a photo copier or a fax machine. It sounded great.

"Moreover," Bernard continued, "if you do not take your medicine, and you get malaria, you will be very, very sorry. Malaria is not fun. And if you get it, we will have no choice but to send you home and it will be the end of your Peace Corps service."

"Why are you threatening us about taking Aralen?" asked Elena. "I mean, I know you've been scaring us all day about all kinds of things, but who *wouldn't* take that medicine?"

"You would be surprised. Some people do not like the side effects, so they stop taking it," he explained. "Aralen can give you headaches, diarrhea, unusually intense dreams, and visual disturbances."

"Wait a minute," Kyle interrupted, "when you say 'visual distu'bances' you mean like hallucinations?"

"Hallucinations are one possibility."

"That doesn't sound so bad. Hell, it might even be fun. What do you say group fawty-faw? Should we trip-out on some Aralen tonight?"

"That's a terrible idea," Bernard answered. "If you have an allergic reaction or an overdose, you could experience seizures or even cardiac arrest."

"That sounds awful!" Elena exclaimed.

"It does sound pretty awful," Bernard agreed, "but allergic reactions are very rare. And malaria, I assure you, is worse. Just take the medicine when you're supposed to, and you'll be fine."

11

On the last day at the training center, we met individually with the Spanish teachers. They assessed our skill level and assigned us to one of three groups: beginner, intermediate, or advanced. I took Spanish for four years in high school, but I'd been a terrible student. Based on the few words I managed to retain, the teachers put me in the intermediate group. Kyle and Elena, to my delight, were also placed in the intermediate group. For the next three months, we would live in *Cerro Verde*, a small town in the watershed of the Panama Canal, just a few hours west of the capital city.

That night, after the girls had retired to their dorm and we were in ours packing up and preparing for bed, Kyle made an announcement: "I'm gonna take my Aralen tonight . . . and I'm gonna take two of 'em."

"You're serious?" I asked.

"Shaw," Kyle answered. "I'm hoping I'll have one of them dreams Bana'd was talkin' about."

I'd known Kyle for only a couple of days, so I couldn't tell if he meant it or if he was just trying to get a rise out of the rest of us. "You're full of shit," I told him.

"Yeah?" he asked, looking me in the eye, unblinking, as he tossed two of the large pills into his mouth and took a long pull off his water bottle.

"Were you at the same lecture as me!?" another trainee asked him. "Didn't you hear all the stuff that medicine can do to you?"

Kyle grinned. "I shaw did. It sounds intrestin', don't you think?"

I couldn't help but like the crazy bastard, and soon we'd be thick as thieves. In the meantime, I looked forward to hearing about his Aralen experience.

Unfortunately, by the time I woke up in the morning, he had already left for our training community. I wondered if he'd had any intense dreams in the middle of the night. Or diarrhea.

Chapter 3 – Less than Gospel

On the way to *Cerro Verde*, Carlos stopped at the supermarket so we could buy gifts for our host families. He handed each of us an unmarked envelope that contained fifty-six dollars in small bills. "You'll get a new envelope each week," he explained. "Give thirty-five dollars to your host-family for your room and board. The rest is your spending money."

I had no idea what to get for my new "family." I couldn't even figure out how much to spend. Three dollars a day for spending money seemed like nothing to me, but maybe that was a lot of money where I was headed. I considered buying flowers, but Carlos suggested food was more practical. Ultimately, I settled on a couple of pineapples.

A short time later, he walked me to the front door of my new home where he introduced me to my host mom. She looked to be in her early forties. She was plump and had a kind face. "*Hola, mucho gusto,*" I said, pushing the outer limits of my Spanish. She smiled. The exchange was mutually shy and awkward. She and Carlos talked for a minute, but they were speaking quickly and I didn't understand anything they said.

The living room was painted mint green. The walls were adorned with family photos, various crosses, and other religious artifacts. The scent of cooked chicken filled the house.

"Juan." Carlos turned to face me. "You will be good here." I wasn't sure if he meant that I was in good hands or if he wanted me to behave myself.

"Ok."

"We will see each other this weekend," he added before turning around and walking back to the Land Cruiser. My colleagues peered out the car's windows and waved goodbye. I smiled at my new mom. A few bald chickens puttered anxiously around, clucking and picking at anything that might prove digestible.

My host-mom gave me a brief tour around the house. My room was attached to the rest of the house, but could be accessed only from an exterior door on the front porch. The room had a lumpy, full-sized mattress on the floor in the corner. A plywood dresser occupied the rest of the small space.

I dutifully unpacked my clothes, not wanting to make a first impression that I was uncomfortable or untidy. I sheepishly placed my clothes into the drawers and arranged my toiletries on top. My mom looked satisfied and disappeared into the back of the house.

What would I say to these people? What could I talk about when I hardly spoke or understood the language? I told myself that I was there to learn and interact with them and that they probably felt just as nervous as I did, so I mustered my courage and walked into the living room. A teenager who hadn't been there when I first arrived sat on a sofa, husking a mountain of beans while watching a soccer game on the television. The grubby sofa had holes in the cushions; the old, boxy TV sat precariously atop a homemade bookshelf.

"Hi. I call myself Juan," I said. "How do you call yourself?" It occurred to me that simple things in Spanish, like asking a name, seemed beautifully circuitous when compared with the English, no-nonsense way of getting the same information. I embraced the flowery formality of

Spanish and its reflexive verbs. But my musings took a backseat when the boy looked up at me and shook my hand.

"Antonio," he answered. His grip felt limp and fleeting, but at least he forced a smile. I wondered if he resented my presence or if he was just shy about having a stranger in the house. Maybe both.

"I can help you?" I asked.

He nodded almost imperceptibly, so we sat in silence, watching television and husking beans. I remembered his name from the information Christine had given me back at the monastery. Antonio was my 18-year-old 'brother.' He was tall and sinewy, but he had his mother's soft, kind face and clear skin. His t-shirt looked a little bit too small and his jeans were faded. His flip-flops were dirty and worn. I wanted to talk to him, but I had nothing to say. More to the point, I had nothing I *could* say. After wracking my brain I asked as casually as I could, "Soccer is pleasing to you?"

"*Está bien.*"

The conversation stalled and the minutes passed slowly. *How the hell are you going to spend three months in this house?* As the pile of husked beans grew higher, I tried to figure out how I'd get through the next three hours, let alone the next three months, but I was eager to get along.

"What are?" I asked, pointing to the shrinking mountain of unhusked beans.

He couldn't hide his smirk. "*Guandu,*" he answered, probably wondering how this idiot *gringo* would teach anyone anything if he didn't even know what *guandu* were.

"Wan-do," I repeated.

16

He nodded approvingly. I felt the need to make more conversation and I would have asked about the town, or the game on the TV, or anything at all, but I didn't have the vocabulary.

The air was still and thick and impossibly hot. I could feel the sweat running down my brow and neck. My shirt stuck to my back. I couldn't understand how anyone could live in that heat, but Antonio looked perfectly cool and comfortable.

A short time later someone knocked on the door and called out my name. I went to the door and saw Meliza, my Spanish teacher, standing there along with the other trainees assigned to *Cerro Verde*. I'd never been so happy to see English-speaking acquaintances.

Meliza had bright eyes behind big glasses. She always pursed her lips in a way that made it seem she was listening carefully and found everything interesting. When she spoke, she spoke slowly, cheerfully, and deliberately.

Meliza used her fingers like little legs and pantomimed a person walking in a circle as she said, "We are going to walk in the town so that each trainee knows where all the other trainees live. You want to come?"

"*Sí!*" I answered gleefully.

"Juan can come with us for a time?" Meliza asked my mom.

"*Está bien.* Will he be home for dinner?" In retrospect, at 24 years old, it was infantilizing for the two women to discuss me as though I were a small child, but at the time it seemed perfectly normal and I was too excited to give it a second thought. I joined my peers and we walked around town. It didn't take long for me to realize that I had it pretty good. Not only did I have a private bedroom, but my house was built of painted cinder blocks. Some of my colleagues were living in mud houses on the outskirts of town. We had a TV and a refrigerator, but they didn't even have electricity. We were rich.

I found my mom and brother sitting on the sofa watching professional wrestling. My mom looked up and hopped to her feet.

"Do you want to eat?" she asked me as she wiggled her closed fingers towards her mouth.

"*Sí. Gracias.*" I prayed for something identifiable.

Much to my surprise, Antonio went into the kitchen and spooned out a plate of food from the pots on the stove. He motioned for me to sit at a small table in the kitchen and he placed a plate of rice, beans, and stewed chicken in front of me. Then he poured me a glass of sugary, homemade orange juice out of a plastic pitcher from the fridge. He sat down and watched me eat.

"It's pleasing to you?" he asked.

"It's delicious. Thank you."

"I cooked it," he boasted, tapping himself on the chest with his index finger.

"You aren't going to eat?"

"I already ate." He smiled and rubbed his flat stomach.

As soon as I finished, Antonio cleared my plate, washed it, and left it in a plastic drying rack next to the sink. Christine had told us that Panama was a country built on *machismo* and that Panamanians generally considered cooking and cleaning to be women's work. Antonio was a head taller than me and twice as muscular. I wasn't about to ask him why he did women's work. My trainers' guidance, I realized, was less than gospel.

Chapter 4 – Oscar the Grouch

After dinner, Antonio invited me to take a walk. He showed me the school, the store, the health center, and the payphone. I understood only one of every ten words, but I listened carefully. And I appreciated his efforts. He suddenly stopped talking and stood frozen on the dark dirt road. I looked at him to see why he'd stopped and he used his lips to point up ahead. Two police officers lowered the Panamanian flag from a flagpole near the center of town. I followed Antonio's lead and we remained still and quiet until the officers had folded the flag and walked away.

On the walk back to Antonio's house we passed the town's only bar. There was an area set up outside for cock fighting, but it looked like it hadn't been used in a long time. I asked Antonio if he wanted a beer by using my thumb to act out drinking a bottle. He held up his index finger and said *"uno"* with a smile and suspicious eyes.

The paint was chipped and fading. The room had no television. No music played.

Three men sat close together at one end of the bar. One had his head down and appeared to be unconscious. The other two hunched over a bottle of clear liquor in front of them. They watched us walk from the door to the bar. They didn't look away until we'd taken two stools. I wondered how they felt about a *gringo* crowding their turf.

"What are they drinking?" I asked Antonio.

"*Seco Herrerano.*"

"It's pleasing to you?"

He crinkled up his nose and shook his head.

Seco, a sugar cane liquor, is the national drink of Panama. And even though it tasted like turpentine, I'd eventually drink gallons of the stuff. For the time being, I'd have to settle for the beers Antonio ordered.

The bartender was in her early sixties. She had dyed black hair, too much mascara, and deep crow's feet around her eyes. The skin on her neck sagged towards her wrinkled chest. It was obvious that she'd been a beautiful woman a long time ago, but she wasn't yet willing to concede the inevitable.

She reached down into the cooler in front of her and put two bottles down on the bar. Antonio started to reach into his pocket, but I quickly placed my hand on his forearm and shook my head.

"*Cuanto?*" I asked.

"Eighty cents," the bartender answered in perfect English. I handed her a dollar and she passed me back two dimes. My three dollars per day would suit me fine.

"You're one of the Americans," she told me.

"That's right. I'm John." Although I liked the idea of speaking Spanish, it was nice not to think about every word.

"I'm Rita. This is my bar."

"It's nice to meet you."

"It's nice to meet you too. I wanted to have one of you live with me. Maybe one of the girls. I have a nice house and I live all alone. I don't need the money, but I would have liked the company. I don't know why they turned me down."

"I don't know either," I lied. A bar-owning spinster wasn't the sort of host-family the Peace Corps looked for. "Maybe it's because your English is too good."

"That's probably it. I used to be married to an American. We're divorced now. He lives in Nebraska. Too cold for me." She shivered at the mere thought of it.

"How'd you meet him?"

"He was a G.I. here before they gave the canal to the Panamanians. I worked as a waitress at the U.S.O. I was very popular with all the soldiers. They used to call me 'coochie.'" She ballooned with pride at the memory. I assumed, and hoped, she didn't know what they'd meant.

She seemed to read my mind, for she smiled flirtatiously and winked at me. Then she moved down to the other end of the bar to see if her other three customers needed anything, swaying her ass from side to side as she walked. I imagined her younger and more beautiful, like Zorba's Madame Hortense, naked, surrounded by admirals who drank champagne from her porcelain tub as she bathed in it.

Antonio looked horribly bored. "Where is our papa?" I asked him. The file the Peace Corps gave me listed a 'dad' in my host-family, but I had yet to see him.

"Oscar is your dad, not mine," Antonio answered solemnly. "My father," he added, "*está muerto.*"

"Oh. I'm sorry."

"It's ok. It's been a long time."

"But Oscar, where is he?"

To my surprise, Antonio used his lips to point to the other end of the bar. Oscar, apparently, was one of the men who had stared at us when we first walked in. He wore a condescending smirk, a navy blue baseball cap pulled low, and a full, well-manicured mustache. He could-n't have been more than five-and-a-half feet tall, but I could see he was strong. Veins popped out of his dark neck and forearms and stood in stark contrast to the heavy eyelids that blinked lazily over his red, watery eyes. I got the impression he spent a lot more time at the bar than at home.

"We should probably go home now," Antonio suggested, loud enough for Rita to hear him. "I told my mom we wouldn't be long."

"That's fine," Rita answered. "Thanks for coming in."

"It was my pleasure," I said. "Have a good night. I'll see you soon."

"Ok. Anytime you want you can to come over to my nice house." She used her thumb to point backwards over her shoulder and I realized she could walk straight into her living room from an open doorway behind the bar. "I make you fried chicken and French fries. You can watch TV or relax in the hammock. It is nicer in there than in the bar. And you can bring your friends."

"I'll take you up on that. It was nice to meet you. Good night."

As we walked home from the bar, I wanted to thank Antonio for dinner, for showing me around, and for waiting patiently for me while I talked to Rita, but I didn't know how to say any of that, so I just said clumsily, "Thank you in order for everything."

"*Está bien*," he assured me. Then he added, while waving his finger back and forth between us, "We are brothers."

Chapter 5 – Aum

I woke to the jarring sound of crowing roosters. With my clothes and towel slung over my shoulder, I made my groggy, grumpy way outside in the pre-dawn light. The shower stall out back was a patchwork of corrugated steel panels, not much bigger than an outhouse. I pulled back the door to find a fifty gallon drum filled with water. The top half of an empty Clorox bottle, with the cap still on it, floated on the surface. *That's odd.* I shrugged to myself and turned the faucet, but nothing came out.

Well this sucks. What do I do now? How long shall I stand here, naked, contemplating this useless faucet?

The Clorox bottle is a scoop! Of course! You figured that out almost as fast as you should have.

Water, I soon learned, was a commodity in *Cerro Verde*. Like most of rural Panama, *Cerro Verde*'s aqueduct was just a gravity-fed series of PVC pipes, so only houses located downhill from the cistern had running water all the time. I took the half-bottle by its handle and scooped up as much water as I could before pouring it over my head. The water – still cold from the night air – crashed down on me and washed away my sleepy daze. Splashing water up into my man-crannies was particularly tricky, but after flinging several gallons of water on myself, lathering up, and rinsing off, I was ready to start my day. *You, John Dillon, will make a fine Peace Corps Volunteer.*

By the time I dressed, my mom had already prepared my breakfast: a hot dog without the bun, a slice of processed cheese, and weak, sugary coffee. I gobbled it up, went back to my room, and grabbed the pineapples I'd bought as a housewarming gift.

"They are for you." I handed my mom the pineapples. "I forget to give yesterday."

"*Gracias*," she answered as she looked at the floor and blushed. Antonio started laughing at me.

"What?" I asked, genuinely perplexed. I couldn't imagine what was so funny about pineapples. Were they laughing at my Spanish?

Antonio pointed under the kitchen sink where four milk crates overflowed with pineapples. Oscar, it turned out, worked at a nearby pineapple plantation. He was allowed to bring home all the pineapples he could carry. I couldn't have picked a worse gift. I shook my head and laughed at myself and said goodbye for the day.

My Spanish class was only a hundred feet away from my house, in a gazebo in the middle of the town's park, but I arrived to find everyone else already there. I took a seat between Kyle and Elena. Elena wore a tank top, and I noticed for the first time that she had a small tattoo.

"What's that on your shoulder?"

"It's the symbol for 'Aum' in Tibetan script."

That seemed pretty cool. I had nothing clever to say, so I smiled at her and tried to be handsome.

"Are you laughing at me?" she asked.

"No, I'm smiling at you."

She looked unconvinced.

The weeks went on like that. Unhurried and hot. We met in the morning in the gazebo and had our informal Spanish lessons. Meliza guided the conversations and we did our best to keep up despite our limited skills.

Every so often we broke into English to joke or bicker and Meliza sweetly scolded us back into Spanish.

We took breaks and pulled oranges down from the trees. Then, in the afternoon, Carlos picked us up in the Land Cruiser. He took us to farms and taught us about the local produce. He also taught us simple techniques regarding planting, reforestation, soil conservation, and organic fertilizers. After a morning of sitting still in Spanish class, I liked sweating and getting my hands dirty in the fields. I ate fresh sugar cane and milked a cow and used a machete, all with varying degrees of success. At the end of the day my mom washed my muddy clothes in the sink behind the house and hung them up to dry.

In the evenings, Antonio served me dinner and kept me company while I ate it. Then we sat in the park and talked with neighbors or played cards. Sometimes I'd go to the bar with Kyle where we'd drink beers and talk with Rita all night.

"What do you think of Elena?" I asked Kyle one night.

"Not as much as you do, but she's kind of sexy."

"What do you mean 'not as much as I do?'"

"I see you tryin' to make eye contact with her."

"So?"

"So, do you try to make eye contact with any of the other girls here?"

"Fair enough." We sat in silence for a minute as we contemplated our beers. "But you know what the ocean looks like on a calm, sunny day? When the reflection is so bright you can look at it for only a fleeting moment? That's what it's like when I make eye contact with Elena."

"Wow. That's deep . . . and I had no idea you were *such* a pussy."

"Now you know." I laughed. "But it doesn't much matter, does it? It's not like I have anywhere to take her. All I need is my host mom to walk in on us."

"You neva know." Kyle shrugged. "Maybe your host mom will get turned on and join in."

"Dude, that's sick. She's my mom."

Kyle had the special gift of making everyone around him comfortable. He was intelligent, hilarious, energetic, and kind, and could tell fantastic yarns about himself without bravado or shame. One night at the bar he revealed to me that his father had been a crack addict. The only thing that helped his mom get through each day was a bottle of Popov and a soft pack of Winstons.

At just 12 years old, Kyle called social services on himself, shattering an already broken home, because he thought it was the only way to save his father's life. The State of Massachusetts became Kyle's parent, so he spent his teenage years bouncing from foster home to group home and back. His call to social services had been both brave and desperate, and it got his father sober for a few months. Eventually, however, his father succumbed again to his addiction and died, homeless, on the streets.

Kyle was only 22 when we met, but he seemed much older. I couldn't understand how he managed to overcome his adolescence, but he did well enough in high school to win a scholarship to Loyola where he played business and studied rugby. Moreover, I admired his care-free, unembittered approach to life. When you've had

26

problems like his, you get perspective on what real problems are. Even though he was two years younger than me, I felt like the little brother in the relationship.

Rita also took a liking to Kyle. A carnal liking. Night after night, Kyle fended off Rita's advances while I played with her dog and fascinated the drunken locals with tales of shoveling snow. Sometimes I thought about Kyle's parents and the problems they had with booze and drugs. I worried that maybe all the drinking we did wasn't good for him, but he was never an angry or sloppy drunk. In fact, he held his liquor as well as anyone I'd ever raised a glass with. And we always left Rita's bar in a better mood than when we arrived. We often invited Antonio to join us. Once in a while he even said yes.

Kyle's host-mom, Mafalda, was a completely different story. She was a 68-year-old woman with nine kids from six different fathers. Sometimes one of the fathers would stay for a couple of weeks, but he always left again. Meanwhile, the younger kids who still lived under her roof ranged in age from seventeen to three. They'd earned a reputation all over town for their wild ways, but it seemed to me the town's folk should cut Mafalda a break. All things considered, she held it together pretty well.

But if anything got Mafalda worked up, it was the thought of me and Kyle at the bar. She claimed that Rita was a witch and it would be only a matter of time before she used her black magic on us. And Mafalda convinced herself that Kyle would come home too drunk one night, under an evil spell, and beat her or rape her. The thought of Mafalda's fat, wrinkled body was enough to make my root wilt, but Mafalda somehow sold Kyle on Rita's dark powers. I was shocked at Kyle's superstitious streak and inexplicable allegiance to Mafalda's dubious dogma, but I had to admit that Rita, with her dyed black hair and thick black mascara, certainly looked the part.

Regardless, we still went to the bar several times a week. The only thing that changed was the farewell at the end of each evening. Kyle stopped bidding me goodbye at the foot of the park. Instead, night after night, he begged me to walk him home. He believed that if I left him alone, Rita would appear from the shadows and whisk him into her lair, or some netherworld, or some such silliness.

"But my house is right next to the bar," I told him. "You live all the way out of town."

"Come on man . . . *please.*"

It was pathetic watching a grown man plead for a chaperone in a sleepy, rural town. But it was also fun. I made him squirm for several minutes before invariably giving in. Then I tortured him the whole way back to Mafalda's house.

"So," I teased as we walked along the dark, dirt road, "will she appear as herself or take on some other form?"

"I don't *know*," he moaned. "I don't want to talk about it. I don't want to think about it. Let's just *go.*" A few minutes later I threw my arm across his chest to stop him in his tracks.

"Wait a minute!" I told him in a hushed voice.

"*What is it?*" he whispered back in a panic.

Then, furrowing my brow and thrusting out my chin, as though to peer into the bushes on the side of the road, I whispered, "What is that? Do you see it? . . . Is that her?"

"That's not cool man."

"But it is kind of funny."
"C'mon. Let's hurry."

Chapter 6 – Antonio Isn't

One Sunday afternoon towards the end of training, Antonio took us on a hike to a quiet part of Lake Gatun, the man-made lake that feeds the Panama Canal. We spent the day there laughing and horsing around, tossing each other off the dock and into the lake, sipping on Seco on a sunny afternoon. Most of us jumped clumsily off the end of the dock or swung from a rope tied to a tree branch, but Antonio, lithe and muscular, dove into the water with perfect form. He climbed back up onto the dock, dripping water, smiling his easy smile.

"Dude," Elena elbowed me, "your brother is *hot*."

I shrugged and pretended not to be envious. Some pretty Panamanian girls were sitting nearby, watching us, whispering to one another and giggling. I managed to trade a few glances with one of them. We exchanged a couple of shy smiles before Antonio caught me.

"She's pleasing to you?" he asked me.

"Yes."

"I know her."

"Really?" With Antonio's help, maybe I could land a date and make Elena jealous.

"You want that I present you?"

"Of course." I'd already grown fond of my Panamanian brother. If he could start fixing me up with local beauties he'd take our relationship to a whole new level.

"I've known her since she was a little girl. She's 15 years old."

"Tell me you're joking." I felt like a lecher.

"And she has a 1-year-old son," he added, just to twist the knife.

"Jesus."

"No. Miguelito." Antonio flashed the knowing smile I'd seen several times a day for the last few weeks.

Antonio graduated from high school, but didn't have money for college. He was smart, handsome, and kind. And he had no future. There were practically no jobs in *Cerro Verde*. Manual labor didn't seem in his nature, so it was hard to imagine him getting work at the pineapple plantation with Oscar. He had no family in the city to help him find a job there. So he spent his days helping his mom around the house or tagging along with us as we attended Peace Corps training at nearby farms. If Antonio's dismal situation bothered him, he didn't let it show. He was a good influence on me.

Late that night, a scratching at my door woke me up from a sound sleep.

"Who's there?" I whispered. The scratching continued.

Once my eyes adjusted to the darkness, I realized that someone was using a twig to try and unhook the wooden latch on the inside of my door. I instinctively jumped out of bed, jammed my foot against the bottom of the door, and pushed the latch back into the closed position.

"What do you want?" I hissed, but he didn't answer. The twig came back through the door and tried to lift the wood latch again, but I pushed it back down and kept my hand there.

"Who's there?" a man's voice demanded. He sounded drunk. *Is he dangerous? Is he out to rob me? Maybe he*

31

wants to fight me and rob me. One can feel that vulnerable only in the middle of a dark, silent night.

"I'm *Juan*," I answered defiantly. "Go!"

"Who?"

"*Juan*. The *Gringo*. Go!"

He thumped the door angrily.

I dashed to the other side of my small bedroom and grabbed my machete. I told myself that if he came through the door I'd have to hurt him. I tightened my grip on the black, plastic handle.

"*Deja me entrar!*" he growled.

"Go," I insisted. I wished I had a better grasp of the language, so that I could tell him to fuck off and get away from my room, but my pidgin Spanish would have to do.

"Who are you?" His voice grew louder.

"*Juan*. Go."

"Who?"

I wondered if I'd be crouched in the dark all night, wearing only my boxers, clutching my machete in both hands, waiting for a drunk to smash through the window for reasons I couldn't figure out. *If I cut this man up, at best, I'll be sent home and my Peace Corps service will be over before it starts. At worst, I'll be the* gringo *boy toy in a Panamanian prison. Let's get on with it then.*

I heard the front door of the house swing open. The porch light snapped on and seeped through the crack around my bedroom door. "Who's there?" my mom shouted angrily. "You . . . get out of here!!! Don't come around here anymore!!!" I heard footsteps run away across the park. Through the window I could see other porch lights pop on. Marina shouted something else into the night, but I didn't understand. "Are you ok?" she called softly through the door.

"I'm fine," I answered, feeling dumb but grateful. "Everything is good."

Mom had come to my rescue.

Chapter 7 – The Pineapple Incident

"Good night, Rita."

"*Buenas noches,* Rita. See ya tuh-marra'."

"Good night, boys. Thanks for stopping in."

I snapped on my flashlight and lit up a sliver of an otherwise moonless night. The beam of light bounced ahead of us as we walked towards Kyle's house.

"It's pretty da'k tonight, huh?"

"Yeah. Real dark. A person could get away with anything out here, don't you think?"

"Like what?"

"Like anything. Like witchcraft. Like a human sacrifice."

"Why you gotta say shit like that? . . . Hey! Turn that light back on!"

"Uh oh. I think the batteries are dead."

"Don't tell me that."

"Fire burn, and caldron bubble."

"What? What are you talkin' about?"

"Nothing. I'm just messing with you. Here, look." I switched the flashlight back on. "You happy now?"

"Sorta."

"Why don't you have your own flashlight anyway?"

"I do. I just leave it at home."

"Are you serious? Why?"

"'Cause I have you to walk me home."

"You're unbelievable."

I delivered Kyle safely to his front door and headed straight home, smiling to myself about Rita and Kyle and my new life. My musings didn't last long. I heard shouts and screams. I recognized my mom's voice and broke into a run.

"You are a disgusting sinner!" Oscar bellowed. Neighbors were gathering to witness the commotion. I pushed through them and bounded onto the porch.

I reached the front door to find Antonio on his hands and knees on the living room floor. Oscar yelled down at him. "You give shame to your mother!" Antonio had blood caked around his nose and mouth. One eye was already swollen shut. "I don't want a *maricon* living in my house!" Oscar swayed back and forth with clenched fists. He looked even drunker than usual.

"Enough!" my mom screamed. "You're going to kill him!" She tried to grab Oscar's arm, but he pushed her away and she fell to the ground. Then he cocked his leg back and unwound into Antonio's middle with his steel-toed work boot. I could hear ribs crack, but Antonio hardly made a sound. He merely sucked air as the wind went out of him.

"*Mi hijo!*" my mom cried. She hugged Antonio around his midsection, trying to cover him up and use her own body as a shield to protect him. But Oscar grabbed my mom by a handful of hair and started to yank her to her feet. He was going to strike her too. I didn't know what to do. I spied a knife on the kitchen counter.

I disregarded the knife, reached under the sink, and grabbed a pineapple by its long, waxy leaves. The sharp spines cut into my palm, but I squeezed only tighter as I swung the pineapple into Oscar's temple with all of my might. The pineapple careened off his brow and rolled to safety under the sofa. Oscar crumpled like an empty duffle bag.

I didn't realize that I still clutched the leaves in my fist until I saw Marina staring at them. She looked as shocked as I felt. But she got her bearings first. She helped Antonio to his feet and took his battered face in her soft hands.

"I'm fine, Mama," he told her.

I shrugged at Marina, dropped the pineapple leaves on the floor, stepped over Oscar, and went to bed.

I needed only a few days in *Cerro Verde* to realize that Antonio was gay, but I hadn't broached the subject with him or anyone else. I wasn't even sure if he'd figured it out himself yet. But he had.

My visitor from the previous night hadn't been looking for me at all. He was Antonio's lover. And in his drunkenness he forgot that Antonio wouldn't be sleeping in his room as long as I lived in the house. When he heard my voice, he probably thought that Antonio had jilted him. And he grew determined to confront the new object of Antonio's affection. My host-mother, along with the neighbors, put it together the moment she opened the door and chased him off. It quickly became the town gossip and the family shame.

When I woke up in the morning, I tip-toed into the house and tried not to make a sound. I expected Oscar would still be on the living room floor, sleeping off the Seco and a possible concussion, but the room showed no sign of the prior night's drama. No drops of blood marked the floor. No pineapple rested under the sofa. I found my mom, alone, sitting at the kitchen table.

"Are you ok?" I asked her.

"We're all fine. Thank you." She forced a smile, served me some lukewarm coffee, and took her seat again. I sipped on the coffee and we sat in awkward silence for a couple of minutes.

"And Oscar?"

"He must have woken up and left in the middle of the night."

"Where did he go?"

"I don't know. Probably to one of his girlfriends." Her cavalier comment about a mistress caught me off guard, but compared to Antonio's public outing, a cheating husband was relatively uncontroversial. Being gay, on the other hand, in a small town, in a devoutly Catholic country, had to be miserable.

I worried Oscar would come back and get rough again. "How long do you think he'll stay there?"

"I don't think he'll be back, ever. He's too proud."

"So what will you do? How will you eat?"

"I'm going to stay with my sister's family."

"Is Antonio going with you?"

"No. They don't have room for him there."

I wondered if that was true. I suspected they just didn't want the town queer under their roof.

The Peace Corps would surely want to know about the turn of events. But if I told Grace what happened, she would find me a different host-family. I liked my mom and I liked Antonio. The thirty-five dollars I paid each week for my room and board was a substantial sum for them, especially if Oscar was gone for good. So I decided to keep the news to myself. I didn't even tell Kyle what happened.

When I got back from class that afternoon, Antonio sat alone in the house. "It's good to see you," I said. He made an effort to greet me, but winced in pain. "How are you feeling?"

"*Mas o menos.*"

"I'm surprised Oscar hasn't come back to kick you out."

"Oscar can't kick me out."

"How so?"

"Because this house doesn't belong to him. It is the house of my grandmother. Oscar can't say anything about it."

That settled it for the time being. Antonio and I stayed in the house together while his mom lived across town at her sister's. I gave Antonio the money for my room and board and he did the cooking and washed my clothes while I went to training each day. My dysfunctional host-family fit me fine.

I didn't know what Antonio would do after I left *Cerro Verde*. He'd still have a roof over his head, but without any income – whether from Oscar or the Peace Corps – the food could last only so long. And the ten dollars per day that I'd get from the Peace Corps once I became a Volunteer wouldn't be enough for me to support myself in my new town and still have something left over to send to him.

I approached Carlos. "You know my brother?"

"Of course. He goes to the farms with us all the time. He seems like a good kid. He's done a pretty good job teaching you Spanish too."

"Right. I think my host-father has it in for him. I'm worried for his safety."

"Why?"

"Well, . . . he's gay. And his step-dad isn't exactly understanding about it."

"I see." Carlos shuffled his feet. "It's not easy to be that way in the *campo*."

"I'm sure it'd be a lot easier for him in the city, but he doesn't know anyone there. Do you know where he might find a job?"

"Hmmmm. I'm not sure, but I'll think about it."

"Thanks. I appreciate it." I couldn't tell if Carlos judged Antonio or if he just loathed getting involved in family politics

Carlos must've picked up on the half-heartedness of my gratitude or seen the consternation on my face, for he added, "in the meantime, you can tell him that he can stay in my apartment if he keeps the place clean for me. But he'll have to find a place of his own within a few weeks."

"Thank you, Carlos. You might be saving his life."

"Don't mention it." A broad grin stretched across his face. "Besides, training you clowns keeps me on the road most of the time anyway. It'll be good to have someone I can trust looking after my place."

Chapter 8 – Jack and the Giant Beach

We spent the last week of training in Panama City, undergoing a battery of medical tests. Shimmering glass and steel buildings towered downtown and stood in stark contrast to the rural communities where we'd spent the last three months. It was the last time for a while that we'd get the chance to hang out with fellow Americans or have regular access to simple conveniences like drug stores or electricity.

The Peace Corps was kind enough to arrange some sight-seeing tours for us while we were there. During our last week of training, however, Panama's rich history was lost on us. Instead, the city's importance lay in its quality restaurants and decadent dance clubs. On our first night in town, Kyle, Elena, and I went out to a pub called the *Pavo Royal*. We threw darts while a live band played CCR and Grateful Dead songs. Kyle and I took turns cuddling with Elena on a couch and we laughed until midnight. Then we made our way to *Bacchus*, a Technicolor trance club. Kyle met some guy on the dance floor who sold him some ecstasy.

"You know," Kyle pointed out, "it's already pretty late and we only got two pills for the three of us."

"And?"

"So we should go to the ba'troom and crush 'em up and snort 'em. They'll hit us fasta' that way."

"Thanks, but no thanks," Elena answered. "I'll wait for you two out here." She wore an amused smile.

I didn't want to leave her alone. "You'll be ok by yourself for a couple of minutes?"

"I'll be fine."

"We'll be right back," I assured her.

"I can handle myself. Go have your fun."

Bacchus' unisex restroom had a large, crowded antechamber filled with sofas and mirrors and sinks and commotion. But each toilet was located in its own little room behind a full-sized locking door. This was, undoubtedly, a restroom designed for hedonism. We waited our turn.

A door swung open and I found myself face to face with three beautiful women. One wore a silver sequined dress. All three had high heels and long, jet black hair. I stared too long. The one in the sequined dress made eye contact with me and casually dabbed at her nostril with her middle finger.

A few minutes later Kyle and I walked out of the bathroom and found the club had become a different place. The music got louder; the dancing grew wilder. Popping strobe lights confused everything. The club heaved and pulsed. I spotted Elena dancing by herself in the crowd; her hands twirled high above her head.

She shrieked with delight when she saw us, as though it had been a year. We frolicked on the dance floor, dodging florescent clothes, LED-encrusted jewelry, and glow-in-the-dark yo-yos. Beads of sweat ran down sunglass-clad faces. The *campo* was just on the other side of the bridge, but it was a world away.

A man who looked to be about our age stopped Kyle. He was lean, had dark hair, and wore tight black clothing like most every other guy in the place.

"You're nawt from aroun' 'ere, ah you?" he shouted over the music in a strong British accent.

"How can you tell?" Kyle shouted back, creasing his brow and feigning utter confusion. With blonde hair, blue eyes, and a green Hawaiian shirt, Kyle attracted attention everywhere we went. In a place like *Bacchus*, where all the other patrons dressed like Versace models on acid and spent untold fortunes on hair products, Kyle looked all the more out of place.

"I come 'ere all da dime and I don't believe I've ev'uh seen you befaw. Beside, you don't . . . blend," the man answered politely, oblivious to Kyle's sarcasm. "My name is Jack. Welcome to Panama."

"Are you Panamanian?" Elena asked him as she tossed her hair over her shoulder and batted her eyelashes. She was taken with the accent. After all, a girl from Feather Falls couldn't tell the difference between cockney and Queen's English. Jack grinned from ear to ear and took Elena's hand. I was fairly sure he'd introduced himself to Kyle only to meet Elena. I hated him.

"I am. Well, my mum is Panamanian, but my father is Bri'ish. I grew up in *London*," he explained, making sure we understood the importance of "London."

"Are you visiting family then?" I asked him, hoping he'd be on the next plane back to England.

"Not exactly. I moved 'ere dree months ago to study adminisdra'ive engineering."

"What's administrative engineering?" Elena asked.

He laughed. "I don' quite know, but I'll be sure to dell you when I fine out." The four of us returned to the dance floor for a while. "Say," Jack yelled over the deafening bass, "would da dree of you like to come back to my place and smoke a liddle mar-ee-wana?"

Back at his apartment, Jack put some records on his turntables and played DJ for us while we smoked his pot. I passed the joint to Elena. To my surprise, she accepted it, handled it deftly, and took a big hit. *So much for a Mormon teetotaler.*

Jack had never heard of the Peace Corps, but once he realized how we intended to spend the next two years, he was fascinated. More than fascinated, he was dumbfounded. He couldn't believe that anyone would voluntarily head off into the mountains to live in poverty. "Yaw really naught goin' to have 'lectricity?" he repeated over and over. "But how'll you watch telly or listen to trance?" Despite my jealous instincts, I was beginning to find him quite likable.

"We won't," Kyle answered.

"Well, you'll 'ave to 'ave some form of distraction while lost in the wil'erness."

"I guess we'll read a lot," I suggested.

"Please. That sounds bloody awful! We can do beh'er 'an 'at." He went to his freezer and tossed me a large bag of pot. "This is the same stuff you've been smoking. They call it 'Panama Red.' Now you'll 'ave sumpin' to wile away the hours when yer out in the boonies."

"What do we owe you for that?" Elena asked worriedly. We hardly had enough money for cab fare back to the hotel.

"Nothing. It's a present. It's not every day I get to party with some Yanks."

"Wow!" I said. "Thanks a lot man. That's really kind of you."

"Don't even mention it. Drugs are so cheap in this country . . . and we have loads of pa'ies," he boasted. "Last week I met a German couple. They got stoned on my couch and started goin' at it right in front of me. I think they must have been on ex too. They got completely naked. I couldn' believe my fuckin' eyes. Den dey looked over at me and asked me to join 'em."

"Did you?" Elena asked – with a little too much enthusiasm.

"I did. But it was a little weir'. Things sta'ted to get hot and heavy. I was making out wif the lady when he unbuttoned my trousers. The next thing I know, I'm kissing his lady and he was sucking on my willy."

Elena shot me a glance that seemed to say, "is this for real?" Whatever small crush Elena had developed for Jack, it was gone. I felt relieved that I didn't have to hate him anymore.

"I didn't try to stop him either," Jack continued, "I let him go . . . er . . . how should I say this? . . . I let him go . . . all the way." Then, after a long pause, he asked nervously, "Do you think that makes me . . . gay?"

I didn't know what it made him, but it was damn entertaining.

"I mean, I was thinking about her the whole time," he added defensively.

Kyle pursed his lips and raised his eyebrows and looked everywhere but at Jack. Elena was looking at her feet. "I can't say I've ever been in that boat," I said, after taking a contemplative hit from one of the joints we'd been passing around.

A few hours earlier we were carrying plastic specimen cups filled with our own shit through the streets of Panama City to the local lab so we could figure out if we were fit enough to go save the world; now we were accepting large amounts of Panama Red from a stranger who wanted us to help him figure out his sexuality. The Peace Corps was already living up to its motto; it really *was* the toughest job I'd ever love.

Fortunately, before I had to counsel our host any further, some of his Panamanian friends showed up and he quickly changed the subject. The music got louder. More and more guests arrived. When the apartment swelled with bodies and smoke and we had to shout above the music just to hear one another, a final guest arrived. He walked in without saying a word, as though he lived there. He nodded and smiled at friends and strangers alike as he made his way across the crowded room. Then he opened up the messenger bag slung across his shoulder, pulled out a Ziplock filled with cocaine, and dumped the entire contents onto the coffee table. He made Scarface's desk look strictly junior varsity.

Kyle dove into the veritable beach, snorting what he could right off the table. Others came by, kneeled next to the table, snorted a couple of lines, and disappeared back into the crowd.

"I've never tried cocaine before," I confessed to Kyle. I was nervous about the proposition. Pot and ecstasy were hijinks. Cocaine was *drugs*.

"Well this is the time, my man. Do you have any idea how much this much coke would cost at home?"

"No."

"Neither do I," he howled with delight. "But I know it'd be a *fortune*! And I know you'll probably never get an appatunity like this again."

I took the largest pinch I could between my thumb and forefinger and fell back into the couch. Then, with my other hand, I stuck out my thumb as far as it would go and dropped the cocaine into the little pit that formed at the end of my wrist. Some of the powder dropped onto my lap, but there was so much that no one cared or even blinked. The extravagance was half the fun.

"Rub some on your gums," Kyle suggested. "You'll like it."

He was right. After a few hours of fast music and faster conversation and debauchery in general with total strangers, Elena and I had to drag Kyle out of there. We thanked Jack and took a cab back to the hotel.

We stumbled in at about seven-thirty in the morning. Our colleagues were already up and bathed and chipper, applying bug spray and suntan lotion and eagerly asking us where we'd been and how did it go.

"Where's everybody going?" I asked.

"*Barro Colorado*," Elena answered. "Christine set it up for us."

"She set what up for us?"

Elena sighed. "It was all explained yesterday at the office. You don't listen to anything they tell us, do you?"

"I listen to what you tell me."

"We need to get to the port on time or we'll miss the boat."

"Port?"

"Just go get ready."

I managed to shower and grab a handful of dry cereal before I found myself in the back of a cab.

"*Vamos al puerto en Gamboa*," Elena told the driver.

46

"So what is *Guarro Colorado* anyway?" I asked.

"*Barro Colorado*," Elena corrected me.

"That's what I said."

"It's an island. Sort of. Like a hundred years ago, engineers built a dam in the Chagres River to make the Panama Canal. The flooding made a big lake, and what used to be hilltops became little islands. One of them is *Barro Colorado*. It's the Smithsonian Institute's Tropical Research Institute. Scientists come from all over the world to study the bugs and plants and stuff. I think it's supposed to be like a real life Jurassic Park."

"You're quite a nerd; I mean, uh, 'history student.'"

"Whatever. Jerk. I read most of it in <u>Lonely Planet</u> yesterday. Christine said it's usually closed to the public, but the Peace Corps pulled some strings for us. It's going to be cool."

We caught the ferry just in time and got to *Barro Colorado* and we walked. And then we walked some more. And then we went up lots of stairs and then some more stairs and then we walked into another time altogether.

Howler monkeys berated us from 300-year-old trees. Endangered *conejo pintados* scurried through the brush within a few feet of us. Brightly colored frogs, otherwise extinct on earth, went about their business, oblivious to the sanctity and safety of their tiny island universe.

On the return boat ride, I leaned over the railing, spaced out into the wake, and got myself dizzy in the rippling foam. Elena found me there.

"Wasn't that place amazing?" she beamed, looking vibrant and fresh.

47

"It was, but I'm not feeling so hot."

"Go to sleep then." She sat down on the deck and patted the inside of her thigh, as though to offer me her lap as a pillow. I lay down and nestled my head in the crook of her leg. The engine's hum sent vibrations through the hull of the ship and I drifted off into deep, dreamless sleep.

"John, we're back." I felt the back of Elena's fingers rubbing my cheek. "It's time to wake up," she whispered softly in my ear. I had no idea where I was.

But when I opened my eyes, I found her face only inches above mine. Her long curly hair hung down past her cheeks like curtains that cloaked us from the rest of the world. It was one of those moments that is far longer when remembered than it ever was in reality, where romanticized details become crisper with each passing year.

Elena.

Chapter 9 – Bittersweet Notion

The Peace Corps swore us in as Volunteers at the ambassador's house. We shared the same nervous excitement one feels when graduating from high school or college, but this time we stood in front of the flag, raised our hands, and took an oath:

"I, John Dillon, do solemnly swear that I will support and defend the Constitution of the United States against all enemies, domestic and foreign, that I take this obligation freely and without mental reservation or purpose of evasion, and that I will faithfully discharge my duties in the Peace Corps by working with the people of Panama as partners in friendship and in peace."

A lump formed in my throat as I recited the words. I'd always been a sucker for solemnity. A small, but passionate audience burst into applause. We gorged ourselves on *hors d'oeuvres* and attacked the open bar.

The idea of getting on a bus by yourself with everything you own to go somewhere you've never been in a country where you don't speak the language, knowing that you're going to stay at your remote destination for a good long while, if you even find it on the first try, is daunting. Our collective consciousness agreed not to think about it until the morning. So we hopped from club to club. We laughed and danced and drank.

Elena, Kyle, and I left the last club around two in the morning and shared a taxi back to the hotel. Kyle reasoned that we should split up the bag of weed that Jack gave us before we went to bed, just in case we didn't see each other the next day. It was a bittersweet notion.

"You two can keep it all," Elena offered.

"You shaw?" Kyle asked her.

"Thanks, but I'm sure. I don't want it in my site. I'll just smoke one last joint with you two, if that's ok?"

Elena came back to the simple room that Kyle and I shared. The room had two twin beds, a TV, and a small air conditioner. I sat on my bed while I rolled up a joint.

"I'm gonna go for a run in the mawnin'. It'll be good to stretch my legs befaw my bus ride." Kyle's community, *Cacique*, was a sleepy fishing village only a few hours away on the Caribbean coast. The idea of going for a run after a night of drinking and smoking and dancing never occurred to me, but he swore it helped him sweat out the toxins.

No sooner had we finished smoking than Kyle climbed into bed and shut his eyes. I promptly fished a bottle of *Ron Abuelo* from his backpack, unscrewed the cap, and took a long draw straight from the bottle.

"Can I have some of that?" Elena asked.

"Of course." I'd never seen her drink before. Despite our adventures in Panama City, Elena drank only water whenever we went out to the clubs. But Elena was full of surprises.

We sat cross-legged on my bed, facing one another. Elena and I passed the bottle back and forth. I could smell the sweet scent of the rum on her breath. My eyelids grew heavy.

"Do you ever miss California?" I asked her.

"No. Not Feather Falls anyway. I'm *never* going back there."

"Why?" The harsh edge in her voice took me by surprise.

"I mean, I miss my two little sisters, but I haven't been back in years. I don't know if I'll ever see them again."

"That seems a little dramatic, don't you think? Why don't you just go see them sometime?"

"My parents. They think I'm a bad influence. They don't want me around my sisters. Not that I'd visit my dad anyway."

"Why?"

"I hate him."

"C'mon, hate? That's a little harsh, isn't it? Besides, it's hard to believe anyone could consider you a bad influence."

"You don't know my parents. They were *very* strict."

"How so?"

"Well, for starters, I never had any boyfriends in high school. And when I say 'boyfriends,' I mean friends who were boys." The idea that Elena never had a boyfriend seemed preposterous. She was a beautiful woman. And she carried a warm heart and an easy smile. Surely she had her share of admirers back home. "It's true," she insisted, as though reading my mind. "No one even asked me to prom, so I didn't go."

"Now you're just breaking my heart."

"I didn't give it much thought at the time. It was just my life. I was *very* sheltered. I didn't even have my first kiss until I went to college."

"How can that be?"

"Don't get me wrong. I wanted to date in high school, but my parents forbade it. I was barely allowed out of the house. I had to go to seminary every morning before regular school, so I had to get up at four-thirty in the morning, six-days-a-week. I'd get home from school at the end of the day, have to do my homework, have dinner, and go right to bed so I could get up in the morning again for seminary."

"What's seminary?"

"It's basically extra school for Mormons. It sucks. Anyway, after high school, I went to BYU Hawaii."

"I didn't even know there was such a place."

"It's awesome. I learned to surf and snorkel. I went hiking and mountain biking all the time. Hawaii is amazing.

"During my freshman year, after Bradley Nowell from Sublime overdosed, Bud Gaugh and Eric Wilson came to Oahu to mourn. They rented a house on the North Shore. Each night they jammed on the beach around bonfires. I'd go and listen to them and party all night. It was also the first time I ever kissed a boy, or drank, or anything."

"That sounds like a good first kiss."

"It was." She blushed before the color quickly disappeared from her face. "Everything was going great until my junior year. I was working at my part-time job, selling coconut milk to tourists out of a stand by the beach, when my father shows up out of the blue." She took another swallow off the bottle and passed it to me. Her smile was gone.

"Your dad? From California?"

"Right."

"You didn't know he was coming?"

"I didn't have a clue, and he didn't even say hello. He just tells me where he's staying and that I should go there as soon as my shift ends. I was totally freaked out. I had no idea what was going on." She pulled the bottle back from me and took another big swallow.

"How did he even know where to find you?"

"Wait. I'm getting to that. After he left, I was nervous as hell. I finished my shift, wondering the whole time what the hell was going on, and then I went straight over to his hotel and up to his room. I remember it like it was yesterday. He was sitting in an armchair by the window. The sun was setting behind him. 'Is everything ok?' I asked him, 'Is mom alright?' 'No,' he said, 'Your mother and I know what you've been up to and we're very disappointed.' I didn't have any idea what he was talking about and I told him so. 'Don't play dumb with me!' he shouted, 'We know you've been drinking and doing drugs and dating a drug dealer who you *have sex with*!'"

"He sounds nuts!"

"Well, he is . . . , but he wasn't totally off base either. I mean, my boyfriend did sell a little grass and I did sleep at his place sometimes, but the way my dad put it, he made me feel so cheap and small. I just stammered, 'I don't know what you're talking about.' His face got bright, bright red. 'DON'T LIE TO ME!' he yelled. I thought he was going to explode. He'd never hit me before, but he looked like he was about to beat the shit out of me. I'd never been so scared in all my life. I just answered, 'I'm not lying to you Dad. I swear.' I shouldn't have said that though, because then he yelled, 'THEN WHAT ARE THESE?' and he threw a big manila envelope at me.

When I opened it up, it was filled with glossy 8x10 black and whites."

"Get out of here!"

"I swear to God. He'd hired a private investigator to keep tabs on me for who knows how long. There were pictures of me drinking and kissing. There was a picture of the front of my boyfriend's house. There were records of where I'd been and what I'd done, down to the last minute. It was creepy and unbelievable all at the same time. I was speechless."

"That's the craziest thing I've ever heard."

"Wait. There's more. He said that he'd already gone to the dean of the university with the photos and had me expelled. It didn't matter that I had straight A's. Then he told me that since I'd been expelled I had no reason to stay in Hawaii. He said that I could go home with him right then and there or I shouldn't ever think about going home again."

"So what did you do?" I was horrified. And captivated.

"I looked him right in the eye and I said, 'Fuck you dad, fuck your photos, and fuck your religion!' I'd never seen him look so shocked. I still remember his stupid mouth dropped open in disbelief. He never imagined his little girl could talk to him like that. He was so flustered and angry he couldn't even speak. Not that I would've let him. I walked out of the room and slammed the door and I haven't seen him since."

"You're like a rock star!"

She laughed. "Not so much. I'd been too angry and everything had happened so fast that I didn't think it through. My father had been paying all my bills. I was broke. My part-time college job didn't cover much of anything."

"So?"

"Well, first I went straight to my boyfriend's house. I figured he'd help me out until I got on my feet, but he turned me away at the door."

"What? Are you serious?"

"Completely. My dad threatened him. He told my boyfriend that unless he agreed to never see me again, my dad would call the cops and report him as a drug dealer."

"So what did you do?"

"I couldn't pay my rent. I didn't even have money to eat. I was literally starving. So I did what I had to do. I found a job in Honolulu. I started . . . dancing." The last word trickled out her mouth almost inaudibly. If I hadn't been hanging on her every word, I might have missed it.

"Dancing? You mean like stripping? You?" I took another pull off the rum bottle and so did she.

She nodded as she swallowed. "People usually get weird when I tell them that." I was grateful for the warning and made a conscious effort to keep my tongue from falling out of my mouth. She continued. "It didn't take me long to realize I was good at it. In no time I saved up enough money to pay for a flight back to the mainland, so I flew to San Diego. I started dancing there too and I made enough money to get an apartment and buy a car and get a degree in marine biology from UCSD. Thanks to dancing, I graduated debt free. I even had time to play on the club soccer team."

"And you haven't spoken to either of your parents since that day at the hotel in Honolulu?"

"I've spoken to my mom on the phone a couple of times, but I haven't actually seen either of them. They don't even know I'm here. At least, I don't think they do. For all I know, they've got a private investigator watching me here too." She laughed self-consciously. Then she hiccupped and covered her mouth with her fist. "Excuse me," she muttered, still holding her hand to her mouth. She got up and walked briskly to the bathroom.

As fascinated as I was with her story, I was even more fascinated that she could laugh it all off. Elena had always struck me as innocent and uncomplicated. But I couldn't have been more wrong. I wanted to know her better.

Then I heard the sound of a dog hacking up a hair ball, followed by the splattering sound of liquid hitting liquid, and encored with a pitiful gasp of relief. The cacophony repeated itself a few more times. I was shocked that such a beautiful creature could make such obscene sounds.

I tapped lightly on the bathroom door. "Can I come in?" I asked cautiously.

"I guess so."

Elena was on her hands and knees in front of the toilet. I held her hair while she finished puking and then I helped her to her feet. She swayed before me with a beaten, sorrowful expression. I fumbled through my Dopp kit and tried to keep from laughing at her.

"It's not funny," she protested.

"I know it's not," I lied. "Here, take this." I handed her a spare toothbrush and my toothpaste and pretended, for both our sakes, not to notice the speck of vomit on the corner of her mouth. "Take a minute to clean yourself up." I shut the door behind her, sat down on the edge of the bed, and watched a Mexican variety show on the room's small TV. A bunch of adults were dressed as elementary school students. They sat at desks in a mock classroom and told jokes every time the teacher asked a question. I couldn't understand the jokes, but I got the distinct impression they were terrible.

A couple minutes later Elena walked out of the bathroom with perfect posture and her chin held high, avoiding eye contact and disregarding my very existence. She moved towards the bed with an ironic air of supreme dignity as though to deny she'd just been sick or, for that matter, ever experienced inelegant bodily functions. She might've even pulled it off, but she wasn't wearing any clothes.

Elena sat down next to me without saying a word, all the while maintaining that perfect posture, like she'd practiced it for years by walking around with books balanced on her head. "Are you alright?"

She gave no response. Her eyes were empty. Her body was there, but no one was home.

I took the opportunity to admire her. Her breasts weren't very big, but I liked them. They were full and perfectly round. I'd never seen such round breasts.

Her nipples were hard from the air conditioning. I reached out, as though in a slow-motion dream, and I slowly brushed one with the tip of my thumb. She didn't even flinch. I thought about pushing her down on her back and burying my tongue inside her shaved snatch. The notion gave me a hard-on and I felt embarrassed for a moment, but she was utterly oblivious to me or anything else. I wanted to have my way with her, but I only stared.

After a minute, I snapped out of my trance and pulled a t-shirt out of my bag. "Come on. Time for bed." I took hold of her elbow and she responded like a sleepy, obedient toddler. First I helped her get the t-shirt on; then I pulled back the bedspread and told her to get under the sheets. She dutifully followed my instructions, but never said a word. She rolled away from me and onto her stomach. I was pretty sure she didn't have anything left to puke up, so I tucked her in and let her be. I gathered her clothes up off the bathroom floor, folded them up, and placed them on the foot of the bed.

"Goodnight Elena." I took a pillow off the bed and lay down on the floor. She was already snoring.

"You pussy," Kyle whispered, breaking the silence.

"You're *awake*?"

"Damn right I'm awake. And I was hopin' you'd give me a betta show than that. Afta all I'd done to give you alone time with her. Pathetic. Talk about a wasted appatunity."

"But she's too drunk," I protested.

"Too drunk fa what? You should be ashamed of ya'self. Yaw a disgrace to men everywhere."

"Whatever."

"Guh'night, you little bitch."

"Goodnight, you prick."

Chapter 10 – Cold Scrambled Eggs

KNOCK. KNOCK. KNOCK. *"Buenos Dias!* You want I clean your room?"

"What?" I rolled over and smashed my face into the leg of the bed. My cheek shot alarms to my half-asleep brain. *"Goddamnit!"* I shouted.

Instinctively, I reached to check for blood, but my hand wouldn't cooperate. It flailed like an unattended fire hose and slapped into my ear before flopping clumsily across my shoulder, awash in a blaze of fried nerves that punished me for spending the last several hours sleeping on top of my arm. My ankles cracked in protest as I scooped myself off the floor and struggled to my feet.

A shocked housekeeper stood frozen in the half-open doorway. We locked eyes. Mine grew narrow; hers went wide.

"Good morning, *señor*," she whispered. "You want I clean your room?"

"Am I bleeding? It feels like I'm bleeding."

"No *señor*. You no bleeding. I come back later. Ok? Bye." She backed out of the room and shut the door. I surveyed my surroundings.

My bed was made. My t-shirt, folded neatly, sat atop the fluffed pillow. "Are you *mocking* me?" I demanded. The bed didn't answer. Neither did the t-shirt.

Kyle's bag was gone, so I figured he already left for his community. Elena, however, couldn't possibly be on the road yet. Not if she felt half as bad as I did.

I staggered into the bathroom, looked in the mirror, and found a weary stranger scowling back at me with deranged hair and puffy, blood-shot eyes. He was an ugly bastard, but he looked more or less how I felt, so I concluded with some measure of confidence that it was indeed me. I patted my cheek with my fingertips and surveyed the damage. The maid was right: I wasn't bleeding. I'd sure have a nasty bruise though.

A shower didn't make me feel any better. My stomach was weak and swirling. My temples pulsed. When I brushed my teeth I had to clutch the sink with both hands to keep from throwing up. I nursed three glasses of tap water out of a disposable cup and then pulled some clean clothes on. Hangovers, it occurred to me, were much worse in Panama.

The thought of a bumpy bus ride with shoddy shocks made my stomach churn. I could already hear crying babies, squawking chickens, and loud accordion music blaring from the bus' blown speakers. Food was the last thing I wanted, but it was going to be a long day. I had to eat something. Maybe a yellow hockey puck.

The hotel had a small restaurant, so I made my way slowly downstairs. I was glad to see Elena sitting by herself at a four-top. She wore a cotton dress and big sunglasses. She had one elbow propped up on the table so she could cradle her forehead in her hand. The plate of eggs in front of her looked untouched. I couldn't tell if she was staring out the window or sleeping.

"Good morning," I croaked as I pulled out a chair and took a seat across from her.

"Oh. Hey."

"How are you feeling?"

"Awful. You?"

"About the same."

"What happened to your face?"

"Just a run-in with the maid."

"I'd hate to see what she looks like." After a long pause, she added, "Why did we do that to ourselves last night?"

"Because we're invincible. You ready for *Quebrada Brava?*"

"I'm ready to *be* there. I'm just not ready to *get* there."

"Huh?"

"Do you have any idea what it takes to get to my site?"

"I guess not."

"It's going to be a nightmare. First, I have to take an hour-and-a-half bus ride to *Chepo*. Then I have to lug all my crap from the bus station to the port and find my town's only boat."

"Your town has its own boat?"

"Don't get too excited. It's just a dugout canoe with an outboard motor. Supposedly the captain will be waiting for me. I guess I'm just supposed to ask around for the guy that goes to *Quebrada Brava*." She shrugged.

"I'm sure you'll find him," I said, trying to sound encouraging.

"That's the least of it. After I meet the boat we have to go downriver for a couple of hours until we hit the Pacific Ocean; then we travel along the coast for a few miles before we finally reach another river. After traveling up *that* river for a few more hours, we *should* be there."

"That sounds pretty involved," I admitted. It sounded fucking awful.

We sat in silence as I imagined Elena, hungover, sitting on a hard wooden plank for hours on end as the canoe bounced in the water and she choked on thick gasoline fumes wafting out of the outboard engine. It seemed like a truly miserable way to start one's Peace Corps service, but I knew Elena was excited about getting out there. She'd been talking about it for weeks.

Quebrada Brava was populated by the Wounaan, one of Panama's seven indigenous tribes. We learned all about them in training. The women wore big flowers in their hair, ornate necklaces that hung loosely over their bare chests, and colorful cotton skirts. And they painted themselves with intricate designs using inks mixed from jungle fruits. I loved imagining Elena in that getup. A big red hibiscus flower tucked behind her ear. Shells and beads and other jungle treasures dangling over her pert breasts. Pocohontas eat your heart out!

But the Wounaan were also some of the most impoverished people in all of Panama. The Peace Corps had never sent a Volunteer to *Quebrada Brava* before, so Elena would have her work cut out for her. She already knew her village didn't have potable water, and the town's health center rarely had any medicine or anyone who knew how to use it. Elena embraced the idea of such an adventure, but as we sat in the restaurant and quietly contemplated our uncertain futures, I couldn't help but worry about her.

I looked around at other patrons busily scarfing down their bacon and pancakes and slurping their cereal. Surly waitresses refilled coffee cups as busboys heaved over-flowing rubber trays filled with dirty dishes. They were all totally oblivious to *Quebrada Brava*, the Wounaan, and the dangers Elena would face in just a few hours. I didn't want her to go.

"You were asleep on the floor when I woke up," she said, breaking the silence between us. "I guess I stole your bed. Sorry about that."

"Don't sweat it."

"You must've been pretty uncomfortable on that tile. Did you get any rest?"

"I was out cold. I was so drunk I could've slept on broken glass. It's my head that's killing me."

"Mine too. I guess I was pretty messed up last night."

"Yeah." We both fell silent again. After a minute the waitress came by. I ordered a cup of black coffee and an ice water.

"I woke up in one of your t-shirts. Did anything happen last night? You know, between us?"

"Not a thing," I assured her.

"Really?"

"Really."

I picked up her fork and ate a couple of bites of her cold, scrambled eggs. I knew I wouldn't see her again for a long time. "You don't remember anything?"

"I remember coming back to the hotel, but that's about it. Did I embarrass myself?"

"Not at all." I wondered whether it was a lie. She might've been embarrassed if she knew about all the puke and nakedness, but I was only impressed.

"That's a relief." She managed a weak smile. "And thanks for lending me your t-shirt."

"Anytime," I said.

I meant it.

63

Chapter 11 – Timshel

On the bus ride to my town, I thought only of Elena. And I had to cover my lap with my backpack to hide it from the other passengers. I remembered Kyle calling me a "little bitch" and I wanted to punch myself in the groin for passing up the opportunity to explore Elena's body. I wondered when I'd get to see her again.

Compared to her, I would be living in a thriving metropolis. I was going to *Los Altos de las Cascadas*, a *latino* community nestled in the mountains of *Coclé*. I expected I'd receive a warmer welcome in *Los Altos* than Elena would receive in *Quebrada Brava*. I'd be the second Volunteer in my site, so my town had an idea of what to expect. It would probably take Elena a while just to prove she was human. And unlike Elena, I'd have my own house from day one. I couldn't wait to smoke pot and masturbate with impunity.

When the bus to *Los Altos* turned off the Inter-American Highway and started to climb, sprawling pastures seemed to stretch out forever on either side. But as the hours passed, the mountain grew steeper, the pastures became forests, and sporadic homes began to appear on both sides of the dirt road. When there wasn't much more mountain to climb, we passed a general store, a school, and a large, open-air pavilion that I guessed was some sort of town hall. The school and the store were on opposite sides of the road from one another. I saw a payphone in front of the pavilion, right where the Peace Corps said it would be.

"Excuse me," I said to the driver, "Is this *Los Altos de las Cascadas?*"

"Yes."

"Do you know where Kevin, the *gringo*, lived?"

"Yes." He laughed derisively. It didn't seem like a funny question, but at least I knew I was almost home.

"Please leave me at the house of Kevin."

"Ok, but he's not there. He left."

"I know. My name is Juan. I'm his replacement. I'm going to live there."

The driver dropped me off only a mile from the top of the mountain and pointed in a general direction. From what the Peace Corps had told me, I knew my house had two rooms, a corrugated steel roof, and sat in the middle of a small pasture. And, like the rest of town, it didn't have electricity or indoor plumbing. It didn't take long to find it.

Because the house sat in the middle of the pasture, there weren't any trees to block the view. I could appreciate the mountains in the distance and the low hanging clouds that obscured their peaks. Also, from my porch, I could look down on the dirt road and see anyone who happened by long before they reached my front door. My closest neighbor was at least five hundred feet away. At $20 per month, it seemed like a pretty sweet deal.

As I walked up the path to my new home and dusk settled in, I could hear the bus turning around further up the road. I reached my door and looked back just as the bus rolled back past my house and down the mountain. I waved to the driver, but he didn't wave back. He only stared and smirked. He seemed to find me amusing.

I wondered what Kevin had left behind for me. Even though Kevin and I had never met, he was well aware that a Volunteer would be arriving in *Los Altos* right after he left. And like all Peace Corps Volunteers around the world, he'd once made the long, lonely journey to his new home for the very first time without knowing any of his neighbors or having any strong sense of what the next couple of years would hold for him. In that light, I figured Kevin could relate to my anxieties, would have at least some empathy, and think to leave a few things behind. At the same time, I knew he didn't owe me anything.

Apparently, he felt the same way. My cupboard was bare. In fact, there wasn't even a cupboard. The only thing left in the house was the pungent smell of dust and mildew. Kevin had gone and sold *everything* for beer money. He hadn't left so much as a fork, a candle, or even a few matches.

According to the town gossip, as I'd find out soon enough, he had been a lazy drunk who spent most of his time arguing with bus drivers in the town bar and harassing young women anywhere he could find them. Indeed, he was known for getting so drunk that he'd stomp around the road and yell out into the night between bouts of sobbing over a Panamanian woman who'd spurned him.

Although Kevin had undermined the Peace Corps' objectives and ensured my first few days in my new home would be fairly uncomfortable, I was grateful to follow such a derelict. It would've been nice if he'd started at least one project in his two years there, so that I could hit the ground running by swooping in and keeping it going, but at least he'd set the bar low. By comparison, I'd seem industrious if I accomplished anything. Perhaps more importantly, the town was already familiar with the concept of Peace Corps, if not its practice. I had a huge head start.

I'd deal with the issue of furnishings the next day. In the meantime, I needed to find a way to feed myself. It hadn't occurred to me to bring food with me for that first night, so I made my way down the road back towards the main part of town, intending to rely on the kindness of strangers.

Not long into my walk, I encountered the ugliest dog I'd ever seen. He couldn't have weighed more than twenty-five pounds, though he should've weighed closer to forty. His ribs protruded through the sparse white hair on his chest and he had no hair at all on his hindquarters, leaving his pink, wrinkled haunches exposed to the elements. A tuft of thin hair sat atop his head like an un-kempt Mohawk and patches of more white hair covered the rest of him. And he had tiny dark pupils in the middle of eyes so light blue they were almost clear. Those eerie eyes dominated his disheveled appearance and created the expression of constant surprise.

Worst of all, he was twisting around in frantic cir-cles, trying to get at a plastic shopping bag that stuck half-way out his puckered asshole. I could only assume the bag had once held something at least remotely edible, that he'd found it in the street somewhere, swallowed the whole thing down with reckless abandon, and then managed to pass it only halfway out the other end. The sight of that candy-striped plastic bag hanging out his anus combined with the look of sheer panic on his face was perhaps the most disturbing thing I'd ever seen in nature. The image still haunts me to this day. There are some things in life you can't unsee.

"Sorry dog, but you're on your own with that one. I promise I won't tell anyone about your embarrassment though." I quickly took my leave and didn't look back.

After twenty minutes I arrived in the main part of *Los Altos*. Children played in the street. Accordion music wafted over radio waves and through open front doors. While my house on the outskirts of town seemed still and quiet, the center of *Los Altos* crackled with life. I picked a house at random, mustered my courage and my hunger, and stopped a few feet shy of the front porch.

"*Buenas noches!*" I called out.

"*Buenas!*" a voice called enthusiastically back. A moment later a young woman who couldn't have been more than eighteen or nineteen stood before me.

"I call myself John. I'm the new Volunteer from the Peace Corps."

"You wait." She showed me the universal sign for stop with the palm of her hand. Then she disappeared into the house. As I stood in the front yard, tapping my feet and feeling self-conscious, some young children peeked around the side of the house to look at me. When I noticed them, they shrieked with delight and ran off. An older woman, perhaps the younger woman's mother, suddenly appeared in the doorway. She looked me up and down as she wiped off her hands with a dish towel.

"Good evening," I said. She took my outstretched hand between her damp thumb and forefingers. It was more of a touch than a shake. "I call myself John," I repeated, "I'm the new Volunteer from the Peace Corps."

"Much pleasure," she answered flatly, as though she didn't really mean it. She didn't even tell me her name. She wanted to find out what I was selling. And for a moment I did too. What *was* I selling? Peace? America? Capitalism? I didn't have time for such philosophical thoughts. I needed food.

"Pardon. I arrived and I no have nothing. Can I eat here tonight?" I didn't have the vocabulary to formulate a more polished, less forward approach. Luckily, it didn't matter.

"Of course. Pass forward." She led me inside the modest front room that served as both living room and dining room. The blue paint was peeling. A picture of Jesus had been cut from a magazine and pasted to the wall. A wooden dining room table with four chairs was pushed into one corner. It looked like it had been a nice set a long, long time ago. A TV hooked up to a car battery sat on top of some milk crates. There was no other furniture. "Please, sit." She disappeared behind a curtain that covered the hallway to the rest of the house.

As I sat alone at the dining room table I thought to myself, *Wow. That was easy.* I wondered how I'd react if I was back in the States and a foreigner showed up on my doorstep asking for dinner.

A few minutes later, the matriarch reappeared and served me a plate piled high with white rice and diced tripe.

Shit.

As famished as I felt, everything about tripe – the sight, the texture, the very idea – riled my gag reflex. I wondered if I could get away with feeding the stuff to the family dogs on the sly, but I knew that wouldn't work. All the children had gathered around to watch me eat. Besides, I couldn't, or at least wouldn't, play the ingrate on my very first day in town; and I was, I had to remind myself, starving. The slimy strips of something's pock-marked, stinky stomach would have to do.

First, I turned to the unobjectionable, dry white rice. That went well enough. But once the rice was gone, I had to face the tripe. The children crowded closer.

"You like it?" I asked them, expecting they'd scrunch up their noses and curl their lips to echo my thoughts. But, to my surprise, they all nodded eagerly with smiles and wide eyes. For a second, I thought they hoped to trick me into eating the slimy, unchewable rubber tubes, but they weren't that savvy. They practically licked their lips.

"You want some?" I offered. One of them dared to nod and give me a glimmer of hope, but his cousin promptly dug an elbow into his ribs.

"You already ate," she reminded him, "that's for him. Don't be selfish."

The young boy tucked in his chin and lowered his eyes to the floor in a showing of self-reproach. I was in this alone.

Resigned to my fate, I laboriously cut the *mondongo* up into teeny-tiny pieces. Once I'd cut each piece down to the size of an aspirin, my procrastination could go no further and I had to face the task at hand. One by one, I swallowed each tiny piece with a big gulp of water. Every few minutes I'd drain my water glass and ask one of the children to fetch me another. They'd never seen such a well hydrated gringo. Sure enough, I managed to clean the whole plate that way. I felt like a genius. The technique would prove handy over the next two years.

After dinner, the matriarch returned from the kitchen and served me a glass of cool, sweet coffee.

Despite my contempt for tripe, I had nothing but gratitude for my hostess. It wasn't the best meal I ever had, but it might have been the most generous.

"Thank you for dinner."

"Don't worry yourself. I call myself Alejandra. Welcome to *Los Altos*."

We had a hard time understanding one another, but I gathered that she was the secretary at the local school. Because she had one of the town's few steady jobs, the hassle of preparing me dinners probably wasn't worth the modest income I could provide. Nonetheless, Alejandra agreed to let me eat dinner with her family every night; in exchange, I would pay her fifteen dollars a week. I thanked her, bade her a good night, and strode back up the road to my house, feeling full of myself for surviving my first night in my new town.

Once inside my dark house, I got to work blowing up my thin Therm-a-Rest. I lay the mat on the dusty, concrete floor, pulled a sheet up to my chin, and put my headphones on. As I listened to *Dark Side of the Moon* and drifted off to sleep, it occurred to me that my new house, like all great houses, needed a name. I envisioned Falling Water and Hearst Castle, Monticello and Vizcaya. And as my body began to sink into that dopey place between awareness and sleep, the right name swaggered across my mind: *Timshel*.

Chapter 12 – They Killed Nomé

"*Buenas!*" a man's voice called out, waking me from a deep sleep. It took me a moment to shake free the slumber and get my bearings. I rose slowly, stiff from a night on the concrete floor. Fortunately, I'd slept in my clothes, so I didn't have to scramble to get presentable. I combed my hair with my fingers, stretched my back, and made my way outside to greet my visitors.

Two men stood at the edge of my porch. They both held their straw hats in their hands and smiled. The older one was missing several of his front teeth. "Good morning," he said, "We heard that you arrived yesterday." He had bushy, ungroomed eyebrows and short gray hair. His deep, craggy face evidenced a hard life, but his eyes were soft and mellow. Both men looked bathed and fresh which is more than they could say for me. They were *real* farmers and had probably been up for hours. The older man handed me a corn tortilla and a hardboiled egg wrapped in a paper napkin.

"We brought you breakfast."

"Very kind. Much thanks."

"I call myself Jose Ojo," the older gentleman said. "This is my son-in-law, Eduardo." Eduardo had shiny black hair that covered his forehead and a pencil-thin mustache. He had a big smile filled with good teeth and he eagerly took my hand. Other than Jack, our half-British friend who didn't really count, Eduardo was the first Panamanian to give me a decent handshake.

"We wanted to work with *Señor* Kevin while he was here, but we never realized that goal. Perhaps you would be willing to visit our farm sometime."

72

"Of course I would. Thank you for inviting me."
Throughout training, I heard tales of Volunteers who had
to spend weeks, if not months, in their communities
before anyone would even talk to them. Here I was, only
one day in, and I'd already been invited to someone's
farm. It felt good.

"Also," Jose continued, "we imagine that you are
missing things. If you would like, Eduardo will take you to
town in order to help you." Eduardo nodded, as though to
confirm his father-in-law's offer.

"*Gracias.*" I felt lucky that a couple of my
neighbors had reached out to me so fast, but my skeptical
side questioned their angle. Would Eduardo expect me to
pay for such services? It didn't seem that way, but I didn't
know the protocol, or the going rate. It could get awkward. And even if he didn't want cash, they'd already made
clear that they wanted my help at their farm. After all, I
was the local agriculture expert. What a joke.

These men had been farming their whole lives.
And so had their fathers. And so had their fathers' fathers.
Meanwhile, I'd been born and raised in Philly. The closest
I'd come to botany was playing Frisbee in Fairmount Park.
The closest I'd come to farming was picking apples at an
orchard in Pennsylvania Dutch country during an elementary school field trip. Like many of my colleagues, I didn't
join the Peace Corps because I had some expertise I had
to share with the world. Some of us joined because we
wanted to have an adventure or because we didn't know
what we wanted to do. Some joined to see the world.
Others joined to hide from it. In the end, it didn't matter.
We had gone. And those who didn't quit would grow
strong and make change despite themselves.

Regardless, Carlos had taught me a bit about rice farming, organic fertilizers, and contour planting. I could share those techniques with my neighbors right away. Beyond that, I'd have to read a lot and experiment. Eventually, I'd teach myself about animal husbandry, seed preservation, and a host of other subjects related to sustainable agriculture on a tight budget. If any of my suggestions didn't work out, I'd bullshit my way though the failures. I'd blame my limited language skills or remind my neighbors that I'm from the States where the climate and soils are different. We would just have to modify our approach and try again. Wink, wink.

Eduardo and I waited on my porch for a bus to rumble by. "We're going to a town called *Penonomé*," he explained. "It's the capital of our province: *Coclé*." Eduardo beamed with pride as he talked about his home. "*Penonomé* is located on the Zarati River. When we get to town I will show you a place where the *gringos* once put a medallion into a stone. The stone says it is the center of our country. The *gringos* did that," he repeated, as though if the *gringos* did it, it had to be true.

"Very interesting."

He nodded. "I went to school until sixth grade," he boasted. "I still remember everything they taught me. My teacher told us that the Spanish settlers founded *Penonomé* on the ruins of an ancient indian village. *Nomé* was the name of the chief of the indian tribe. You get it?"

"Not really."

"They killed *Nomé*." He smiled and nodded with raised eyebrows as he waited for it to sink in. Then it dawned on me that "*Penó Nomé*" literally means "Nome was punished." I gave Eduardo the benefit of the doubt

74

and assumed he was smiling about the play on words and interesting history lesson rather than the execution of an indigenous leader. After all, like most everyone in *Los Altos*, Jose and Eduardo's faces showed they had plenty of indigenous blood running through their veins.

Once in *Penonomé*, Eduardo pointed out the post office so I could mail a couple of letters. Then we made our way to the market place. The Peace Corps had given me $300 for "moving-in" money. Some of my peers would need that money to build themselves houses, but since I had the rental deal squared away, I could blow it all on furnishings. I felt embarrassed spending so much money in front of Eduardo, and I didn't want him and the rest of the town getting the idea that I was filthy rich. But there was probably no escaping that anyway. Even if I was dirt poor by my own standards, I was pretty wealthy compared to almost everyone in *Los Altos*. Only the bus drivers and store owners earned more money than me.

In less than two hours I acquired the material elements of a life: I bought a mattress, a set of sheets, a towel, a set of plastic hangers, a two-burner propane stove (along with a large tank of propane gas), two pots, one frying pan, a spatula, a pasta strainer, two sets of cutlery, two sets of plastic flatware, two wooden tables, and two wooden chairs. I also bought a shovel, a pick-axe, a rake, a hammer, nails, a handsaw, some fence wire, a tape measure, two kerosene lanterns, and some candles. I felt insecure buying so much stuff in front of Eduardo and I wished I could have pulled it off alone, but I was glad to have the tour guide and he didn't seem to take offense. In fact, I would have forgotten the kerosene lanterns if Eduardo hadn't suggested them. He also encouraged me to buy a *sombrero* for working in the fields. In retrospect, I think he enjoyed the spending more than I did. His broad smile, nonjudgmental demeanor, and endless patience reassured me that he was a good man. I was lucky to have such a good-natured ally so shortly after arriving in town.

After we finished shopping, the bus to *Los Altos* stopped at all the different stores I patronized before it headed out of town. I felt embarrassed that all the passengers had to wait while the driver's assistant loaded my newly acquired stuff onto the roof of the bus, but no one seemed to mind. No one was in a rush.

As soon as we returned from *Penonomé*, Eduardo helped me carry my belongings up to my house before he bid me goodnight.

"Eduardo, thank you. You help me much."

"Don't worry yourself."

"How much do I owe you?"

He smiled a smile that communicated more than words ever could; the thought of charging me for his help had obviously never crossed his mind. He mulled the concept over for a couple of seconds. I felt both dirty and dumb.

"You don't owe me anything. Welcome to *Los Altos*. Good night."

"Thank you Eduardo."

I lit up the kerosene lanterns so I could see what I was doing and I got straight to work. One of the tables became my kitchen; the other would be both my desk and dining table.

I didn't have any closets or dressers, so I made the most of the walls. I used as many nails as I had excuses for. My machete hung from a nail. My shovel hung from a nail. My pots and pan hung from nails over the kitchen table. My Phillies cap and new *sombrero* hung from nails in the rafters. By the time I finished, even my hammer was nailed to the wall.

Next, I went outside, found a nearby tree, and cut down a long, straight branch about two fingers thick. Then I took two pieces of nylon string and tied them very loosely around opposite ends of one of the rafters. I hung each end of the branch inside the nylon loops and *voila*: I had a place to hang my hangers.

Lastly, I lay my mattress down on the floor and hoped that nothing would cozy up next to me in the night. I was short on furnishings, but long on possibility. *Timshel* was quickly becoming a home.

The next morning, I asked around town until someone directed me to a man who could sell me some wood.

"Good morning," I called out from his gate at the edge of the road.

"Good morning," a voice called back.

A shirtless man walked out of the house and greeted me in the front yard. A woman and young girl stood in the doorway behind him. Random bits of lumber were piled neatly all over the property. A chainsaw leaned up against the front wall of the house. I knew I was in the right place.

"I call myself Juan," I announced so they could all hear as I shook the man's hand. "I'm the new Peace Corps Volunteer and I arrived to the community this week."

"Welcome. I call myself Enrique. This is my wife, Marcella, and my daughter Lucila." His wife smiled and nodded at me. The daughter just stared with disbelieving eyes. "How can I attend to you?"

"I need a bed."

"You want me to build it or you just want the wood?"

"I just want the wood."

I had never built anything in my life, but I looked forward to the opportunity. Enrique cut the wood from several long planks that lay under a tarp against the side of the house. He marked off straight lines with a string soaked in oil and then he pulled the start rope on his chainsaw. He must have sensed my ignorance, or maybe he just assumed no *gringos* knew anything useful, because after he cut the wood, he laid all the different pieces out on the ground and showed me how they fit together to build a bed.

"How much do I owe you?"

"Six dollars." I paid him and started to gather up the wood. "Wait," he called, and beckoned me to the house, "give me a minute." He said something to his wife that I didn't catch before she turned and disappeared into the back of the house. As I stood in his doorway wondering what was next, I admired a bookshelf in the front room. A few minutes later his wife handed him a bag of oranges which he then handed to me. "They're good for juice," he told me.

"Thank you. Very kind. Can you cut me wood for something like that too?" motioned towards the book-shelf.

"No problem."

As I carried my lumber on my shoulder and made my way back home, I doubted my furniture would look as sharp as Enrique's, but I was up for the challenge. I took my hammer down off the wall and got to work. *Even the simplest of beds takes some time to build. Don't think about the finished project. Don't worry about what the whole thing will look like when you finish; instead, focus on one nail at a time.* I knew that some people, like Enrique and Eduardo, could probably hammer the nail home in one smooth stroke, but I couldn't. *Best to concentrate on each swing of the hammer. Don't get caught up on what you can't do; don't get too pleased when you hit the nail well; don't get too angry when you hit the nail badly. Don't even imagine how it will turn out, for what I imagine is just that: imaginary. Best to concentrate on the stroke at hand. Focus on the moment and a positive outcome will follow.*

Of course, none of that stopped me from screaming profanity and kicking the pile of wood and hurting my toes when I missed the nail and smashed the hammer into my thumb. My frustration raged to near-insanity as I had to re-straighten nail after bent nail. I recalled my own advice and simmered back down, only to boil over, over and over. Finally, the piece of shit was finished. It looked like the whole bed might come crashing down if I broke wind in the wrong direction. The bookshelf wasn't much better. But I had a rickety place to rest my head and a precarious place to put my books.

Sigh.

Chapter 13 – Naked Little Face

Even though Alejandra cooked my dinner most nights, she was usually too busy attending to the kitchen to spend any time with me. Instead, her younger sister Lola kept me company at the dinner table. Lola was 19 years old, less than five feet tall, and couldn't have weighed more than ninety pounds. She had deep chocolate eyes and freckles and a decent sense of humor. Each morning, she woke up at four to catch the *chiva* and take the three-and-a-half-hour ride to *Penonomé*. She was studying to become an elementary school teacher at the university there. I admired her dedication. I also admired her small, perky breasts. And I liked to stare at her ass when she walked. She could wiggle it in a way American girls never did. I spent a lot of nights making love to myself as I imagined what she looked like naked.

"How's your work going?" Lola asked me one night as I ate my dinner.

"Ok, I guess. I work with the Ojo family sometimes, but I would like to work with more than just one family."

"Have you been to *El Futuro* yet?"

"What's that?"

"It's a cooperative here. It just started."

"No. I haven't even heard about it. What do they do?"

"I don't know much about it really. I think they're building a farm. The government bought the land for them and gave them tools."

"That sounds really good. I've heard a lot of people here say the Panamanian government doesn't do anything."

"It doesn't. Groups like this start up all the time. The government extension agents visit a couple of times at the beginning and hand out some seeds or some tools, and then they never come again. Once the handouts stop, the members of the cooperative start to bicker and the farm dies. Still, I thought you should know about it."

"Maybe this one will be different," I suggested. "Maybe I can help them. Do you know where it is?"

"I think so."

"Will you take me?"

"I have to go to school tomorrow, but if you can wait until the weekend, I'll show you."

On Saturday morning, Lola came by my house with her two little nieces. We walked twenty minutes up the steep road before Lola stopped. I could barely keep up with her.

"This trail leads to the house of the president of the cooperative. His name is Mateo. The farm is right behind his house. I'll see you at dinner tonight, ok?"

"You're not going to introduce me? I don't know anyone here," I protested.

"I don't want people talking about me. I don't want Mateo getting the wrong idea about you and me either."

"Just from walking me here?"

"This is a small town. You know the expression . . . small town, big fire."

"Alright, thanks." Lola turned and left as I braved the steep path to Mateo's house. "Good morning," I called as I reached the house, out of breath. A naked baby played with a toy car on the front porch.

"Good morning," a man called back. He had short white hair and looked to be in his sixties. He was barefoot and shirtless. His gnarled, calloused feet looked thicker than the soles of my boots and I got the impression that his brown, round paunch had seen its fair share of sun during the last half-century.

"My name is Juan. I'm the new Volunteer of the Peace Corps. I'm looking for Mateo."

"I'm Mateo."

"Much pleasure. They tell me that you're the president of the cooperative. I hope that you will show me your group's farm."

"Of course."

Working with the men, I told myself, would be a good way to earn their trust, but I knew the Peace Corps hadn't sent me there to provide manual labor. Instead, my job was to teach about environmentally friendly, sustainable farming. I stayed up late each night and read books on horticulture, vermiculture, and agroforestry. Although I'd never put the techniques into practice, they seemed straightforward enough and I was pretty sure I could explain them correctly. I crammed as much technical information into my head as I could.

For the next few weeks I tried to help them build the place. At first, I could last only an hour or so. Panama is barely nine degrees north of the Equator, but that fact doesn't really sink in until you've rid a hillside of brush with a machete in one hand and a clearing stick in the other. And the sun was only part of the problem. The brush we cleared grew tall, over our heads, and swallowed us whole. Razor-edged leaves scratched my face and neck and bare arms. Thousands of thorns tore my clothes and ripped my skin.

Eventually, we cleared all the brush. A trickle of water flowed lazily through the bottom of the valley. Hillsides stretched up and away on both sides. We had our canvas. I implored the men to let me help develop the farm's layout and much to my surprise, they agreed.

We dug out the land to broaden and flatten the narrow valley bottom. It took much less time than I'd imagined. The amount that could be accomplished by ten men using only machetes, pickaxes, shovels, wheel barrows, and strong backs was extraordinary. They had no idea they were dirt-moving artists; for them it was just another week of manual labor.

I, on the other hand, could work for only a short time before my red, raw palms would swell. Then my blisters burst and my hands began to bleed. At that point, I'd swallow my pride and say goodbye and leave for the day. I felt like a sissy, but the men never treated me with disdain. Rather, they seemed to appreciate my willingness to work alongside them. I think they also liked that I was learning how hard their work was. And they never mocked my fragility, at least not to my face. But I grew more accustomed to the sun with each passing day. Soon, the blisters turned to calluses. I'd last two hours at a time, then three, then through lunch like the other men. After a few weeks my skin browned and toughened; my forearms grew thick and sinewy. My back was strong. I'd swing a pick or a shovel all day long like the rest of them. I felt fierce.

During that time, however, I had my first Aralen dream. I was a senior in high school again, but I'd transferred from my public alma mater, Lower Merion, to attend Episcopal Academy, an expensive private school and one of our cross-town rivals. I was new and awkward and attempting to play football in preseason try-outs. But I was graceless on the football field. I dropped balls and tripped over my own feet and felt generally stupid.

None of the other players let me sit with them in the posh dining room where the school served us lunch. I sat alone at a table and watched the other boys laugh at me. I envied their shouting and their horse-play. I hated them for excluding me from it. I had transferred to the school only to play football and it was going horribly wrong. I suddenly realized what I'd given up by leaving Lower Merion, the prom, and graduation. In short, I'd forsaken the warmth of familiarity. The feeling of sadness was overwhelming. I hadn't felt such profound insecurity since my early teenage years.

I woke to the sound of flapping wings. Something had inadvertently flown inside my house and couldn't find its way out. Since it was the middle of the night, I figured it was probably a bat. Any sensible bird would have been sound asleep. I hated bats. I knew that most bats ate only fruit or pollen or insects, but knowing that some of them were carnivorous gave me the heebie jeebies. And I couldn't tell the difference between one bat and another. But my dream had defeated me and I felt too exhausted to challenge my uninvited guest. Besides, bats were farmers' friends; they pollinated flowers and spread seeds and ate insects. I was safe inside my mosquito net.

The sound of his beating wings woke me up a few more times throughout the night, but I told myself that he'd eventually find his way back outside. Each time I drifted back to sleep. In the morning, however, when enough sunlight had penetrated my house, I saw that the bat was *inside* my mosquito net.

His startled, naked little face peered down at me. He didn't even have the decency to wear fur. He flew desperately from one side of my bed to the other where he'd inevitably get his nasty, short claws stuck in the mosquito netting. Then he'd crawl up the netting to the seam at the top and fly back to the other side before doing it all over again, glaring angrily at me all the while.

His hideous, frenzied expression was too much to bear that early in the morning, so I dove out of bed and crashed onto the floor. I scrambled to my feet and danced frantically on my tip-toes, flapping my arms like a deranged chicken as I held up the corner of the mosquito net between thumb and forefinger. "Get the *fuck* out of here!" I yelled at him.

Finally, after what felt like an eternity, but couldn't have been more than a minute, the tiny beast found his way out of my bed. He was still in my house, but at least he was outside of the mosquito net. With my head pulled down into my shoulders like a frightened turtle, I clumsily dressed and fled. He'd have to find his way out of my home and back to his roost all on his own. Bastard.

Chapter 14 – Dangling Receiver

On my three month anniversary in my site I made myself what had become my usual breakfast: a two-egg, tomato and onion omelet. The eggs often came for free from the farmers I worked with, but if I didn't have any I could just walk down the road to the general store and buy them for a dime each. I always had to buy the onions at the store because it was too hot and humid to grow them in *Los Altos*; they always seemed to rot before they were ready for harvest. The tomatoes, however, came straight from my own garden and gave me great pride.

As I was sitting down to my meal, a young boy arrived, out of breath, panting on my doorstep. He was no more than 7 or 8 years old. I'd never seen him before.

"You have a call," he gasped.

"You're sure?"

"Yes. Come," he beckoned.

I'd written the number of the town's lone pay phone on the Peace Corps' emergency contact form, only because the office had required it. I hadn't bothered giving the number to anyone else because the phone was too far from my house to serve any practical purpose. I hoped nothing terrible had happened, either at home in Philly or within my Peace Corps family.

I stumbled after him in my flip flops as we ran down the dirt road. A few grubby children gathered around the phone, for this was high entertainment in *Los Altos*. They were going to get to listen to the *gringo* speak English, a feat they found uproarious. I pushed past them and grabbed the dangling receiver.

"Hello?"

"It took you long enough." I recognized the voice right away. Elena.

"How are you?" I huffed, out of breath from the run. The children around me covered their mouths and giggled to one another.

"You sound out of shape," she teased. "Anyway, I'm in the neighborhood and thought I'd say hi."

"Right."

"No, seriously. There's a beach in your province called *Santa Clara*. It's beautiful. I found it last night. I'm at a place called 'Excess.' Can you come meet me here?"

"Yes."

"I'll wait for you then."

I ran all the way home and stuffed a few things into a daypack. Then I stood at the side of the road and waited impatiently for a bus to come through. I caught a break forty minutes later when an ambulance came barreling down the mountain. The lights and sirens were off, so I assumed it was returning to *Penonomé* after an uneventful call further up the road. Then I wondered if there was a corpse in the back.

I stuck out my arm and waived my index finger up and down and I got lucky. The ambulance stopped in front of me and a cloud of dust swirled up around the tires. Two men – the driver and his colleague – looked at me through the passenger side window to see what I wanted.

"Can you give me a ride?"

"Where are you going?"

"Only the highway."

"It's fine. Come."

"Many thanks."

I walked around back of the ambulance and to my surprise, when I opened the door, I encountered not a cadaver, but a toothless, old woman strapped to the gurney. She was like an ancient baby, drooling and detached. Two more women, who I gathered were her daughters, tended to her and wiped her mouth. I'd never seen any of them before. After saying hello and taking my seat, I decided I wouldn't speak unless spoken to.

Half-way down the mountain, the old woman seemed to notice me for the first time. Then she stared out the back window with wide, glassy eyes as the landscape disappeared behind us. I followed her gaze and imagined she thought she'd died and was being driven into the next world, escorted by a pale-faced *gringo* angel and her two daughters. She looked scared, so I tried to give her a comforting smile.

After the bizarre, bumpy, three-hour ride down the mountain, the ambulance dropped me off on the shoulder of the Inter-American Highway. I shut the doors and thumped the side of the ambulance with the palm of my hand to let them know I was clear. Then I waved goodbye as the ambulance kicked up more dust and sped away towards the hospital in *Penonomé*.

It didn't take long for me to catch a bus going in the opposite direction and I arrived in *Santa Clara* just forty minutes later. "Excess" wasn't too hard to find. Only the place wasn't called "Excess." It was "XS." The word play made sense in English, but in Spanish the sign didn't read "Excess." It said *"equis ese."* The name made no sense to any of the locals. Maybe that was the point.

A tall concrete block wall enclosed the four acre property. In the middle there was a restaurant with a large patio out front. To the side of the patio there was a pool and a huge, open-air *rancho* with hammocks strung up. It looked like a comfortable place to lounge in the shade and read a book or take a nap. There were three modest guest cabins to one side of the restaurant and plenty of spots where a backpacker could set up a tent if he was low on cash. Parrots, toucans, ducks, cats, and a monkey named Yoda populated the sprawling grounds. A good-natured Doberman named Joy kept them all in line and watched over the place at night.

The bar itself was a classic American sports bar dropped into the tropics. The legs of the tables had been cut and sanded to look like baseball bats. Glass table tops covered trading cards and ticket stubs and other random bits of memorabilia. Every inch of the walls was covered with photos and posters and pennants. The owners had every sport and team covered with an obvious bias for the Pittsburgh Steelers.

A grizzled Vietnam vet named Dennis owned the place. He had a wispy blonde mullet, mischievous blue eyes, and a U.S. Marine Corps tattoo on his forearm. A bushy mustache anchored his tan, leathery face and gave him the appearance of a walrus that had spent too much time toiling in the sun. Later he'd tell me that he built the place with his wife, Sheila. She was so tall and thin that she looked like she might shatter if she tripped and fell. She kept her waist-length hair tied back so it didn't get in the way when she was flipping the best burgers in the province. The two of them met out in Las Vegas when he worked on the tarmac at the airport and she danced at one of the big hotels. Then one morning, during a particularly ambitious bout of pillow talk, they decided to discard their lives, buy an RV, and travel south. They didn't stop until they found the land that would become XS.

At one time the property had belonged to Manuel Noriega's bean counter. But in 1989, the U.S. Army drove through the front gate and destroyed the place as part of Operation Just Cause. After the invasion, locals looted the property for everything it was worth, down to the tile and wiring, before it was left in disrepair for several years.

By the time Dennis and Sheila's RV pulled up, nature had reclaimed what was left of the main house. Trees sprouted through the floor and rose nearly to the ceiling. The place was fit only for the iguanas and bats and mice that had made the place their home.

Because the property was so disheveled, Dennis and Sheila had bought it for a pittance. The concrete block wall alone, reasoned Dennis, made the property worth buying. If nothing else, the place was secure.

Chapter 15 – The Size of Rhode Island

By the time I arrived at XS, the manicured grounds revealed no indication of their historic past. I walked thirty yards down the long gravel driveway and found Elena sitting alone at one of the patio tables. She was absorbed in a book, so I walked to the bar, quietly ordered a beer, and watched her read. I didn't want to disturb her just yet. She was too nice to look at.

After several minutes, she looked up from her book and noticed me.

"Hey!" she called. "What are you doing over there?"

"Just admiring the view."

"I'm glad you made it," she said, ignoring the compliment. She got up and gave me a warm hug before I took a seat at her table. "I already have a room here. There's plenty of room for both of us. I figured we could split the cost and save some cash."

"Alright. Thanks. You looked pretty absorbed by whatever you're reading."

"I'm into it." She held up the worn cover to show me a yellowed, dog-eared copy of The World According to Garp. "I found it in the Volunteer lounge on my way out here. It's really good. I'll give it to you when I'm done. Have you been reading anything lately?"

"Mostly I've been writing. I've been reading some too though. I just read The Grapes of Wrath again. It's even better when you read it down here, in the hills, amidst the *campesinos*. Sometimes it depresses me though."

"It's not exactly an uplifting book. I remember it from high school."

"I know, but that's not really what I mean. The book itself is extraordinary. It breathes with real people and textured scenery, and above all, it has purpose. It's truly genius. I read it and sigh."

"So you'll never be Steinbeck?"

"To put it kindly. But I love sitting in that house in the hills and writing for hours on end. Sometimes I get so excited that I drop my pen and jump from my desk and dance with my shadow as it flickers on the wall. It probably sounds crazy to you, but I've never been so happy as when I'm living in the soft glow of my kerosene lamp."

"It does sound a little nutty, but I'm glad you're so happy out there."

After several weeks in *Los Altos*, the sound of English set to Elena's tune poured over me like cold, liquid music. Her voice was soothing and hypnotic. I found myself grinning from ear to ear. I had thought I'd been happy in *Los Altos*, but as I sat there with Elena, giddy like an idiot, I realized what profound happiness really is. I had to concentrate just to stay in the conversation.

"How's it going out there in *Quebrada Brava?*"

"Oh," she answered contemplatively, seemingly taken aback by the simple question. "It's . . . hard."

Our world deflated just a little.

"The men assume I don't know anything and the women don't seem to trust me. They seem to think I'm going to steal their husbands or something. The only people who even talk to me are the kids." Her voice revealed an unsettling chink in her otherwise unbridled enthusiasm. "I've been trying to teach some English to

92

some of the kids," she added cheerlessly, "but that only takes up a few hours a week. Mostly, I just read books and write in my journal."

"That actually sounds kind of nice," I offered, trying to inspire her characteristic optimism. "And I'm sure they'll warm up to you once they figure you out."

"I thought so too, but it gets old. I didn't join the Peace Corps to read books. I want to do *something*. But like I said, the men don't believe there's anything I can teach them, so I'm not sure why I bother. Besides, most of them aren't interested in learning anything from a blonde, *gringa* girl."

"What *are* they interested in?"

"Mostly they just want to shrimp and fish and clam. They clam a lot. The rest of them spend their days hunting with spears, blowguns, and arrows dipped in poison extracted from venomous frogs."

"That sounds pretty badass actually."

"It is pretty badass," she agreed. "And it was fine once upon a time, but I'm afraid it can't last. Their resources are disappearing. The *colonos* are taking over."

"*Colonos*?"

"*Colonos* are what the people in my town call the cowboys from the *Azuero*. They've already clear-cut their own land in western Panama," Elena continued, a sharper edge creeping into her voice, "so now they're moving into *Darien* and *Panama Este*. And when they're not ranching, they're logging. The forest where I live is supposed to be protected land, but the Panamanian government doesn't have the resources to enforce the law. The honest cops are too busy chasing drug traffickers or Colombian guerillas and the rest of them are too busy getting bribed. That means there's something like twenty people to protect 600,000 hectares at the national park in *Darien*. It's insanity to think *twenty* park rangers can patrol a piece of land that big."

"That does sound pretty ridiculous."

"And many of the rangers don't even have vehicles or radios, let alone guns. We're talking about a place that's like *twice* the size of Rhode Island!"

"It's like we live in different countries."

"Well, that's one of the things that's so amazing about Panama," she added, lightening up just a bit. "You know there are more species of plants and birds in this country than in the rest of North America *combined*?"

"No. I didn't."

She must've seen the consternation on my face because she stopped and took a breath. "Look, it boils down to this: these cowboys have brought their chainsaws and their cattle into some of the most pristine tropical rainforests in the world and no one is doing a damn thing about it. They illegally cut down trees that are hundreds of years old in order to harvest the lumber and plant grasses and let their cattle graze there. After the cows ravage one field, the cowboys move to another area, set up another temporary camp, and hack down even more trees."

"That doesn't sound good."

"It's not good. What frustrates me the most is that the *colonos* don't even seem to realize there's anything wrong with what they're doing. They don't understand that when the trees go, the water goes too. They'll wonder why their farming and ranching isn't as good as it used to be. And with no water, of course, then the insects go, and the fish go and birds and animals go too. Maybe by then they'll get it, but by then who cares? The damage will be done and the ecosystem will be gone forever! And what if some exotic plant or funky bird in the jungle they're decimating holds the cure to cancer or AIDS? These cowboys might be screwing the entire human race and no one is doing a damn thing about it."

"I guess that's why they need you."

"I don't know. Maybe. Sorry to get all psycho on you."

"It's fine. You've probably had it bottled up for a while."

"On the bright side, my house should be complete in a few weeks, so that should be an improvement." She regained control of her voice and emotion. "What about you? What's it like in *Los Altos*?"

"Everything's good. I like my town." I didn't want to tell her how easy it had been for me. By comparison, my community's development issues seemed insignificant. Also, Alejandra and Jose and Eduardo had been so receptive to my arrival. I told her about *El Futuro* and a few of the workshops I'd put together, but I kept it brief. "Oh, I almost forgot, have you seen the new pirate movie?"

"Have you been listening to anything I've been saying? I live in the middle of a jungle that no one has even heard of."

"It's rated Arrggghhhhh!" I growled as I twisted one hand into the shape of a hook and used my other hand as a patch to cover my eye.

"That's terrible," she answered. But she laughed. It always made me happy to hear her laugh. I was also glad to get her mind off of *Quebrada Brava*.

95

An old man who sat by himself at a nearby table was chuckling at my feeble joke. A mesh baseball cap sat atop his otherwise bald head. He held a can of Budweiser between both hands and rested it on his paunch.

He called over to us, "I couldn't help but hear some of your conversation. You kids are in the Peace Corps I take it?"

"That's right."

"Good for you. May I buy you a round?"

"Absolutely," I said.

"Thank you," Elena added. We got up and moved over to his table. We introduced ourselves and he told us his name was Doug Butler.

"Hey Dennis, get these kids a beer on me."

"What'll you guys have?" Dennis asked.

"I'll have an *HB*," Elena answered.

"Me too," I added. "These tables are really cool. Where'd you get 'em?"

The table tops were thick slices of a felled tree trunk. They were about one foot thick and four feet in diameter. The base of the table was a thinner piece of tree trunk. Both the top and the base had been sanded flat and varnished, but Dennis' customers could still count the tree's many rings. The tables were beautiful in their simplicity.

"I made them myself. The trees used to line the Inter-American Highway, but the government cut them down when they widened the highway. In typical Panamanian fashion, they just left the trees on the sides of the road when they were done. No one seemed interested in doing anything with them, so I figured I might as well try to make use of the free wood." With that he shrugged and turned to get our beers. It sounded like Dennis could teach the cowboys out in Darien some lessons on wasting natural resources.

"I like your macaw," Elena commented. "He's beautiful." I hadn't even noticed him, but sure enough, just past the edge of the patio, a large, blue macaw shimmied from side to side on the tree branch above his open cage. "I'm surprised he doesn't fly away though. Do you clip his wings?"

"There's no need. He doesn't know how to fly."

"How can that be?"

"An old woman here in *Santa Clara* got him when he was just a baby. She had two of them actually. The one you see there, Paco, used to have a wife. The old woman kept both of them in a small cage their whole lives, so they never learned how to fly. That's why I just leave the cage open. He sleeps in there, but he spends most of the day just walking around in the branches of that tree." Dennis crooked his thumbs into his armpits and shimmied from side to side on the patio doing his best macaw imper-sonation.

"Anyway, the woman who owned the birds got older and she couldn't take care of them anymore. Her kids were all grown and lived in Panama City, so they asked if we'd take the birds. Obviously we said yes, but we didn't know what we were getting into. When the birds got here they were underweight and had big patches of missing feathers. They were awful looking. We gave them vitamins and supplements. We did everything we could think of, but they didn't get any better. And they were mean. We had to warn the tourists not to go too near to them because we were afraid they'd bite someone's finger off.

"We had a vet come out and take a look at them. He told us they were at least thirty years old, but he couldn't say for sure. He also swore that apart from their appearance, there wasn't anything wrong with them. We had our doubts, but what could we do? Then, a few weeks later, we came outside one morning and the female was dead in the bottom of the cage."

"That sucks," Elena answered.

"Not so fast." Dennis smiled.

"Huh?"

"Paco's ol' lady dropping dead was just what the doctor ordered. Within a couple of months, all of Paco's missing feathers filled in. His chest puffed out. He strutted around with a new lease on life.

"It turned out the only thing that had been bugging those birds was the stress of living with each other. Who knows how many years she'd been nagging him. I've never seen such a relieved bird. In fact, that bird never said a single word the whole time his wife was around, but now he hardly shuts up. He can speak Spanish and English and he must be twice as full of dirty words as he is full of those big bright feathers. He sits up in that tree all day and laughs at my customers who look for him in his empty cage. And as to snapping at fingers, he's so mellow now that he even lets me scratch his neck."

"No way," Elena said.

"Way. I'll swear to it too." Dennis raised three fingers as though to give us his Scout's Honor. "Sheila?" he called into the restaurant.

"It's true," Sheila confirmed, "but I'm sure Paco nagged her plenty too. Dropping dead was the poor lady's only way out."

"It kind of makes you think," Dennis added, raising his eyebrows at Elena before winking at me. Before Elena had a chance to protest or point out that we weren't even a couple, Doug spoke back up.

"So you guys are on the front lines?"

"Well I don't know about that," Elena answered.

"Yes you are lassie. Believe me, I know. I served two tours in Korea and two tours in Vietnam. Seventh Cavalry." As Dennis served us our beers, he looked me hard in the eye for an exaggerated moment, as though to say "recognize who you're sitting with young man."

"You two," Doug said as he pointed at each of us in turn, "*are* the first lines of defense."

"Well thanks," I said, "and thank you for *your* service." He nodded and raised his can of beer as though to toast the sentiment.

"Your parents should be proud of you for the sacrifice you're making," he added.

"It doesn't *feel* like much of a sacrifice," I told him.

"I think you're on to something there," Doug answered. "After all, there are different kinds of wealth, right? There's money and there's time. We've chosen time."

Chapter 16 – Black Stars

That night Elena and I walked down the road to the empty beach and took a swim in the ocean. We floated on our backs in the warm, calm water and stared at the stars. Every time we moved, the water lit up and trailed off our limbs in a tremendous blue glow, as though someone had broken open a Phish concert and poured it into our bath. I'd never seen anything like it. Elena explained that they were blooms of bioluminescent dinoflagellates, tiny plants which live in the sea and obtain energy from sunlight during the day. For a kid from Philadelphia, it was other-worldly. Elena couldn't help but laugh at my wonderment. We walked back to XS and air-dried along the way.

"You know," I told her as we walked along the dark road on a quiet night, "I've had a really good couple of weeks in *Los Altos* . . ."

"I can tell," she said, cutting me off before I'd said my piece. "It sounds like you have some good projects going. I knew you would."

". . . but this is by far the greatest day I've had in this country."

"*Really?*"

The surprise in her voice caught me off guard. And as happens sometimes, the moment settled and hovered and lasted for much more than a moment. Sound stopped and movement stopped for far longer than a moment. And when I finally turned to look, I found her staring at me with big, soft eyes, as though trying to make sense of what I'd just said. She couldn't find it in herself to believe that a day spent only with her could be that great.

And that sort of modesty was just one of the many things that made her so special.

When we got back to XS the bar was closed and everyone seemed to have gone to bed, so Elena and I sat on the foot of the bed in our room and smoked a joint. Elena seemed to get more loquacious the more she smoked, whereas I became a paranoid introvert, too stoned for the intricacies of human interaction. I reduced my end of the conversation to smiles and nods, afraid that if I dared say anything I would reveal the imbecile I knew myself to be.

Elena told tales and giggled at her own funny jokes. I laughed with her and met her eyes to show my appreciation. Her eyes betrayed all the modesty of her unassuming, hunched-up body language. Her posture said she was sweet and innocent, but the eyes told me she could have her way with me. I imagined she was gifted in the arts of love.

I tried to tell her a story, but I held her gaze too long and got dizzy and lost my speech and had to look away so she couldn't read the thoughts I imagined I wore too obviously. I could see lightning bolts flashing in her pupils. I wondered what she could see in mine.

She bit her lip and looked as though I might not want her. It made me adore her. I summoned the courage to put my hand, ever so briefly, on her knee. She jumped suddenly to her feet.

"It's getting late. I'm going to take a shower."

"Sounds good," I answered, but I was really thinking, *shit . . . you mistook her charm and the fun we were having for romance and seduction and now she thinks you're creepy and she has to share a room with you.*

Even if the window of opportunity had opened a crack and let in the fair breeze of possibility – and I wasn't sure it had – I imagined my presumptuousness slammed that window shut before the winds of passion could cross its frame. When Elena walked into the bathroom with her towel slung over her shoulder and her soap and shampoo clutched against her chest, I could feel whatever magic had been in the room wash out behind her, like a wayward astronaut blown off the face of the moon, tumbling backwards, head over heels, into cold, dark space.

I felt very confused as I lay down on the bed and stared at the ceiling. Had I mistaken her inherent goodness for something more? Either way, I knew there was no place on earth I'd rather be than our modest motel room at XS. And that was before she stepped out of the bathroom wearing only a smirk.

But she was definitely not the same woman who had stumbled senselessly from a different bathroom in a different hotel at a different time in our lives, for a rush of blood surged to her face and the only way she could think to hide it was to climb into the bed, throw her arms around my neck and give me a hard, passionate kiss that lasted until we were both gasping for breath. We made out for what seemed like an hour. Then she wriggled down to the foot of the bed where she climbed between my legs and took me in her mouth. I put my head back and lost my fingers in her wild, curly hair. *She likes you too.*

A few minutes into the bliss I noticed the mirror on the back of the open bathroom door. I watched her undulating ass and the treasure between her legs in the reflection of the mirror as I simultaneously watched her beautiful face appear and disappear and reappear under her untamed locks. And her obliviousness to the mirror and my private musings made it all the more salacious.

And then the tension. Flashing black stars.

Elena wiping at the corner of her mouth with the top of her thumb.

Thick, cloudy slumber.

In the morning, I woke to find Elena's naked body sleeping peacefully with her back turned to me. I propped myself up on one elbow and stared at her curves and lines and perfect bottom. When I couldn't wait any longer, I cupped her ass in my palm and whispered light kisses on the back of her neck.

She woke up slowly and shrank away from the tickle of the kisses before she climbed out of bed and ran daintily to the bathroom. It occurred to me only then that she'd allowed her pubic hair to grow back. I liked it the other way, but I couldn't hold her grooming habits against her. *Quebrada Brava* surely wasn't the easiest place to perform such maintenance. I lay back and listened to her pee and brush her teeth; I relished her morning sounds.

I climbed out of bed when I heard the shower get going. Elena's Peace Corps-issued life preserver sat on the floor next to her pack. The Peace Corps required her to wear it when she made the river trips in and out of her village. But none of the locals used a life jacket, so Elena never wore hers. She didn't want to be the only person on board strapped into a floatation device like some sort of idiot princess. Nonetheless, she carried it for show; she couldn't be seen traveling without it if she were to bump into Grace or Christine or any other members of the staff.

I figured someone should get some use out of it, so I pulled it on and crept stealthily into the shower. She was rinsing her hair and didn't see me until she opened her eyes. Then she laughed an easy, joyful laugh that I never tired of.

"I don't think you'll need that in here."

"But I'm not that strong a swimmer," I explained.

"I'll keep an eye on you."

I kissed her on the mouth as she soaped me up. Her coarse pubic hair felt good in my palm. I had a couple of fingers inside her before she pulled away and turned her back on me. She bent over for me and placed her palms flat against the wall under the shower head. So I poked around for a moment and found her and she let out a little groan.

"I won't move," I told her, "just back up on me."

She pushed slowly towards me and took me until I was all the way home. Then she started to rock her hips back and forth and arched her back so that her belly was nearly parallel with the floor. Her wet blonde hair stuck to her scalp and fell down past her shoulders. I unclipped the buckles on the life preserver so I could enjoy the view sliding in and out of her, but I liked the view too much and I could barely hold on. I wanted her to have more, so I bit my lip and pulled away, letting it cool down a bit and catch its breath in the open air.

Elena spun around, confused. She wanted to know what was wrong, but she looked down and saw I still had a hard-on. The look in her eyes was like nothing I'd ever seen before. I couldn't tell if she was relieved or furious. "Don't ever take it out again," she warned me.

I pushed her up against the wall and reached under her legs with both hands and hoisted her up so she could wrap her legs around me and I was inside her again. She threw her arms around my neck and I had to press her into the shower wall to keep from dropping her. She thrashed about and came again and again. We exchanged deep, sloppy kisses until I couldn't take it anymore.

"It's ok," she panted, "you can finish inside me. . . . I'm on the pill."

She didn't need to tell me twice.

Chapter 17 – Meaty Paws

Back in *Los Altos*, I woke up with a head cold. I ran out of eggs. The neighborhood kids had lost my Frisbee.

You've worked hard lately. You deserve a day off. After all, it's not like you have to punch a clock. Relax around the house. Get well. You've earned it.

After breakfast, I decided to get high. For obvious reasons I couldn't smoke in the hammock on my porch in broad daylight, so I took a seat at my desk. Because it was relatively dark in my house and I was up on a hillside, I could see out and admire the view, but passersby couldn't see in.

To my disappointment, I found all my rolling papers stuck together. The inescapable humidity got to them because I hadn't yet learned to store them in a sealed plastic bag. So I cautiously pulled them apart to make sure none of them ripped. That would be tragic, for I couldn't exactly buy more at the corner store.

After separating the papers, I slowly rolled up a thin joint with a bit of the Panama Red that Jack gave us. Kyle had burned through his share within a month, but I smoked only a hit or two each night, thereby preserving the precious gift. A perfect joint, like the one I just rolled, could last a week. I leaned back in my chair, put my feet up on the desk, and admired my work for a moment before striking a match on an overcast morning.

Rolling green mountains, covered with lush primary forest, waited impatiently in the distance beyond my door. They beckoned me to explore them. I wondered what mysteries hid beneath their seamless tree canopy.

The sky had threatened every day for a week, but I didn't think there was much chance of a storm. I hadn't seen a single drop of rain since my arrival in *Los Altos*. It would be a cool, peaceful day.

The THC filled my lungs and passed into my blood stream where it flowed through my veins and found its welcome way into my brain. I thought about friends and family and they brought smiles to my face. I wished they could be there. I'd show them my house and the farm and they'd get a kick out of it all. I was stoned . . . immaculate.

I was lost in my imagination when I noticed that a young woman carrying an infant approached my gate. I barely managed to put out the joint and light some incense before she reached the house. She couldn't have been more than eighteen. She had a boy's haircut and dopey eyes and big cheeks and she said her name was Roxana. I pulled my only two chairs out onto my porch and invited her to sit down.

"I'm Mateo's oldest daughter," she explained.

"Much pleasure," I said, hyper-conscious of my thick Philadelphia accent. The Spanish words fell clumsily out of my mouth. *Keep your shit together. She has no idea how stoned you are.*

"*Los Altos* is pleasing to you?" she asked. I liked that question; I knew the answer.

"Quite. The people fall well with me and the farm is going to be beautiful." I couldn't make the words sound quite right, but I liked my word choice. I felt like a poet. Roxana looked pleased with my answer. I was pleased she was pleased.

"You know," she responded, "I too work at the project. Sometimes I cook lunch for all of the men."

She hung out for a while and I continued to play with the language, but I wondered what she wanted. Her baby had a big head and bug eyes and a tiny, skinny body. He looked like a green olive on a tooth pick. Roxana had a smooth caramel complexion, but the child looked nothing like her. I wondered if he was an alien. I was inventing the child's mysterious origins when Roxana made an abrupt offer: "You want that I clean your house?"

Well, that was unexpected. But I brought it on myself. The day before, while working at *El Futuro*, I mentioned that my house was a mess and I didn't have much time to clean it. I didn't mean anything by it; I was just trying to make conversation. The men had told Roxana I needed help.

"That's very kind," I said, "but I can do it myself." I couldn't tell if she was offering her services free of charge or if she was looking for a job. If she wanted cash, I couldn't afford to pay her. And even if I had the money, the idea of a Peace Corps Volunteer with a maid didn't seem quite right.

Regardless, I didn't want her fiddling through my private things. Maybe she'd find my stash and tell the whole world about it.

"No thank you."

"Why?" she asked indignantly, as though my refusal was an incomprehensible personal affront. She suddenly sprung from her seat with defiant eyes and snatched up the broom that leaned against the house in the corner of my porch. With her baby in one arm and the broom in the other, she started to sweep the dust that I attended to less than I should. Meanwhile, the baby never took his creepy, bug-eyes off me.

"I prefer to do it myself," I explained, "but I thank you."

Roxana didn't seem to believe me, so she shrugged and kept on sweeping. Resigned to the domestic assistance, I moved from the chair to my hammock and pretended to read a book as I wondered what I'd say if she demanded payment for her services. The wind began to kick up.

Roxana suddenly spun on her heels. "*The breeze,*" she observed. Her eyes grew wide; her expression suggested she offered more than idle conversation. I didn't get the message.

The sky turned the color of unpolished silver. The wind became fierce. Massive rain drops started to batter my steel roof. If it hadn't been ninety degrees, I would've believed tropical hail pelted my house. Winter had arrived.

The dirt path that connected my house to the road became a raging creek. *I'm the local agriculture expert and this girl can read the weather better than I can. At least all the real farmers will be pleased by the turn in the weather.* Then it dawned on me: *Oh no. I'm stuck here with her.*

The sound of the rain drowned out the radio and Roxana and I had to shout just to hear one another. We'd find a subject to discuss, like how I could stand to be so far away from my family, or whether I liked Panama, or the size of her family, but every few minutes we exhausted the topic, the conversation died out, and we found ourselves sitting in awkward silence. Her baby, who'd been patiently resting against her chest as he peered around my property, had finally had enough. He began to cry. Without hesitation or embarrassment, Roxana took out her plump, floppy breast and stuffed it in the baby's mouth, flashing me a glimpse of her swollen, brown nipple. After getting his fill, the baby fell fast asleep.

"I can put him in your bed?"

"Of course."

Could I have said no? I wasn't about to tell Roxana she had to go home in the middle of a downpour. So she placed her child in my bed while I gazed at the sky and wondered how much longer I'd be trapped with my houseguests. When she returned to my porch, empty-handed, she revisited the topic of domestic chores.

"I love to take care of a house. I love to cook and make sure everything is nice and neat."

"That makes one of us. But I manage."

"You may be a *gringo*, but all you men are the same." She smiled. "Show me where you cook."

Reluctantly, I led her inside and showed her the wooden table where I kept my two-burner gas stove and my plastic dish rack. I then spent the next ten minutes defending my life style on every level, from my method of washing dishes, to my assertion that I'm quite content with so much alone time, to my position that I'm perfectly capable of doing my own laundry. No matter how much I assured her that I liked my life, I couldn't placate her. "But you said you don't like to take care of the house," she protested. I grew weary of the discussion and rested my palms on the top of the table. She was killing my buzz. What a waste of a joint.

Suddenly, she made her move. Her meaty paws took hold of my arms. She shut her eyes and pursed her fat lips and tried to pull me towards her. I felt my triceps tense under her grip and I remained very still, as though trying not to startle a rhino.

I told her, "No!" in a tone fit for scolding a puppy.

She opened her eyes to reveal genuine confusion. I imagine I looked just as confused. After a long silent pause, she asked only "Why?"

Her eyes pleaded with me, but she maintained her firm grip. If I didn't give in, would she try to take me by force? She looked fairly sturdy. A wrestling match could get ugly. "It's a very bad idea for me to have a girlfriend here in the community," I stammered. "Besides, I already have a girlfriend."

I'd never referred to Elena as my girlfriend before. I liked the sound of it. I liked the idea of it. I wondered how Elena would feel about me describing her as my girlfriend.

"Why doesn't she live here?" Roxana asked suspiciously.

"Because she lives with the *Wounaan*. She's a Peace Corps Volunteer like me. She has a job to do." Roxana nodded reluctantly and looked as though she might cry.

"Besides, I have to live and work here. I'm happy and I'm comfortable. I'm going to be here for two years. So far, this community treats me well." She looked ready to protest and still clung to my arms. I talked faster. "If I have a girlfriend here," I continued, gaining speed with each syllable, "I know that one day she might not be my girlfriend anymore, but I'll still have to work with all the families and I'll need to have good relationships with all of them. If I end a relationship, it could be a problem." She pouted, but she seemed to get it. "I explain myself?" I asked, just to make sure.

111

She nodded again and finally released me. Her eyes welled with tears. My stomach sank with pity, but I still turned my back on her and walked outside to get some fresh air. For all I knew her family had sent her on this mission, for their collective benefit, to try and net the *gringo*. Even though I lived in the dark and shit in a hole, I had far more prospects than any of my neighbors. I was, after all, American, and Americans, as every *campesino* knows, are very rich. Roxanna had already been shamed as a young, single mom in a tiny town. Now she had to go back home, having failed at love yet one more time, and explain to her family that I wasn't interested.

It was too early in the day for so much reality.

"Are you going to live with your girlfriend when you finish here?" she asked me.

"I don't know."

"Do you love her?"

"Yes," I answered definitively, not because I felt sure it was true, but because it seemed like the clearest path to the end of our conversation.

A few minutes later her son woke up. It stopped raining and they left. Some neighborhood kids came by that afternoon. They'd found my Frisbee.

Chapter 18 – Two Feet

I flagged down a bus as it lumbered past Timshel. The driver's assistant opened the door to greet me.

"Juan, *qué tal?* Are you going to *Penonomé* today?"

"Maybe. Do you know where the Ministry of Agriculture Development has its closest office?"

"You want MIDA?"

"*Sí.* Do you know where it is?"

"There is a big office in *Penonomé*, but the closest one is in *Anton.*"

"Can you guys drop me there?"

"Come."

"Good morning," I called out as I walked inside the MIDA office. A few ancient metal desks, a pair of file cabinets, and some uncomfortable looking wooden chairs occupied the small one-room building. There were no computers; only one desk had a phone, and it was a rotary at that. A calendar from the local hardware store adorned otherwise bare walls. The room needed a new coat of paint and pale fluorescent light bulbs white-washed everything. It was hard to imagine how any inspired work could happen in a place like that.

"Good morning," the only man in the office called back. He rose from his desk to greet me. I reached out to shake his hand and my palm disappeared into his large, thick mitt.

"I call myself Juan. I'm the new Volunteer of the Peace Corps in *Los Altos.*"

113

"My name is Victor. Much pleasure. Welcome to our province."

"Thank you. You work with MIDA?"

"No. The extension agent from MIDA is not here right now. I work for *Triple-C*. Can I help you?"

"I wanted to introduce myself today to the MIDA person, but also, I needed to ask him for a favor."

"Tell me."

"I want to start a vermiculture project in *Los Altos de las Cascadas*, but I don't have the worms."

I had never even heard of vermiculture before I left the States, but Carlos had taught us about it during training. He explained to us that earth worms convert organic waste into nutrient-rich poop because the worm's gut facilitates the growth of fungus and bacteria that are beneficial to plants. Best of all, the worms multiplied at magical rates. One pair of adult California red worms could produce one egg each week, and each egg contained up to twenty babies. A few dozen worms would turn into a full blown refuse-munching army in just a couple of months. I could feed them the cow manure from the pasture outside my house, along with mango peels, banana peels, and other food waste from my kitchen. In a real pinch, I could even feed them paper.

"I can help you," Victor said. "Come with me." After leading me to a beat-up government pick-up truck, Victor drove ten minutes outside of town and pulled over alongside a barbed wire fence. Victor got out of the truck, walked over to the fence, and put his boot down on the bottom strand of barbed wire. He pulled up on the top strand to allow me to climb between the two wires without tearing my clothes. Once I was on the other side,

I returned the favor. I had no idea where we were, or whether we were trespassing, but Victor didn't seem too concerned. He led me to an open-air shack in the middle of a tree farm. Old fishing nets covered the shack's corrugated steel roof and reached all the way to the ground.

"So the birds can't get in," Victor explained as he held open one of the nets. "Take what you need."

I pulled out a small cardboard box that I'd brought with me and tossed in a few handfuls of soil. Then I picked through the table and found more than fifty worms in just a couple of minutes.

"Wow. That was easy. Thank you for your help."

"At your service. If there's anything else I can do, you let me know."

Someone in *Los Altos* once joked to me that getting a job in the Panamanian government was like retiring with a nice pension. But Victor seemed interested in more than his paycheck. I was lucky to find him.

"Can I invite you to breakfast?" I asked. "I know a place in *Santa Clara*."

XS was only fifteen minutes down the highway. Victor looked at his watch and seemed to calculate appointments in his head, as though he wanted me to know he thought twice about goofing off while on the clock. He needn't have bothered. He already earned my loyalty.

"Why not? We can talk about the worms while we eat," he suggested, perhaps to justify the diversion. We climbed back into the pick-up.

"So you don't work for MIDA, but you work in their office?"

"Correct. I work for *Triple-C*."

"I heard you mention that before. What is that?"

"*Triple-C* is like a part of MIDA, but it's only for *Capira, Cocle,* and *Colón.* We help the farmers in those areas to organize cooperatives and grow more food."

"Why just those three parts?"

"It's a special project. Funding came from an international grant."

That seemed strange. *Why would an international grant only reward those three areas?* What's so special about *Capira, Cocle,* and *Colón?* Then it hit me. *That's the Panama Canal's watershed.*

"Does it have something to do with the Canal?"

"No," he answered definitively, and even though I had no idea whether Victor just helped me steal somebody's worms, he struck me as an honest man. Still, I wasn't sure I believed him. Maybe he just didn't know.

Container ships had become so large that the Canal's locks couldn't accommodate them, so the big ships bypassed the Canal and made the long trip around the horn. If Panama wanted the Canal to stay relevant, and profitable, the Canal needed to get bigger. But any expansion of the canal would mean flooding hundreds of little communities within the watershed. The people from those communities would have to go somewhere.

Maybe *Triple-C* existed to make sure other towns had the ability to absorb the relocated folk. If that was the case, I understood why they'd want to keep people like Victor, and the famers he helped, in the dark. After all, why anger the *campesinos* who'd be flooded out any sooner than absolutely necessary? Regardless, I was in no position to challenge the powers behind the Canal. I was just glad for Victor's help.

After tall stacks of pancakes with syrup and bacon, he dropped me at the turn-off to *Los Altos*.

"Many thanks Victor. We'll see each other soon."

"It's good. See you later."

Back in *Los Altos*, I went straight to Eduardo and showed him my bounty. He seemed enthusiastic about the idea, so we sat down at the kitchen table and I drew him a picture of what we needed to build. "I know how to do this," Eduardo answered. "It's easy."

Eduardo led me a half-mile through the forest to his father's house. His dad was one of the few people in the area who had a stand of bamboo plants. I never understood why more people didn't plant bamboo.

During my late night studies, I learned that bamboo had been used for centuries in East Asia as building materials, in gardens, and even as food. In common conditions, it can grow two feet a day. Two feet! And to grow it, you just take a cutting from an already existing plant, stick it in the ground, and it takes root.

Eduardo and I carried the hollow tubes of timber on our shoulders and brought them back to *La Tranquilidad*. We cut the wood into short pieces with a hand saw and then used our machetes to split those sections lengthwise, so they were nearly flat. In just a few minutes we'd cut down bamboo, carried it home, and turned it into a number of thin planks.

117

We got to work nailing the planks into the sides and bottom of the frame Eduardo built. Next, we lined the inside of the box with porous rice sacks that would allow the soil inside the box to drain, but keep the worms from sneaking out. We placed each leg of the box into an old coffee can and filled the space between the legs and the edge of the cans with used cooking oil. That way, ants couldn't climb the legs of the box, devour the worms, and frustrate our plans.

We filled the box halfway to the top with cow manure, rice husks, discarded cardboard, and fruit peels. Lastly, we added the worms. After a few weeks, when the worms had eaten all of their food, we'd push all of the castings to one end of the box and fill up the other end with fresh food. Within a couple of days, the worms would migrate to the new food and we could harvest the organic fertilizer without losing our precious worms.

In just one day, with the help of a government extension agent and the enthusiasm of a neighbor, I completed my first Peace Corps project. And it cost only the labor and the price of the nails. A few days later, Eduardo helped me build a smaller version for my front porch.

Chapter 19 – Bonito

The men from *El Futuro* buzzed past me as I gasped for air and struggled down the muddy trail. My shoulder screamed under the weight of wet lumber. They made three trips for every one of mine. I felt weak. I lost twelve pounds in a month.

But as the weeks went by, the farm took shape. We built fish ponds and rice paddies. We also built a chicken coop and a pig pen. Then we added ducks to the fish pond and started an iguana project. The men planted tomatoes, corn, green beans, guandu, squash, yuca, papaya, and plantains.

I learned enough from Carlos to know that soil conservation would be an issue with hillside farming, so I studied up on the subject. Then I went to the farm on a day when only two of the men, Perdomo and Efrain, worked there. They were both about my age, but already had wives and multiple kids.

I helped them water some crops and harvest the ripe tomatoes. We took a short break and sat underneath a mango tree to escape the sun for a few minutes. Perdomo climbed up into the tree and tossed a couple of ripe mangos downs to me and Efrain. Using my pocket knife, I cut away the large pit and popped the fragrant fruit into my mouth. The sweet juices exploded on my tongue.

"How the mangos fascinate me," I said.

"Do you have mangos at your house in *gringolandia*?" Efrain asked me.

"Unfortunately not. They don't grow there. It's too cold in the winter. We have to buy them in the supermarket."

119

"How much does a mango cost in a super?" Efrain had asked me these same questions at least half a dozen times since I started working at *El Futuro*, but he never tired of hearing the answers. I never tired of giving them.

"One dollar," I told him.

"It can't be!" Perdomo exclaimed with a big smile. Efrain nodded, as thought to confirm that it was indeed crazy. In Panama, mangos grew everywhere. They fell to the ground and rotted by the thousands.

"It's certain," I assured them. "Mangos are a delicacy up there. It's not like here. You guys are lucky."

"We should collect up all the mangos and take them to the *gringos*," Perdomo said. "We'll be rich."

"I wish we could," I said.

"But you have other fruits there, right?"

"Sure. Lots of them. Apples grow well where I was born. Pears too."

"I like apples."

"Me too," Efrain agreed.

After the small talk, I got down to business. I explained how tropical rainstorms wash away topsoil. Using a stick, I drew a picture of a hillside in the dirt to illustrate the importance of planting rows of crops in contours with the hillside, rather than in straight lines that would facilitate runoff. Once they began to think of the hill as a curved, three dimensional object rather than a flat plane, they seemed to catch my drift.

I also explained how certain plants with deep root structures could hold the hillside together. If they planted a row of lemon grass or valariana between every few rows of crops, those plants would trap the soil that would otherwise wash down the hillside. They'd have to give up a few rows of crops to accommodate the live barriers, but after a few years the hillside would form natural terraces, thereby saving countless hours of otherwise backbreaking labor.

We got to work and built a simple A-frame level out of three thin branches, three nails, a small rock, and a piece of string. We tied the rock to the end of the string and hung it from the apex of the A-frame. The rock acted as a weight, allowing us to determine whether we were planting in a contour line. We marked the curve of the hill with dozens of stakes we cut from nearby *Balo* trees.

I ran home and dug up some lemon grass and valariana from my own garden and ran back to the farm. From the rice tanks at the bottom of the valley, all the way up to the top of the hillsides, we planted alternating rows of lemon grass and valariana every five meters. That would leave plenty of room for crops. We even planted some in the earthen berms of the fish tanks and rice paddies to help hold them together. By the end of the day I was filthy and exhausted. Dirt covered my clothes; my fingernails were black and I had soil and sweat caked all over my skin. I loved it. It's good to be connected to the Earth.

The next morning, feeling full of myself, I woke up late with the knowledge that the whole cooperative would work that day. Perdomo and Efrain had probably woken up extra early to arrive at the farm first so they could explain what I had taught them. I imagined all the

121

men would be busy planting their crops in the contour lines that we had marked off the day before.

So many Volunteers seemed to have trouble in their communities getting anything done. I felt lucky to have wound up in a town full of receptive people. But I knew it was more than just luck. I'd convinced these men that I was credible. I'd worked hard to earn their respect and their trust.

When I arrived at the farm, I found all of my *Balo* stakes pulled out and thrown into the bushes. The lemon grass and valariana that I'd supplied from my own garden had been torn out and discarded.

"What happened?" I demanded.

No one answered. Perdomo and Efrain wouldn't even make eye contact with me. My stomach felt empty with disappointment, but the heat in my ears and cheeks betrayed only feelings of rage. My limited Spanish escaped me.

"We to need meeting," I seethed.

"The men are busy right now," Mateo answered casually. His refusal to acknowledge my frustration made me only more furious.

"When we can have meeting then?"

He looked me straight in the eye with a look of utter innocence. "Tomorrow morning?"

I looked around the property at the torn out stakes and grasses. It would have hurt less if they'd torn out my pubic hair.

"What *time*?" I asked through gritted teeth.

"Like . . . at nine?"

"We'll see one another tomorrow." I stormed off across the farm without looking back. Some kids ran up to me as I marched back to *Timshel.* They wanted to play hide and seek, but I was in no mood for games.

I spent the rest of the day reading in my hammock. Every few pages I had to turn back to where I started, for my mind drifted from the book in front of me to the men and the farm. I wasn't sure if I was angrier at them for disregarding my hard work or angrier at myself for thinking I'd connected with them.

The occasional farmer walked past with a heavy, overflowing basket of yuca or firewood strapped to his back and a machete dangling from his hand. We'd exchange a nod or a wave or a *salomar* as he trudged on with a smile, uphill, under the weight of his burden. *Attitude is everything.*

By the time dusk settled in, I felt a new perspective on the situation. I'd been naive to think that I could change the way they farmed overnight. At the meeting in the morning I wouldn't scold or pontificate, I'd just explain the importance of soil conservation. I'd prevail to their sense of logic. These were, after all, men who wanted what was best for their families. That had to mean preserving the land for their children's children. Perhaps Perdomo and Efrain lacked the understanding or the confidence to explain the importance of the techniques.

When I arrived at *El Futuro* in the morning, only Roxana was at the *rancho* where the men held their meetings. She plucked a chicken with a smirk on her face. Two men watered crops in the distance. They looked up when I arrived, but returned to their work when they saw it was me.

"Where is everyone?" I demanded.

"How so?" she asked innocently.

"The *meeting*. There's a meeting this morning."

"No, the meeting is this afternoon at four. The men are all attending to their own farms this morning."

"Of course they are," I told her in English.

"What?"

"Nothing. We'll see one another at four."

When I returned at four, no one was there. Even Roxana and the two men had left for the day. I stormed up to Mateo's house.

"*Buenas!*" I shouted. Mateo came to the open door, yawning and scratching his belly.

"*Juan*," he asked, "where were you this morning? I thought you wanted to have a meeting?"

"I was *here*."

"No you weren't."

I spent weeks working alongside him and his men, sweating and bleeding. I thought I'd earned some respect, but I'd been mistaken. I was so angry I couldn't even speak, so I just turned and walked away.

A couple of days later I finally got the men to-gether. I explained the importance of soil conservation and contour planting and nitrogen fixation, but they only half-listened with slack jaws and vacant eyes. No one said a word.

"Don't you guys get it?" I barked. "I'm here to help you. You tore up all of my work without even discussing it. Besides, if you don't use these techniques, the land you're farming will be useless in a few years. The rain will wash away the good half of the soil and your chemicals will burn up the rest. I know you've been doing things the same way for a long time, but it can't last. You can't cut down trees forever. Eventually there won't be any trees left to cut and you'll have to use the same soil year after year."

An old man with white hair and patronizing eyes piped up. "We can't eat *trees*," he sneered. "We can't eat *grass*. We're not cows." He wanted me to understand that the idea of using up valuable crop space for anything besides food was beyond idiotic. His friends laughed at me.

"You can't eat soil either," I countered. "Should we get rid of all the soil too?" I thought I made a good point, but it didn't register. The old man just folded his arms and stared at me. The look in his eyes told me he thought I was so stupid that he wouldn't even give me the dignity of a response. I wanted to pick up a shovel and start smashing stuff, but I knew I was beat. "Good luck then."

And with that, I trudged home.

The next day I went over to Jose's house and asked if I could help out. They welcomed me in and we spent the day digging up tree trunks and stones from a hillside they'd recently cleared. The back-breaking work always felt the most honest. I could feel the stress from *El Futuro* running down my brow, neck, and arms in fat beads of sweat.

125

At the end of the long day, when I finally arrived home, I discovered my porch was covered with strange, black, kidney-shaped stains. Each marking was a couple of feet in length. I couldn't comprehend what had happened. Was it some sort of hex? Witchcraft? Who did it? Why?

The lock on the door seemed untouched. I carefully entered the house, expecting the worst, but everything seemed to be in order. As I undressed and showered, I tried to make sense of the scene on my porch.

That's when the dog arrived – the same dog that I met in the street my first night in town. Much to my relief, he'd managed to get the bag out of his ass since the last time we crossed paths. Unfortunately for him, however, he had traded that particular variety of misery for a different one: somehow, he managed to get himself drenched in what appeared to be motor oil.

The strange shapes on my porch weren't the product of witchcraft, but the evidence of a dog that had decided to lay down there. He'd obviously decided that he would try to get all the oil off by settling down on a half-dozen different spots on my porch. His strategy was largely unsuccessful. He was truly pathetic and his surprised blue eyes made him look all the sadder. I pitied the beast.

I tried to approach him, but he scurried back and flinched. Life had taught this dog to expect a beating. The last thing I needed was a bite from a sick, frightened dog, so I backed off. I went inside and grabbed the five-gallon bucket that I used to wash my laundry. I also opened up a can of tuna fish and placed it in the grass just beyond my porch.

The dog was reluctant to believe his good fortune, as though the free meal had to have a catch, but when he felt I was at a safe-enough distance, he forgot all about me and greedily lapped up the tuna. I took the opportunity to sneak up from behind and douse him with a bucket of water. With just one bucket, I managed to wash off a lot of the oil. He looked shocked, but he always looked that way, so I couldn't tell if he was grateful for the tuna and the impromptu bath or if he wanted to know why I'd played such a dirty trick on him.

"I was doing you a favor," I explained. He looked skeptical, but he didn't run off either. Instead, he returned his attention to the easiest meal he'd had in a long time, trying to lick whatever remnants of taste there might have been off the sides of the spotless tuna can. Without all the motor oil, those sickly haunches re-revealed themselves to the world.

It occurred to me that he looked better covered in oil. "I think I'll call you *Bonito*." As the ugliest dog I'd ever seen, the name seemed perfectly ironic. He didn't seem too impressed. Maybe he understood that I was teasing him. Either way, he scurried off across the pasture and out of sight.

Chapter 20 – Dignity Battalions

That night at Alejandra's house I told Lola about Bonito. She thought the name was funny, but not nearly as funny as me freaking out about the oil stains. Lola explained that people dipped dogs in motor oil to treat them for mange. I was no vet, but that seemed like a pretty good way to kill your dog. Then again, I supposed killing your dog was an effective way to cure mange. In any event, the mange explained Bonito's bare ass, but left another mystery in its place: the misguided oil treatment suggested that somewhere out there, Bonito had a master.

Lola had become my closest friend in *Los Altos*. I didn't do any work with her or her family, and she never showed up at my house and tried to put the moves on me. It was just friendship, with no ulterior motives, and I valued our early evening conversations. After I told her about Bonito, I complained about the situation with the men at *El Futuro*.

"You still don't get the Panamanian joke, do you?" she asked me.

"I guess not." If dismantling my hard work and disrespecting me in the process was a joke, I found it utterly unfucking funny. I'd never get that joke. Regardless, Lola and I had been getting along particularly well that night, so I broached a subject that I'd always wanted to ask about. "What do you know about the invasion?"

"What do *you* know about it?"

"It was about Noriega, right?"

"Yes. Do you know anything about him?"

"I know he was a general. And a drug dealer. At least that's what the news in the United States said. I was in middle school at the time, but I remember it a little."

"He was more than that," Lola told me. "Before he made himself a general and took control of the military, he was the head of Panama's secret police, and everyone here knows he worked for the C.I.A. too. But he was totally paranoid, and he made everyone else paranoid too."

"What do you mean? What did he do?"

"He created these things called Dignity Battalions. They were sort of like the police, I guess, but they didn't have any real training. Almost anyone could be in a Dignity Batallion as long as they were loyal to pineapple face. The people in the Dignity Batallions turned in anyone who questioned Noriega's leadership. Neighbors stopped talking to each other because they were afraid they'd be accused of plotting against him. People were afraid. At least for a while."

"Then what happened?"

"*Gringos* happened. In 1988, you stopped paying your canal fees and you froze all the Panamanian assets in *gringo* banks. Even Noriega couldn't fix elections after that. When his presidential candidate lost the next election, Noriega had the winner beaten by thugs in broad daylight in the middle of the street. Then the *loco* declared war on the United States."

"I remember that."

We learned about it during Peace Corps training. On December 20, 1989, the U.S. military used 26,000 troops to attack Panama with Sheridan tanks and Apache helicopters. The invasion removed Noriega from power and put him in a jail in the United States, but it also left thousands of civilians dead and it destroyed large sections of Panama City. They called it "Operation Just Cause."

I knew a lot of Panamanians were angry about all the collateral damage. It was too much force to catch one man. Moreover, because the poorest parts of the city were made of wood, many of those neighborhoods burned to ashes, leaving residents with only the clothes on their backs. Some argued that Noriega loyalists, rather than U.S. soldiers, had set fire to the homes, but that meant little to a family left with nothing. After all, even if it had been Noriega's people, it wouldn't have happened at all without the invasion.

I assumed that in *Los Altos* we were far enough out in the *campo*, and Lola was young enough, that the issue wouldn't be too sensitive. I was wrong.

"You all had no right to do what you did," she scolded me. As soon as she said "you all" and lumped me in with the soldiers and the government, I knew I was in trouble. "Your soldiers took this road," she pointed out to the road with her lips, "because they thought it could be used as an escape route from *El Valle*. They wouldn't let us walk down the street in our own town. They had tanks. Soldiers were right here in front of our house, *peeing* on our bushes."

"That sounds scary," I admitted.

"It wasn't just scary. It was disgusting." Lola got up and disappeared into the back of the house. I wished I'd never brought it up. Lola was the last person I wanted angry with me.

After several minutes, she returned with a book about the invasion. Her mother and sister and nephews and cousins all crowded around too. The thin book had oversized pages with big, glossy pictures and relatively sparse text. It looked like a disturbing children's book. The pictures depicted pandemonium. Fire and blood and twisted metal. The book provided virtually no context for the images, but the images were undeniably powerful. Maybe that was the point. One cannot justify such a cause.

At the same time, I wasn't about to get apologetic for an invasion I had nothing to do with. I'd been a child when the invasion happened. The whole family watched me, waiting for me to speak.

"It's a shame so many people lost their houses," I said.

"It's a shame!" Alejandra mocked. "It was your fault!"

How was it my fault? Did they really view me as indistinguishable from every other American? I didn't want an argument, but I wasn't about to kowtow either. Didn't they realize that I'd left my friends and family behind to be there with them?

We'd eaten together every night for weeks. They knew that I was just a volunteer and that I could be back home with my friends and family, working at a real job for a real paycheck. But no, I had traveled all the way to *Los Altos* only to try my best to make their town a better place in whatever small way I could. And even if I wasn't making any difference at all, couldn't they at least recognize the effort?

I wanted to show the world that Americans are normal, decent people who are capable of being good neighbors. But they wanted to lay the ugliness of the invasion, along with any other anti-American vitriol they could think of, squarely at my feet. "Well, I guess every story has at least two sides," I answered.

Within seconds, everyone in the room was yelling at me. I had a hard enough time understanding Spanish when people spoke calmly and slowly and one at a time. With everyone yelling at me all at once, the only thing I understood was their anger. I thought they liked me. "None of us in this room know what really happened in the city and just because a book says something, it doesn't make it true."

"*We* know what happened!" Alejandra glared at me. "*We* know!"

Riling up my neighbors wasn't what I signed up for. The job the Peace Corps had charged me with, the real mission – the public relations – was going horribly wrong. The Peace Corps had its English teachers, and small business volunteers, and environmental educators, but in the end, we were really there to show the world that Americans are good neighbors. I swallowed my pride, pushed my chair back from the dining table, and stood up.

"Thank you for dinner." Without looking back, I stormed out of the house, across the front yard, and back up the road to *Timshel.*

I never understood why Americans are so mocked and disrespected and even hated. I wanted my neighbors, the world over, to understand that we are real people with real families and real laughter and real tears and the same hopes and dreams as everyone else. We go to school and get jobs and get married and have babies. We bury our relatives and we mourn them. We get old and get sick and die just like everyone else. We are more than a few bad administrations. It was bewildering how one American family could screw it all up for the rest of us. I didn't realize that my fingernails had cut into my palms until I unballed my fists and opened the front door.

Chapter 21 – Nelson

I arrived at the cooperative one morning to find an unusual buzz in the air. As I got closer, I saw Perdomo running around the chicken coop, chasing after frantic birds that flapped their wings and squawked in protest. Once Perdomo caught a chicken, he passed it out to Efrain who tied its feet with string and placed it on the ground.

Each time Efrain gathered four chickens, he hung them by their feet from the edge of a long work table. The captive birds dangled upside down and twirled around for a few moments before Mateo sliced open their throats with a large kitchen knife. Mateo passed the dead bodies to Roxana who tossed them in a pot of hot water. After soaking for a few minutes, the feathers became easier to pluck. The rest of the men worked on removing the feathers, weighing the poultry, and stuffing it into plastic bags. The efficiency of their assembly line impressed me, but I couldn't take my eyes off the end of the work table. I watched, spellbound, as the blood seeped into the greedy, sun-bleached soil. Ashes to ashes; dust to dust.

I wondered if the other chickens – the live ones with wide eyes and tied feet – realized what was happening to their brethren. Did they watch it? Could they process what was happening? Did they know that they'd be next? Maybe they just sensed an undefined horrible danger in the air. Or maybe they couldn't think past the problem of their own bound feet.

Mateo woke me from my mind and handed me the heavy-handled knife. As I took the bloody knife from him, he met my eyes and smiled and nodded. I couldn't tell what he was thinking. Was he testing me? Did he question whether I could do it? Or did he just not want me to miss out on the fun?

I couldn't profess vegetarian innocence. I ate plenty of chicken, so I reluctantly took the knife from Mateo's outstretched hand. I grabbed the flailing bird, took a deep breath, and sawed open the helpless animal's neck. Thick blood poured from the torn throat; it beat its wings furiously in a vain attempt to flee the inevitable. *Flap, flap, flap, flap, flap . . . flap, flap, flap . . . flap, flap . . . flap, flap . . . flap . . . flap . . . flap.* The bird writhed in a final act of defiance. And then it was still.

The lifeless chicken hung sadly. All the farmers watched me and seemed pleased. I felt an odd sense of honor as I sat down and helped pluck feathers. It occurred to me only then that I'd always taken for granted how dead the clean, cellophane-covered animals were as they sat on their little Styrofoam trays in the supermarket.

After a couple of months, the strangeness of such experiences became the norm, and my daily routine became effortless. I woke up early, made my breakfast, and worked out with some dumbbells that I'd bought in *Penonomé*. Around seven, after I washed the dishes and swept the floor, I made my way over to one of the nearby farms. On tough days, we swung pickaxes or machetes. On the easier days, we planted seeds or watered crops. The families I worked with usually served me lunch. We sat around the table telling stories and laughing or talking about plans for the future.

At the end of the day, I walked home, climbed into my hammock, and watched the evening light melt into night. As soon as it got dark enough, I lit up a joint. I swung back and forth and listened to music and let thoughts dance inside my head until inspiration hit. I made my way inside the house and wrote in my journal for a couple of hours. When I couldn't keep my eyes open anymore, I blew out the tiny dancing flames scattered about my house.

On Sundays, during football season, I woke up even earlier than usual and got the first bus out of town. I made my way to Santa Clara where XS had football games beamed in via satellite. Dennis cheered for the Steelers and Sheila pulled for the Bears, but the Eagles were the only team for me. Win or lose, I turned to Jack Daniels for company in the early evening. Dennis made sure my glass never emptied.

After twelve hours of booze and burgers and apple pie a la mode and drunken conversation and the roller coaster of close football games, when I couldn't maintain my balance on my barstool any longer, I'd stumble outside and try to set up my tent. Dennis followed me out so he and Paco could enjoy a good laugh.

"What's that goddamn bird doing up at this hour anyway? Shouldn't he be asleep by now?"

Dennis laughed. "Don't tell him he's a bird."

"You know, that sonofabitch sounds a lot like you."

"Go figure. Say, how's that tent coming?"

"Fuck this tent. I'm sleeping in the grass."

"Don't worry brother. I'll lock the front gate. Joy will keep an eye on you. You'll be safe and sound."

In the morning, Sheila would make me an early breakfast before I hit the road back to *Los Altos*. Those Mondays in *Los Altos* were tough. And it had little to do with my blinding hangovers. XS symbolized an insurmountable disconnect with the community. Even if I lived amongst them, and like them, there was a world of places and experiences and ambitions that lived inside of me that my neighbors would never know or dare to dream possible. They probably imagined all Americans had yachts and helicopters and mansions. They couldn't understand why anyone in their right mind would voluntarily leave their loved ones to live alongside strangers in relative squalor when I could be back home, working for cash to spend on myself and my family. Sometimes I couldn't understand it either.

Regardless, my 'real' life seemed like a secret I needed to keep even if I didn't understand exactly why. In the end, I knew no matter how much time I spent with the people of *Los Altos*, no matter how much I liked Jose and Eduardo and Lola and their families, and no matter how much they seemed to like me, they'd never really know me. I'd never felt so alone. And I loved it.

There were no smiles or scowls from family and friends and roommates and lovers to serve as signposts along the way. My place in the world was undefined. For the very first time, I didn't have to measure up to anyone else's standards or approval. I got drunk on the freedom that came from feeling proud or sexy or smart or tough only in my own eyes. And if I felt none of those things, I'd done it to myself. I imagined plenty of people already felt that way, but for me it was a new sensation. I liked who I was. I liked even more who I was becoming.

Adults rarely came to visit me at my home, but four or five of the neighborhood kids always seemed to be around my porch in the late afternoon. I enjoyed their company as I tended to my garden or relaxed in the hammock. They played tag and sang and asked me to say words in Spanish so they could laugh at my accent. Sometimes they told me innocent children's jokes that I rarely understood. I ran around with them as I tried to teach them to throw my Frisbee. They were terrible at Frisbee, but they didn't care. They found everything fun.

Nelson hung out around my house too, but he rarely ran around with the other kids. Instead, he contented himself playing with my radio and looking for small tasks outside in the yard. He'd find a good stick and use it to prop up a droopy tomato branch in my garden or he'd ask me for my file and sharpen my machete for me. Our association was built on little conversation, but I enjoyed his company and he seemed to enjoy mine. He was always the last to leave, often staying until just after sunset.

One afternoon, using a piece of scrap wire he found in the road, he fixed a loose hinge on the door of my shower stall. He didn't know I was watching him from afar.

"Thank you. That was clever."

He smiled bashfully at the compliment. "You need someone to cut your grass?" he asked hopefully.

"No, thank you." I allowed the grass in my garden to grow too long, but I'd get to it sooner or later.

"Ok. I'll see you tomorrow then." And he ran up the road towards his house.

Nelson came back the next afternoon with a small machete. Undeterred by my rejection the day before, he bent down and started cutting the grass just on the other side of the fence from my garden. With one hand on his thigh, he bent low at the knee and started slicing the grass with his machete in short, quick motions, as though to say, "see, I can do this; I'm not just a kid asking for a hand out."

I liked his determination and low-pressure sales tactic, so I gave him the job. He came by once a week and cut my grass for two dollars. The men in town earned only three bucks a day plus lunch for a morning's worth of labor, so Nelson had a pretty good gig. I sometimes felt guilty about giving a kid that much money for relatively little work, but I loved watching him run off to the store to spend his earnings. He could have spent it all on candy and soda and gum, but he always returned with a bag full of bread and a proud grin. "For my mother," he explained.

Chapter 22 – Coatimundi

I walked to the payphone to leave a message for Elena. She was on her way to *Los Altos* to visit me for my birthday. We usually met in the city every few weeks where we'd get a cheap hotel room, shut the curtains, and hide from the world for a blissful day or two. In *Los Altos*, we wouldn't have A/C or lights, but I couldn't wait to show her the life I had built there.

Because she'd never made the trip before, I told her I'd meet her at the bus station in *Penonomé*. Then I went home and watered my plants, swept up, and showered. The bus started to rumble past my house, so I ran into the middle of the pasture wearing only a towel, waiving and screaming like a lunatic. The bus stopped and waited for me to get myself together. I stumbled onto the bus with untied boots and an unbuttoned shirt.

"*Gracias*," I said to them all. "My *gringa* would have killed me if I'd missed the bus."

"You're going to see your girlfriend?" the driver asked.

"I sure am, and I'm going to bring her back to my mansion." I said it loud enough for everyone to hear. The driver rolled his eyes. The passengers giggled and laughed. I couldn't imagine a bus full of passengers exhibiting such good-natured patience back in the States.

Once in *Penonomé*, I ran some errands. I bought an ice cream cone and a tape measure and a toilet seat. I went to the post office and once again they told me I had nothing.

"But this is terrible," I protested. "I know that people have sent me things and they never arrive here."

"Wait a minute." The clerk went into a back room and poked around an avalanche of boxes and produced two packages with my name on them. The first one, from an old friend back home, arrived three months earlier. It contained a fresh journal and a touching letter. It also included some photos and some stickers, "for the kids in your town." The second package came from my mom and arrived only a few weeks earlier. Inside, I found a water-color she painted and framed. The glass in the frame didn't survive the trip, but I was still happy to have it. I had one more thing to nail to my wall.

I waited for Elena at a restaurant by the bus station. I re-read the letters and admired my gifts; before I knew it, Elena arrived.

"Happy birthday, gringo."

"Hey. Thanks for coming."

Once she settled in and we ordered lunch, Elena caught me up on her life.

"I started working with a small group of women in my village. They make the most beautiful baskets out of palm tree fibers. They weave crazy designs into them too. Here, I drew some pictures."

Elena pulled a sketch pad out of her pack and passed it to me. The pad contained page after page of colorful drawings. Many of the drawings showed the same basket from different angles.

She pulled her chair around the table so we sat next to one another and could look at the drawings together. Her arm pressed against mine as she leaned in over her work. I could smell her clean hair as she flipped it back over her shoulder. I looked away from the sketch pad to appreciate the sight of her smooth, tan neck.

141

"The women showed me how they make the dyes from different mixtures of plant and soil extracts. It's really cool. They also use Tagua nuts and Rosewood to make intricate carvings. Here, check these out." She turned a few pages to some more sketches.

"You drew these? They're really good. You're a natural artist."

"I don't know about all that, but you're sweet to say so."

"Have you tried making a basket?"

"I started one, but I don't have the concentration for it. The women spend four or five hours a day, every day, making them. The really good ones take months and the weaving is so tight they can hold water. I think I'd like to finish one before I leave here though."

"So what do you do when they're weaving baskets for hours on end? Do you just sit around topless with them and dish dirt about the guys in town?"

"For starters, it's not a big deal to be topless in their culture. Being topless as a woman is the same as being topless for a man. When it's too hot they'll take off their shirts."

"So you're parading around topless for these dudes, all hot and sweaty on summer days? You're liable to drive me into a jealous rage."

"No, jerk. I haven't gone native. At least not yet." She winked at me. "But I have taken a couple of the women to the city. We've made some relationships with tourist shops. The tourists have no idea who the Wounaan are, but they seem to like to buy their baskets. I think it'd be cool, one day, if we could eventually use the baskets to raise money and attention for eco-tours to the community."

"And you think it's a good idea to get them hooked on the city? What if they abandon the town altogether?"

She shrugged. "I thought about that too, but the way I see it, the money allows them to buy seeds, or tools, or food, or even medicine. And they're making money in a way that rewards and promotes their culture. The way things are going, with all the cowboys and the deforestation, they'd have to leave their homes anyway. At least this way they're keeping their history alive. And maybe selling their artisan stuff will bring more attention to their problems and they can preserve their lands for a while longer. Besides, I don't really see it as my place to make those decisions for them. I'm there to help them realize their goals, whatever they might be. If they want me to help them make money, I'll do it."

"It sounds like you've come a long way out there."

She smiled with closed lips and satisfied eyes in a way that suggested she had more to tell.

"What is it?" I asked.

She blushed.

"Come on, tell me."

"The women's group gave me a present."

"Cool. What did they give you?"

"Have you ever heard of a *coatimundi*?"

"A what?"

"*Coatimundi*. The locals call it a *gato solo*, but it's not really a cat at all. It's related to a raccoon."

"And they gave you a raccoon? That sounds like a pretty crappy present. What if it scratches up your face in the middle of the night? I've always been partial to your face."

"Dork. It wasn't a *live* coatimundi. One of their husbands hunted it. But no; they didn't give me a raccoon. Not exactly."

"'Not exactly?' What does that mean?"

"Well, they didn't give me a whole *gato solo* . . ."

"They just gave you part of it?"

"Right. They gave me its . . . penis bone."

"Did you just say they gave you a penis bone?" I didn't know if I was more disturbed about the present or that this poor animal had a bone in its penis.

Elena giggled uncontrollably. Her cheeks turned bright red and she avoided eye contact with me. "Supposedly," she said, "it's a powerful aphrodisiac. The women consider it highly coveted stuff. They say it's like natural Viagra. They told me to crush it up and put it in your drink."

"You've told them about me?"

"Of course I have," she answered casually, as though it was the most natural thing she'd ever said. "I talk about you all the time."

A sudden rush passed between my shoulder blades and through my belly. Then she added, "Why do you think they gave me a penis bone?"

"Hey! I don't know what awful lies you've told these women, but my performance has been pretty darn stellar if I say so myself!"

"Well, if you say so, then it must be true . . . stud." Diamonds sparkled in her pupils. The little minx was teasing me.

"Shit, I'll give you the best two minutes of your life right here on this table if you don't watch yourself." I pulled her out of her chair and onto my lap and I tickled her until she couldn't breathe. Her knees banged into the bottom of the table, overturning the water glasses and sending silverware crashing to the floor. People at other tables looked at us as though to say "goddamn *gringos*."

"Stop!" she pleaded. "You're embarrassing me."

The waitress came by with a dirty look and a wad of paper napkins.

"*Desculpa*," I said to the waitress, but I wasn't really sorry. I was having more fun than anyone else in the room . . . and maybe the country. Elena stood up to smooth out her sarong and I gave her a smack on the ass.

With her back still to me, she continued to smooth out her skirt as though nothing had happened. When she finally turned around, she bent over me and stroked my chin. "You might want to reconsider taking that penis bone after all, Mr. Confident. It's gonna be a *long* night for you. I'm not feeling forgiving either."

I adored her.

Chapter 23 – Pins and Needles

We paid the check at the restaurant and found a bus back to *Los Altos*.

"So, are you ready to visit *Timshel?*"

"What's that?"

"My estate."

"Did you say Tin Shell?"

"I might as well have. Are you ready for it?"

"That depends. Why do you have a toilet seat with you?"

"You never know what might happen. It's like the Boy Scouts say, 'be prepared.'"

"Seriously," she said rather sternly, "why do you have a toilet seat?"

"Because I never bothered buying one for my out-house."

"So what do you do?"

"I've managed to survive with just the concrete rim for the last few months. But I won't have your perfect bottom subjected to such misery. I want you to be comfortable. Besides, you have to sit down a lot more than I do."

"You're such a romantic," she teased. "I got you a present too. After all, you're the birthday boy."

"You didn't have to get me anything."

"I didn't feel like I *had* to get you something. But I wanted to." She pulled a small, rectangular box out of her pack and passed it to me. "Sorry about the wrapping paper." She'd wrapped the box in an issue of *La Vaina*, the newsletter written and published by Peace Corps Volunteers in Panama.

146

"I don't mind the paper at all. I actually kind of like it. I just hope it's not another penis bone."

"Just open it."

I unwrapped the gift to find a nifty-looking aluminum pen. "It's great. Thanks."

"It's not just a pen."

"It's not?"

"Nope. Check this out." She took the pen back from me, clicked a tiny toggle button on the top of it, held it close to her mouth like a microphone, and said, "John eats penis bones." Then she clicked the button again.

I must've looked perplexed, for Elena laughed at me, showed me the top of the pen, and said, "Look, see this button here? To record you slide the button this way. To play it back, you push it this way."

"John eats penis bones," the pen announced in Elena's clear voice.

"Wow! That's really cool. I've never seen anything like it."

"At first, I had no idea what to buy for your birthday. I was wandering around *Cinco de Mayo*, wondering what to get you, and I couldn't come up with anything. But then I found this in an electronics store on *Via España* and I knew it was perfect."

"Now, anytime I'm alone and missing you, I can listen to you tell me I eat penis bones."

"You could, but that's not really what I envisioned. I know you love to write. And I imagine you hiking around *Los Altos* or traveling to *Penonomé* on the bus and coming up with all kinds of good ideas but not having a chance to write them down. Now you can take notes with this pen and you won't have to worry about forgetting stuff before you get back to your house."

"I think this is the most thoughtful present anyone's ever given me." I'd been feeling silly all day, with the horse-play in the restaurant, the talk of penis bones, and the general euphoria that went along with seeing Elena for the first time in too long, but her present really touched me. She must've picked up on the shift in my attitude, for she twisted in her seat so she could sit with her back against the side of the bus and get a better look at me.

"I knew you'd like it," she said, looking entirely too pleased with herself.

In the late afternoon, after we arrived at *Timshel* and settled in, we walked down the road to visit *La Tranquilidad*. I introduced Elena to Jose and Maria and the rest of their family. They welcomed her with smiles and hugs and kisses, as though they were meeting their son's fiancée for the first time.

"John has taught us so much," Maria told Elena.

"That's not really true," I answered, "but they're very kind."

Maria showed Elena the farm and all the work we'd done together.

"John is the king of kings," Maria added at the end of the tour. I laughed. She was laying it on way too thick, but I appreciated the effort. As we said goodbye and began to take our leave, Maria gave Elena some fresh flowers straight from the gardens of *La Tranquilidad*.

Fresh flowers in hand, Elena and I made our way to the center of town. We had dinner at Alejandra's house and played hide and seek with the kids until the sun was nearly down.

At dusk, as we walked back up the road towards my house, Nelson found us. He walked alongside me so I was between him and Elena. With his relatively short legs, he had trouble keeping up. He leaned forward every few minutes to try and peek around me and get a glimpse of Elena's blonde curls and green eyes. He'd never seen anything like her.

"Is that your *señora?*" he asked eagerly.

It was a tricky question. Elena most certainly was not my *señora*. We'd never even talked about whatever it was we had or didn't have, but if I answered "no," I'd brand Elena a whore and the whole town would know it by morning. Most people didn't have casual sex in the *campo*. And those who did weren't obvious about it. Many of my neighbors hadn't been wed in the church because they couldn't afford it, but any couple that shared a roof was married in most people's eyes.

"Yes, she is my *señora*," I answered definitively. I kept my eyes on Nelson to avoid looking at Elena, but I could feel her smile searing into my cheek.

"Aww, you're so sweet," Elena ribbed me in our native English.

"What did she say?"

"She said she's crazy about me."

Nelson gave me a big grin to show me his approval. Elena hooked her arm through mine and we walked the rest of the way home with little conversation.

When we arrived at my front porch, Nelson hopped into my hammock, crossed his hands behind his head, and settled in as though he intended to spend the next several hours with us. I appreciated his friendship, but I had other plans for the evening, so I unlocked the front door and tossed him a piece of hard candy from a bag I kept on my desk. "Nelson, thanks for accompanying us, but I want to be alone with my *señora* now."

"Ok," he answered cheerfully, without protest. "It was nice to meet you," he said to Elena. "Good night," he called over his shoulder as he ran down the path, down the road, and out of sight.

"I like him," Elena told me.

"He's a smart kid."

"Well it's obvious he thinks you're the coolest guy ever."

"Like I said, he's a smart kid."

While Elena showered, I lit my kerosene lamps and a couple of candles and I put on Mark Farina's *Mushroom Jazz.* The light flickered on the walls and gave the house a cozy glow. A few minutes later, standing in my room with damp hair, wearing only a towel, Elena began to kiss me.

She slipped her tongue deep inside my mouth and backed me up against my desk. Then she pushed me away and let her towel fall to the floor. I told myself to burn the moment into my mind to make it live forever.

I lifted her up onto the desk so she sat facing me. I undid my belt and unbuttoned my pants, letting them fall to the floor, and pulled my cock through the fly of my boxers. She spread her legs for me and leaned as far back as she could until the back of her head leaned against the wall. She gripped the edge of the desk with both hands as I pushed myself inside her.

She closed her eyes and bit her lip and let out a long groan that was too sexy and I came almost instantly. But I fought through the tingle and kept plugging away. Though I'd already cum, my erection showed no signs of death. My stupid cock was numb like a rubber dildo. I could work it in and out of her all night. After twenty minutes, the batteries in the tape deck began to die. The music warbled into slow motion and then gave out completely.

When my poor penis felt fit to burst aflame and I thought I couldn't endure a minute more, Elena moaned and shook and shuddered and came and came, delivering lurching orgasm after orgasm. The savagery of her grunts took me by surprise and aroused me anew and I blew a load into her that I didn't know I had before I fell against her, exhausted, gratified, and buried my face in her neck.

"Did you finish?" she asked me innocently.

"Like you wouldn't believe."

I felt my penis slowly soften inside her. Finally, it slipped out on its own accord. We both flinched at the shock of separation.

When I came back from the shower, Elena was already asleep. I blew out the lamps and candles and climbed into bed next to her. I pressed my chest against her back and appreciated the way my limp dick felt mashed against her warm, bare ass. The top of my thighs pressed against the bottom of hers; I wrapped my arm around her and placed my palm flat on her stomach.

"Thanks for visiting," I told her as she slept. I wanted to say more, but nothing else came out. Maybe next time. I gave her a squeeze goodnight and rolled over and shut my eyes.

In the morning, I cooked omelets with cheese and onions and some homemade guacamole. I also squeezed some oranges that I'd picked up at *La Tranquilidad*. It made me happy to prepare such a good meal for Elena. I wished I could do it more often.

After breakfast, out on my porch, Elena trimmed my beard with a straight edge razor. I watched her eyes as she studied my chin with furrowed brow and decided where to clip. I found something sexy about trusting her with a blade so close to my throat. I was getting drunk on the intimacy of the moment.

"You really need to pay more attention to this thing," she told me.

"But then you wouldn't trim it for me."

"I'll trim it for you."

After a while the bus came. She climbed aboard and waved goodbye. I watched the bus go around the bend and out of sight. *Los Altos* felt very, very quiet.

Night after solitary night, Roxana's question – "do you love her?" – swam around my fishbowl head. I swung back and forth in the hammock as tiny frogs chirped desperately in the soggy pasture outside my house, each with the frenzied hope of finding a fleeting lover for nothing more than a quick hump-hump to sow a seed before doing it all over again one moon later.

And should I decide that yes, I most definitely love her, as I had so many times, why should I tell her? For whose benefit? Hers? Mine? To make her feel more secure? To satisfy my own need to express myself? Or more pathetic yet, to hope to hear her say it back? No matter what it was, or what it wasn't, I knew enough to know that time was all I had, and my favorite kind of time was the kind spent with her. Did the labels matter?

Besides, there was no context for our intimacy. Our romance was so far off the map, literally, that it seemed impossible to hold it up to the light and figure out if it was real. We'd spend an intense night or two together and then go back to our separate lives for weeks at a time. Usually, the weeks apart gave me the opportunity to idealize her and endow her with imaginary virtues and unlikely sentiments. But on my clearer days, I had to wonder if Elena would be as important to me, and I to her, if we weren't so far from home, lost in the woods and surrounded by people who didn't quite understand us. Then again, maybe she didn't even think about me that much when we weren't together. Maybe she was better at compartmentalizing her life and living in the moment. Maybe she could build a better bookshelf.

But none of that mattered because the precious time we had together was perfect, so I tried to slow the r.p.m.'s and grasp those moments and live inside them as long as possible in an otherwise vast series of melting moments. And I thought of my neighbors in *Los Altos* who struggled every day just to feed their families and I cursed myself for such self-absorbed preoccupations. And then I wondered what the hell I was rambling on about and realized I'd been smoking way too much weed lately.

Chapter 24 – Empty Vessel

My neighbor, Virgilio, knocked on my door at six o'clock in the morning.

"Will you lend me your pick and your shovel?" he asked me. "My father-in-law died last night."

"Of course. I'm sorry for your loss."

He nodded stoically, took the tools, and walked off.

I'd never met his father-in-law before. I'd never even seen him. Still, I felt I should pay my respects, so I dressed quickly and headed up to Virgilio's house.

I stepped through the front door and found a roomful of silent mourners. The corpse, surrounded by burning candles, lay on a table in the middle of the room. I studied the dead stranger in front of me – his nostrils stuffed with cotton, his cheeks covered with rouge. He looked like he was made of wax. *Are you there? Are you anywhere? Can you hear my thoughts? I hope you don't mind that I came. Did you have a good life?*

I wanted to feel sad, but I didn't. For me, the body was just a nameless, empty vessel. I didn't even know his family. Not really.

I found an empty chair in the corner and tried to be inconspicuous. Save for the occasional sniffle, the only sounds came from somewhere outside the house. A hand saw sighed back and forth as it chewed through wood; a hammer nailed fresh cut planks together.

I imagined I was supposed to pray for the guy, but I'd never been one for prayers. My mind wandered to issues of etiquette. *Am I welcome here? Maybe I shouldn't have come. If I didn't come, would they think I'm rude? It's hard to know what to do sometimes.*

After I paid my respects, I walked down to the cemetery to help dig. The grave was nearly finished by the time I arrived. The men nodded to me in solemn salutation.

A man stood in the bottom of the hole and looked up at me. He wiped his brow with the back of his wrist. Without asking if he wanted a break, I reached down into the grave and offered my hand.

Once he climbed out, I took his place, clawing at the bottom of the grave with the pick axe. Then I passed the pick axe to a man standing over me and he handed me the shovel. I jabbed at the hard clay with the point of the shovel. It was much more difficult than moving topsoil on the farm, but I managed to make a bit of progress. I could feel the men's eyes on me, evaluating my contribution. *This, John Dillon, is the strangest moment of your life. You are a long way from Wall Street.* After several minutes of toil, my arms felt like rubber. Sensing my fatigue, someone else took over.

When the work was finished, I collected my muddy tools and reached the road just in time to watch the funeral procession walk by. With my pick and shovel swung over my shoulder, I removed my hat and clutched it against my stomach. I felt like an extra in a Faulkner yarn.

That evening, the whole town arrived at Virgilio's house to kick off the nine-night wake. Virgilio's wife served plates of *arroz con pollo* to the crowd who sat outside in the yard on chairs and rocks and five gallon buckets. It was like a big party with the volume turned down to a whisper.

Bonito slinked through the yard and lay down under a table. He probably hoped that a few scraps would fall his way, but he wasn't that lucky. Without hesitation, Virgilio's teenage son sprang to his feet, grabbed a heavy stick off the ground, and whaled on the pitiful animal. Rather than move, Bonito looked up at the boy with big pleading eyes as if to say, "I won't bother anyone; please let me rest here a while. I'll be good. I won't beg. Please."

I wanted to storm across the grass, snatch the stick away, and crack the bully with it, . . . but I wouldn't get righteous at his grandfather's wake. So I grit my teeth and flinched each time the stick landed on Bonito's hide with a dull thud.

C'mon Bonito, just go.

Finally, when Bonito couldn't endure any more pain or public humiliation, he got up and scurried into the darkness. Some teenagers next to me started to giggle.

"Why are you laughing?" I asked the kids. "You think that's funny?"

"No," one of them lied. "But that dog used to belong to them. Then he got sick, so they don't want him anymore, but the stupid dog keeps coming back." They whispered something to one another and started to giggle again.

The boy's account explained the motor oil. But it hadn't cured Bonito's mange, so Virgilio decided to kick the dog to the street and get a puppy. Dirtbags. I regretted helping them dig their hole. I went home and climbed into bed.

But I couldn't sleep soundly, for the bolts that kept my roof fastened to one corner of the house – after years of torrential winter rainstorms and blustery summer winds – had finally rusted and given way. Whenever the wind got underneath that corner of the steel roof, it lifted up the metal sheet and bashed it back down again.

Each time it woke me, I masturbated and fell back to sleep, only to have the roof bang and crash and wake me up again. So I masturbated *a lot.* I rubbed myself raw. I made a mental note to find some big rocks and place them on the roof.

The little sleep I found passed in thick layers of muddled Aralen dreams. There were wobbly bicycles and noisy casinos and college exams and an endless cast of characters with familiar faces and forgotten names and the constant feeling of being lost or confused or both at the same time as I went about it all in the wrong way. The only constant was my dark bedroom, which at times seemed the most alien place of all.

Chapter 25 – Reality's Handle

I awoke in a pitch black room to sheer, irrational terror and the primal sound of dogs' frenzied barking. *What's out there? What's set off the dogs?* I lay perfectly still, hyper-vigilant, awaiting the next sign of my intruder's arrival. My clock ticked and the spigot dripped; the bamboo wind chime on my porch clinked from time to time. I was certain a bad person crept outside.

A sliver of moonlight reflected off my mosquito net. My door was unlocked and I realized that my machetes were in the other room. My intruder was going to burst through the door and attack me at any moment. Why? I didn't know. I tried to figure out what I might have done or who I might have upset. Maybe it was just about my *gringo* possessions. It occurred to me that bed is too vulnerable a place to be.

I shut my eyes to listen. Something definitely moved about. Then it stopped. Then it started again. I heard a rapping on wood and wondered if I was being threatened or mocked or both. Was someone looking at me through the window?

I slipped out of bed and crept across my dark house, cursing my ankles for giving away my position when they cracked and popped upon contact with the cement floor. It was so dark I couldn't see much of anything, but I knew my house well. I found a machete by feel and could tell by the weight that it was the short one. It wouldn't give me much reach, but it was light and easy to wield.

I peeked through the space in the door. Nothing. I gathered my courage and threw the door open and glared around my porch with the machete held out in front of me. Nothing. I urinated in my garden and marked my territory. "You have lost it," I said to myself. Then I went back to bed.

As soon as I was back in bed I heard something moving again and the sound of knocking on wood. I couldn't help but remember that night in *Cerro Verde* when Antonio's lover tried to pay me a visit. This time my Panamanian mother wasn't going to save me either.

"WHO IS IT?" I bellowed, trying to sound tough.

The movement stopped. Frogs chirped in the distance. I fell back asleep and started to dream again.

Elena was in *Los Altos* and I took indescribable pleasure in watching her interact so easily with the people, especially with the kids. She played hide and seek with the whole town. She ran around someone's yard with her sarong clutched up in one hand to give her enough freedom to move. As I watched her laugh and shriek with the kids, it occurred to me that she'd make a wonderful mother one day. Then it occurred to me that I was thinking about her being a mother. I thought to myself that I'd like this woman to raise my children. I couldn't believe that I was thinking such thoughts. It seemed too fast and too adult, but it also seemed so right.

Then I suddenly became aware that Elena had broken up with me. Just before she walked out on me, she called up an old boyfriend and asked me to listen in on their conversation. He spoke English well, but had a *Latino* accent. He was happy to hear from her. I listened to them flirt. I couldn't understand why Elena would ask me to listen to that. Why would she do such a thing? Didn't she know how hurtful and cruel that was?

I woke up to the sound of rain hitting the steel roof. Then the rain stopped and the dogs started barking again. I lay in bed with my head cold and my exhaustion and I observed my sinuses drain and fill and drain again as I floated in and out of sleep. The barking faded away and I fell into a series of dreams that kept me confused and troubled all night, mixing my past with the present and the totally foreign. I had a slimy grip on reality's handle and the time had less meaning all the time. I felt like an actor on a foggy stage of a theatre I didn't know I'd entered and I wasn't even sure if there was an audience.

Just then, I noticed a big, creepy spider crawling across my bedside table. His body was bigger than my whole hand and his legs were longer than my fingers. I didn't know what he was; I didn't know whether he was dangerous to me or if he was a blessing that kept my house free of other pests. Although it took a lot for the insect world to upset me after a year of being a Volunteer, I'd had a bad night, he'd scared the shit out of me, and it was going to cost him his life.

The chase was on. He sensed the danger and scrambled across the house and under my stove. Because I wielded a machete in each hand I had to hold my flashlight between my teeth. Reluctantly, I lowered my eyes to his level so I could see under the stove, afraid that he'd jump out at any second and latch on to my face as I fell, screaming, to the floor, flailing like a turtle on its back, but when I shined the light underneath the stove, I found him cowering in the corner where the table met the wall. He froze in the light and his eyes glowed fiercely, reflecting the light right back at me in a demonstration of his eerie alien powers. I had to jab the machetes at him at least half

161

a dozen times before I stuck him. He was a quick little bastard, but in the end I proved too formidable an opponent. I hoped he'd been dangerous so I could chalk it up as a justifiable killing.

I woke up in the morning feeling quite insane, sure that sometime in the last few days some gear or cog vital to my very being had cracked. My head hurt. My chest hurt. I swallowed a handful of government-issued pills as I admired the different colors, shapes, and sizes. I wondered if I had a fever. I wanted to be somewhere more comfortable. Somewhere with fluffy pillows and air conditioning and clothes that didn't smell like mildew.

I decided then and there that I wasn't going to take any more Aralen. I lived far away from Panama's malaria infested jungles and coasts. I'd get a bottle from Bernard, put the bottle aside, and mark the months off my calendar. Then, when enough time had passed and I should've been running out, I'd ask Bernard for some more. That way he would think I was still using it. If I knew I'd be traveling to an area known for malaria outbreaks, I'd take the pills for two weeks before I went and two weeks after I got back. Other than that, to hell with it. The Peace Corps' rules be damned.

When I finally went outside I found Bonito sleeping underneath the bamboo worm bin on my porch. I quickly realized that he had been the one lurking around my house in the night. And that he had set off all the other neighborhood dogs. Other dogs – dogs with homes – didn't want Bonito crowding their turf. So he decided he'd bunker down at my place. He must've banged the legs of the box as he scratched at his fleas and got comfortable on my sack of wood ash. That bastard.

I chased him off with a broom.

But he didn't go far. He scampered into my garden, stopped, and looked back over his shoulder with those perpetually surprised eyes, as though to say, "*Et tu Juan?*" I couldn't take the guilt, so I opened up a can of tuna fish for him. He buried his snout in the can and didn't look up again until all of the tuna was gone. Then he gazed up at me, seemingly unable to comprehend the sudden, fortunate turn of events.

"It's alright dude," I reassured him, too tired to be adversarial anymore, "it's for you. Enjoy it." That was all he needed to hear. He ran his tongue around the inside of the can a few more times just in case the tin held some extra flavor. Then he nestled himself back under the worm bin, shut his eyes, and thumped his tail contentedly against the leg of the box. I wondered if he was awake or dreaming. I wondered if he wondered the same thing.

From then on, I always let Bonito sleep on the floor inside the house. I didn't want him setting off the neighborhood dogs or freaking me out in the middle of the night anymore. Besides, he desperately needed a friend. I gave him a can of tuna fish each morning as I cooked my breakfast. Then, in the evenings, he'd stick his nose up in the air and savor the sweet smells simmering on my stove, in a not-so-subtle reminder to give him another can for dinner. Sometimes, I'd get some locally baked bread at the town store and make myself a couple of peanut butter and jelly sandwiches. When I got sand-wiches, Bonito always got one too. Most of the time, how-ever, I left him to his own devices as I made the rounds and visited farms. I didn't know where he went or what he got up to during the days, but little-by-little he gained weight and started to fill out. After a few weeks, I couldn't see his ribs anymore. Finally, on one of my trips to *Penonomé*, I bought him some medicine for his mange and sure enough, his hair started to grow back. He wasn't exactly living up to his name, but at least he was turning into a dog again. I guess I needed a friend too.

Chapter 26 – Bored of the Foolery

I finally got a break from the *campo* and the inside of my mind at In-Service Training, or "I.S.T." as it was known within the Peace Corps. It marked the first time my entire training group had been together since we'd all sworn in and gone off to our respective sites.

The Peace Corps held our I.S.T at a sprawling agricultural center called *Cedeso*. The center had a seed bank, a large nursery, and hundreds of acres of reforestation projects. The property also had a large cafeteria and a dorm, so it was perfect for an event like ours. And best of all, it was only a mile from the beach at *Farallon*.

An airstrip ran alongside the facility, though it hadn't been used, at least not legally, for years. Local beach resorts had intentions to restore the place, but patches of weeds poked through cracks in the tarmac. If the hotels didn't act quickly, the landing strip would serve only the drug runners who landed there late at night.

Back in Noriega's day, *Cedeso* was a military base. In fact, the U.S. military sustained more casualties on that airstrip than anywhere else during Operation Just Cause. The injuries, however, had nothing to do with any Panamanian show of force. Rather, the American paratroopers miscalculated the drop when they jumped out of their planes. Their legs splintered into pieces when they landed on the tarmac. Ouch.

I.S.T offered workshops on a variety of subjects, from public speaking to seed storage to cultural sensitivity. For me, however, I.S.T. was more about the other Volunteers. I loved just being around them, listening to my native English for the first time in weeks, soaking in jokes and stories late into the night. Simple things.

On the third and final night, we all walked down to the beach where we found a bar called *Guavas*. It was just a shack really; the roof was barely large enough to cover the shelves of liquor. But there were a few plastic tables and chairs out front and the drinks were wet and cheap. Pablo, the bartender, was the only other person there. He told us that he and his brother had built the place as a private beach hang-out away from the city, but it turned into a business when customers started showing up.

Pablo claimed to have learned his impeccable English from watching TV in general, and *Rocky* in particular. None of us believed him, but we listened with rapt attention to his stories of drug running and porn star clientele and weekends spent volunteering at prisons and his father who was a Catholic priest. I drank too much Seco and Pablo sold me some weed and I spent the next half hour dry heaving in the sand. I never could handle mixing weed with booze, but I'd never learned my lesson either. Many of my colleagues were in even worse shape than me.

Jeff and Meredith, who were both dating other people, dry humped each other in the sand. On an otherwise dark beach, they'd somehow found the lone splinter of light cast from the tiny bar. The high tide lapped at their clothes and set a scene reminiscent of a Calvin Klein commercial gone terribly wrong. They were oblivious to the fact that *everyone* watched them.

"Hey Kyle," I asked, "You think he's gonna give her the beans?"

"I don't know. Maybe."

"It looks like he might give her the beans."

"We can only hope," he answered. Then he whispered to me, "I just hooked up with Wendy."

"And?"

"We made out for a little while and she jerked me off in the shadows."

"How was it?"

"Not great."

"Hmmmm. I think I'm disappointed with your standards."

"I am too," he confessed.

Everyone was having a good time.

Except for Elena. Ever since she'd exhibited herself at the Hotel Mocambo, Elena had been more careful about getting drunk in a crowd. Unfortunately for me, sober people rarely enjoy the company of drunks. Elena found the scene too juvenile and grew bored of the foolery.

"This is embarrassing," Elena said. "We're Peace Corps Volunteers and we've covered this beach in trash. Look: plastic cups and beer bottles are everywhere."

"Don't worry about it," I told her. "We'll clean up. People are just blowing off steam and having fun."

"I want to head back," she insisted.

"Really? But this is just getting good."

"I want to go to bed. I'm tired."

Sigh.

I hoped to party with the others *and* hang out with Elena, but she forced me to make a choice. And it wasn't much of a choice. I couldn't – or at least wouldn't – let Elena walk back by herself in the middle of the night. I turned my back on the crowd, took Elena's hand, and walked her back to *Cedeso*. At least we'd have the place to ourselves.

Back at the quiet dorm, in the women's communal bathroom, Elena and I showered and got ready for bed. I stood in front of one sink while Elena stood before another. As I brushed my teeth, I looked at her though the reflection of the mirror. She meticulously brushed her long, blonde hair and didn't realize that I watched her. She stared so intently at herself. I wondered what she saw.

We locked ourselves into one of the dorm rooms. Because the rooms had only single beds, we pushed two of them together to form a makeshift double bed. We lay pressed together, facing one another, our skin still soft from the hot shower.

Chapter 27 – A Good Person

Elena curled up next to me in the darkness and laid her head on my chest. I ran my fingernails across her scalp. She started to sniffle.

"I can't do this anymore," she muttered.

"What?" I asked with alarm. "You mean *us?*"

"No. . . . I don't think so. . . . I don't know what I mean."

Only moments earlier, I'd been in that warm, dizzy place that follows satisfying sex and precedes deep sleep, but panic streamed up my neck and the base of my skull before running around my ears and shooting through my temples. Was Elena breaking up with me? She couldn't.

I loved my time in *Los Altos*, but I loved it because I could save it up and share it with Elena in a quiet room away from the rest of the world. The sex was extraordinary, but the intimacy was better. Our communion became more important to me with each passing day.

Her site was on the other side of the country and she stayed there for weeks at a stretch, but she was never far. Her smiles and laughter lived in my imagination and brightened my pace as I walked along my town's many dirt paths. Our conversations and jokes replayed themselves in my head as I blew out the candles and climbed into bed each windy night. I carried her with me, always, in the softest, safest place in my mind.

That her feelings could be anything less than reciprocal inspired instant terror.

"Baby," I asked quietly, cautiously, "what are you saying?"

"I can't take it anymore."

"You can't take *what* anymore?" The dread spread like bone cancer.

"It's too hard where I live," she muttered.

So it's about her site! Thank God!

"What do you mean?" I asked, with a little more confidence.

"The *colonos* wipe out more forest every day."

"Why don't the Wounaan start to fight back? I'm sure you can help them do *something*," I postured.

"Yeah. Maybe."

"Well then?"

She raised her head and looked at me with profoundly sad eyes. "Right now no one's in shape to do much of anything. A lot of my neighbors can't even put food on the table. Thanks to the *colonos* most of them are too sick to get out of bed."

"How is that the *colonos'* fault? People get sick, right?"

"But it *is* their fault." Her sniffles turned to tears. "They come with their cattle and they clear cut everything in sight and they get closer and closer to the Wounaan villages. A couple of weeks ago they cut down the forest upstream from *Quebrada Brava's* water supply. What they're doing is completely illegal, but the government doesn't care about the Wounaan. To them, the Wounaan are just a bunch of stupid, poor indians."

"That sounds a little harsh, don't you think?"

"You're not getting it," she answered impatiently. "Cows shit. And the shit has to *go* somewhere. So it rains and the shit gets washed into the river and gets in the drinking water. Half my town got gastroenteritis. The only reason I didn't get it is because I use a water purifier that the Peace Corps gave me."

"And you feel guilty because you didn't get sick?"

"I don't know. . . . Maybe a little, but that's not really it."

"Then what is it?

"I've told you about Gloriela before. She's one of the women in the basket weaving group."

"Right. I remember."

"Last week her baby, Leo, got sick. He had a fever and diarrhea and he was totally dehydrated. We didn't know if he had E. Coli or giardia or what. Gloriela was really sick too. She was so sick she couldn't even breast feed him. They both needed to see a doctor, but the town's only outboard motor was broken. The captain was in *Chepo* getting it fixed, so the boat wasn't running. There was no transportation in or out.

"But that baby had to get some help," she continued. "He looked awful. He'd been a healthy eight-month old, at least by *campo* standards, but after a couple of days he was skin and bones. He just cried and cried . . . all day and all night. It was like a dry, panting cry that babies with bad colic get. The houses are so close together that we could all hear him all the time. That sound gets to you. It grates on you."

"I can imagine."

"No, you can't," she told me sternly, scolding me with her eyes before she continued. "Finally, I went to Gloriela's house and scooped up the baby. I told Gloriela I was going to take Leo to the hospital. She was too weak to protest.

"But you said there was no boat."

171

"I know. There wasn't. I had to carry him all day through the forest. He hardly made a peep. I was relieved that he stopped his constant crying, but it was also eerie. I was so scared. It took me almost five hours before I reached the road and flagged down a ride."

"Five hours? You must've been exhausted."

"Maybe. I guess. But it never really crossed my mind. There wasn't any choice. He *had* to have medical attention. I got him to the hospital and they stuck an IV in his tiny little arm. It took them so many tries to find his little vein. The poor thing howled as they stuck him over and over again. He couldn't have understood where his mother was or why all of that was happening to him. He must've thought he was in hell.

"I wanted to be by his bed. I wanted to comfort him in any way I could, but they said I wasn't allowed. They said I wasn't family. It made me ill. The thought of him being all alone, sick, in a strange and scary place. I was climbing the walls in the waiting room, trying to get any information I could from anyone who walked by, but my exhaustion must have crept up on me and I fell asleep in the waiting room." Elena's shoulders began to quake.

"It sounds like you'd earned some sleep, especially after working so hard to get that baby to the hospital."

"But it didn't do any good," she gasped. "Nothing I did mattered." Her lip began to quiver and her chin trembled. She struggled to get the rest of the words out as her chest heaved and the sobs choked the air out of her. "A doctor woke me up in the morning. He told me he was 'sorry.' I asked him what he meant; I asked him what he was 'sorry' for, but I knew. I guess I just needed him to say it. Leo had been too dehydrated for too long. He died in the night."

"Elena?"

"I asked to see him. I don't know why. Maybe I thought that if I saw him he wouldn't really be dead. They didn't let me see him anyway. I wasn't family."

A tempest of reality left me dumbfounded and speechless. I wanted to say the right thing or perform some heroic act, but I felt impotent. We lay wordlessly, staring at the ceiling. Plenty of our friends would complete their Peace Corps service after two years of laughter and parties and life-long friendships, but I knew that for Elena it could never be the same.

No wonder she'd been so moody and aloof down at the beach. I felt like an asshole for trying to convince her to stay at the party, but I had no idea what she'd been harboring. No one did. After several minutes, Elena broke the silence.

"Yesterday I was crying so loudly in my house that some of my neighbors came over to see if I was ok. I felt so embarrassed."

"Oh *honey* . . . there's nothing to be embarrassed about. You're a strong person. You're a *good* person."

I meant only to comfort her, but the words hit her too hard and she started sobbing again.

"You really think so?" she asked pitifully.

"Of course I do."

She buried her face in my neck and clutched my t-shirt in her balled up fists.

"He was only eight months old," she pleaded. "I wanted to save him so badly."

"It wasn't your fault."

173

"I know it wasn't my fault. It was those *fucking* cowboys' fault!" she barked, her pain evolving into anger. "But that doesn't make it any easier. You can't imagine what the trip back to *Quebrada Brava* was like . . . knowing the whole time that I had to tell Gloriela her baby was *dead*. How do you tell someone something like that?"

"I don't know how you did it."

"I felt so powerless."

"Don't do that to yourself. It's not like that. There's only so much you can do."

I wanted to say the right things, but I knew I couldn't relate. Tears continued to stream down her scarlet cheeks. She turned her head and wiped her nose across my chest, using my t-shirt as her tissue.

"Sorry," she added, laughing half-heartedly at herself, "that was gross."

"Don't worry about it." I was glad to be a human Kleenex, if nothing else. And I was glad to see she still knew how to smile. I wrapped my arms around her and held her tight.

"I love you," I finally told her. If ever someone needed to hear those terrible, tragic words, she did, right then. It seemed so inadequate, but it was long overdue.

"I love you too," she whispered.

After breakfast, we found ourselves saying goodbye under a covered bus stop on the side of the Inter-American Highway. It was a dismal, grey morning and a constant stream of traffic rushed past us in the rain. I listened to the hypnotic sound of wet tires licking at the asphalt.

"I can't believe you waited until last night to tell me about that poor little kid."

"I didn't plan on telling you at all. I didn't want to ruin the time."

"Oh darling." All she'd endured and she was worried about *me*. "The last thing you should be concerned about is my feelings. What you've been through is too much for *anyone* to keep bottled up. Besides, you can tell me anything."

"I know. Really, I do. Thanks for listening last night. I feel a lot better now," she said dismissively.

We climbed aboard a bus and I lost myself in the passing landscape. It occurred to me that if our roles had been reversed and I'd been forced to deal with *Quebrada Brava*, I'd probably be trembling like a demented butterfly, my arms wrapped around my knees, rocking back and forth and mumbling to myself, hoping that Elena would be there soon to stroke my hair and my back and my ego. *Los Altos* suddenly seemed like a resort town.

After a time, she closed her book and placed it on her lap. She whispered in my ear. "I love you baby. I love you, I love you, I love you." The air in my chest felt crisp and light; we were still drunk on the emotion that had overflowed our dorm room and followed us onto the bus. I looked out the window and watched the rain fall.

Chapter 28 – Tuna Melts

I was reading in my hammock when a white coupe, covered in rust, chugged up the road and came to an abrupt stop in front of my house. Had one of my neighbors managed to scrape enough pennies together to buy a car?

The driver's side door swung open. A tall, lanky figure – a man comically too big for a car that size – emerged from the vehicle. The driver was too far away for me to make out his face, but I knew who he was right away.

I leapt to my feet and ran down the path to greet him. "Antonio! What are you doing here? Are you alright?"

"Relax. Everything is very well. I am here to visit you. May I stay here tonight?"

"Of course. It's good to see you. But how did you find me?"

"Carlos explained to me how to get here. I would have arrived earlier, but I got lost along the way. Some children in town told me where you live and put me back on the right path." He smiled a heartfelt smile. He looked happy. He looked happier than I ever remembered seeing him.

"Come in. I'll make us some dinner."

"You cook?"

"Of course I cook," I boasted. "How do you think I survive out here?" I proudly gave him the tour of my porch and two rooms and pointed out my two-burner gas stove.

"What are you going to cook?"

"I'll make us some tuna melts and French fries."

Antonio crinkled up his nose to evidence his disdain for my culinary inclinations, though he probably never had a tuna melt in his life. He certainly never had one of *my* tuna melts. I made them several times a week in the *campo* and I'd perfected them. It was easy to stock up on cans of tuna when I went to town. And a loaf of bread would last me two weeks before it started to mold. I'd buy a ten cent pat of butter and a slice of individually wrapped cheese from the local store, add some pepper, and I'd be in business.

"How about I cook the dinner," he suggested. "I brought food with me from the city. It'll spoil if we don't make it soon," he added, softening the blow.

"Alright," I conceded. "I'll run down to the store and buy us some Cokes . . . and I'll make us breakfast in the morning."

When I got back from the store I saw that Antonio had made himself at home in my kitchen. It smelled great. He prepared chicken and vegetable shish-kebobs on wooden skewers over a bed of white rice. I was glad I'd deferred to him for dinner.

We ate in silence on my porch. I couldn't be bothered to disrupt the best meal I'd had in months with small talk. But after we polished off the meal and I washed the plates at the spigot outside my porch, I could concentrate on conversing with my houseguest.

"You called Carlos your 'former roommate.' You don't live with him anymore?"

"No."

"Is everything ok?" I asked worriedly.

"Everything is great. Carlos was wonderful to me. He let me stay in his apartment for several weeks. He was almost never there."

"So what happened?"

"At first I had a lot of trouble finding a job. I applied for jobs in offices, but they said I wasn't qualified for even the most basic office work because I didn't have a college degree. I tried to get a job as a waiter, but got turned away again and again. Finally, after searching for about a month, I found work as a prep cook in a small restaurant. A few weeks after that, I saved enough to rent a room in someone's house." He beamed with pride at his success. "Since then, I made enough to buy that car," he added, lifting his chin and pointing to the road with his lips.

All that 'women's work' in *Cerro Verde* paid off after all. I was really happy for him. We played a few games of checkers as Antonio told me about life in the city and I told him about life in *Los Altos*. After a couple of hours I unrolled my Therm-a-Rest and laid it out on the floor.

"You can have my bed," I offered.

"No, that's ok."

"I insist." After all the nights I slept in his bed in *Cerro Verde*, I was glad to finally return the favor.

"Ok. Thank you."

In the morning I made him my perfected omelet, complete with cheese, tomato and onion. To my delight, he liked it. We bid one another farewell and I wondered when I'd see him again.

Chapter 29 – Art

The Peace Corps held its All Volunteer Conference in *Santa Clara* over Thanksgiving weekend. Dennis and Sheila from XS cooked all the food to ensure that we *gringo*s got our stuffing and sweet potatoes and turkey prepared the way it should be. But there was no way XS could accommodate all the Volunteers, so the Peace Corps rented out all of the cabañas at a place on the beach called *Los Girasoles*. When I arrived, I said hello to some people and looked for my room amidst the commotion of staggered arrivals. I found Elena milling about near the office.

"Our room is over that way," she said, pointing towards the back of the property. Then she turned and glared at Kelly, who had only just arrived. "Thanks a lot for stealing our sofa." Kelly shrugged at me and I shrugged back. "We got screwed on our room," Elena told me.

"Ok." I couldn't care less where our room was. My bag was heavy on my back. I just wanted to put it down and take a shower, so I trudged off in the direction she pointed.

I changed into my board shorts and went for a swim. Volunteers were in the ocean, all over the beach, and at the bar. It was like spring break had come to *Santa Clara*. I played volleyball with some Volunteers before eating dinner with Bernard and Christine Katz. After dessert, I excused myself to go look for Elena.

She was out on the dance floor with Alex, another Volunteer. Meringue music blared from the bar's distorted speakers as Alex and Elena danced close together, occasionally spinning one another around and laughing at themselves.

"Can I cut in?"

Alex started to step away when Elena spoke up. "Maybe later," she answered coolly with her nose turned up in the air. "Right now I'm dancing with Alex," she added, as though it wasn't plainly obvious.

"Alright," I told her. "Maybe later." But I walked off thinking, "*well screw you too baby.*" I sulked under the thin layer of skin that separated me from the rest of the world. We hadn't seen each other in a month. I couldn't figure out what I'd done to deserve her disdain.

I found Kyle out on the beach. He was using a Frisbee as a shovel to dig a deep hole. Two other Volunteers were digging with some dinner plates that they borrowed from the restaurant. They'd been out there since the early afternoon, working straight through dinner and the sunset and the moonrise. Their hole was perfectly square, about eight feet by eight feet and nearly as deep.

"What are you guys doing?"

"What's it look like we're doing?"

"It looks like you're digging a hole with dinner plates."

"It's not a hole. It's a combat pit."

"Of course it is."

"You'll see. I'm going to kick some ass in here in a couple of ow'as."

I gave Kyle a hand and pulled him out of the deep hole.

"I'll be back in a little while," he gravely told the other two.

"I'll make sure I bring him straight back."

I bought Kyle a beer and a shot and we watched a great talent show. Bruce's impressions of all the Peace Corps staff were extraordinary, but the offline connection with Elena gnawed at me. When Kyle returned to his pit, I finally sought her out.

"Will you take a walk with me?" I asked her.

"I guess so. Sure."

We walked down the beach without holding hands.

"What's going on?" I asked her.

"What do you mean?"

"You don't seem like yourself. You seem distant. Is everything alright?"

"There are so many Volunteers here who I've never met before, but they all seem to know you."

"That's not so surprising. After all, your site is pretty remote compared to mine."

"But it's annoying. When I meet people, and tell them my name, they say 'oh, like Elena of Elena and John.' I don't like it."

"Is it really that bad?" I asked. I liked the idea of being associated with her. It stung that she didn't feel the same way.

"It's just that I've always been so fiercely independent. Stand-offish even. I feel like I'm losing my independence in this relationship."

"Believe me, you're an independent woman. Look how you handled yourself in Hawaii and San Diego and now in *Quebrada Brava*."

"But these people don't know any of that," she protested.

"So what?" I tried to stay patient and hide my annoyance. "Other people's perceptions are totally irrelevant. How you perceive yourself is what matters. Don't you think?"

"I just feel . . . lost. You seem so confident and together. I'm just confused and . . . unformed."

"We're all 'unformed.' At least we should be, right? We all have hard times and insecurities. Check this out: 'Our doubts are traitors, and make us lose the good we oft might win by fearing to attempt.'"

"What's that from?"

"*Measure for Measure.*" I read the play and scrawled the line across my bedroom wall only a couple of nights earlier.

"I like it." She smiled. It was the first time all day I heard a hint of happiness in her voice.

"I like it too." We sat down on the cool sand, away from *Los Girasoles* and the music and the laughter. "Elena. If you need to search for yourself I'll support that. If I'm in the way of what you need, in any way, I'll step aside."

I didn't mean a word of it.

Elena started crying. "But I don't want to break-up with you," she answered pitifully.

"Good."

"But I don't know *what* I want."

"And you don't need to figure it all out tonight."

I lay back and stared at the stars. Elena lay down next to me and rested her head on my chest and I stroked her hair. We kissed a little bit and I could taste the salt from her tears.

After we finished, we walked back towards *Los Girasoles*. I drank two quick beers before Elena and I stripped down and joined all the naked people shrieking in the ocean.

"Hey, Elena, get over here," Kyle called. "I need a partner to chicken-fight Don and Kerry. . . . Is that cool with you John?"

"Sure," I answered.

Despite my covetous instincts, I wouldn't get in the way of Elena's chance to be an individual. Especially after the talk we'd just had. So I stood aside and smiled a fake smile as she climbed up on Kyle's shoulders. There was splashing and screaming and laughing and I was genuinely glad to see Elena finally having a good time, even if jealousy rippled through the core of my being as I watched her bare ass wrapped around Kyle's neck.

The girls swatted at one another as the guys stumbled back and forth and struggled to keep their footing and the spectators cheered on. Kerry laughed hysterically like it was the funniest thing she'd ever been a part of, but Elena was all business. Elena got her mitts on Kerry and knocked her off balance and Kerry and Don both went flailing into the dark water. The crowd erupted in applause as Elena clasped her palms together and raised them over her head to acknowledge her fans. Kyle, still holding Elena's legs, intentionally fell forward, forcing Elena to splash face-first into the sea.

"Hey!" Kyle yelled, "I lost my necklace." He looked around to find me and then stared straight into my eyes with raised brows and a shit-eating grin from ear to ear, letting me know precisely where he thought his necklace might've gone.

"Watch yourself," I warned him, but I couldn't keep a straight face.

"It really is gone." He shrugged innocently. "I'm just sayin'."

The ocean gave us the chance to breathe and laugh and be with other people for a while, but after it was over, Elena and I found ourselves alone in our sofa-less room.

"I'm sorry about tonight," she said.

"Don't worry about it. You don't need to put so much pressure on yourself. I do wonder though: Why is it so hard for you to stay in the moment?"

"Because I always have to stay two steps ahead."

I thought I knew what she meant. We'd been Peace Corps Volunteers for over a year. The end of our service was closer than the beginning. Every Volunteer thought about the end of their service – at least once in a while – though few knew what waited on the other side.

The Peace Corps warned us that most people found the culture shock upon returning to the States more intense than the culture shock we experienced upon arriving in the third world. But we were all in the same situation. I didn't want to prematurely end the connection I enjoyed with Elena just because she feared the unknown.

"If it's ok with you," she added, "I think I want to spend several weeks in my site. I need some alone time. Do you think we could take a break?"

"If that's what you need."

"This doesn't mean we're broken up," she assured me. "I still love you."

"I know," I answered. But I didn't know.

Thanksgiving dinner, the following night, was magnificent. Our entire training group came together and shared a long table. I tried to do the right thing by choosing a spot between Kyle and Alice, away from Elena, because I assumed that's what she wanted.

A few members of my group had the foresight and thoughtfulness to bring along a case of cheap cabernet, so we toasted countless times, expressing what we were thankful for, first raising solemn glasses in appreciation of our health, our families, our friends, and when we ran out of the serious, but still had more to drink, we raised our glasses again, again, and again, thankful for the wine itself and "group fawty-fuckin'-faw" and not having real jobs or malaria or dengue or diarrhea.

By the end of dessert most of us were falling out of our chairs. I took Kyle to the bar.

"So you really used to take rifles out into the woods and shoot at the moon?" I asked him.

"You gotta shoot at something," he answered with a smile.

"You are art."

"Ok."

"I mean it."

"Yaw drunk."

"Maybe . . . but I also know you. You are art itself. Your medium is your life. It's beautiful. Look at that fucking hole you're digging. From now on I'm going to call you Art."

"That's fine."

I talked in foolish, drunken circles about art and purity and expression. Kyle kindly offered the occasional "yes" or "uh huh" or "right." I knew he only humored me, but I didn't care; as far as I was concerned, I was on a roll.

As we sat at the bar, various women came and went to order drinks. I told them to kiss us. Most of them did.

"I think you should go to bed," Kyle told me.

"I think you shouldn't tell me what to do." I wagged a finger in his face and slipped off the side of my stool.

"I don't think Elena would appreciate you kissing all these girls."

"I don't think she'd give a shit."

"Well I don't want to be here to find out. I'm goin' back to my combat pit. Good night, brother."

"Good night, Art." I wobbled back to my room and passed out.

Elena was already showered and dressed when I woke up in the morning. She sat on the foot of the bed and brushed her hair ferociously.

"Good morning," I croaked.

"It's just that if I spend too many days in a row with *anyone*," she answered, as though she was continuing a conversation that she'd started while I was still asleep, "it takes a toll and usually gets ugly."

"I can understand that."

"I just feel so much pressure. I feel so much is being asked of me by my community. And I feel like I've abandoned my little sisters back home. It's too much. I just can't have more pressure in my relationship too. When I want to leave my site . . . when I *need* to leave my site . . . I need it to be a release. It needs to be relaxing. Not the opposite."

186

"I get that. Are you saying that now you want to break-up with me?"

She sat quietly and looked bewildered for several seconds. "I'm afraid I can't share myself with *anyone*," she explained, as though I shouldn't take it personally. "I can't support anyone else's emotions. I guess what I'm saying is that I can't give you a commitment."

"Have I ever asked you for a commitment?"

"Not verbally."

Sometimes I still try to figure out what that means.

She sat quietly and stared at the wall in front of her as tears streamed down her cheeks. She didn't huff or gasp. Her nose didn't run. She just cried and cried, continuing to brush her hair all the while. I wanted to hate her, but I couldn't. I loved her too much. My head hurt. I was hungover. I just woke up, but I needed a nap.

"So now what?" she whispered.

"Now we're friends, I guess."

"You're my best friend. No one in this country knows me as well as you do." She seemed to think that sentiment would make me feel better. It didn't. "This is twice I've cried in front of you," she added. It was actually the third time, but I doubt she wanted me to correct her.

"So?"

"I don't like to cry."

"It's no big deal. You look beautiful."

"I didn't think you'd handle it so well."

"No? Too calm? Were you expecting bottle-throwing and breaking things and screaming and shouting? I don't think I have the energy for it. I was asleep five minutes ago. And I think I'm still drunk from last night. This is a pretty dirty trick, really."

"It wasn't like I planned this," she protested.
I wasn't sure I believed her.
"Besides, I'm past the bottle-throwing stage."
I wasn't sure I believed that either.

Chapter 30 – Real Pajamas

When I got back from AVC I was in no condition to swing a pick or a shovel, so I embarked on a hike through the forest. I walked for hours, past birds and frogs and lazy creeks. I thought a lot about Elena. I wished that I protested more when she broke up with me. I wondered if there was anything I could have said or done that would have changed the outcome. Maybe I should have jumped on the bed and bellowed and cut off my ear. But I knew that the harder I fought the more she would dig in her heels. She was too stubborn. I just hoped she'd figure out what she wanted. And figure it out soon. And figure out that it was me.

After walking for a couple of hours I stumbled upon a town called *Las Estancias*. It sat atop a jagged peak and looked down on *El Valle*, a picturesque mountain town. Three million years ago, *El Valle* was an active volcano, but it had such a fierce eruption that it blew its own top off, leaving behind a crater five kilometers wide. The crater then filled with rainwater and formed a large lake until one day part of the crater broke open, spilling out its contents and leaving behind a breathtaking, fertile valley filled with waterfalls and streams.

Las Estancias grew around the mountain top and expanded outwards from the center. It gave the town a warmer, more cohesive feel than my town. Although I appreciated my community, *Las Estancias* was the kind of place I would have chosen as my Peace Corps site if I'd had the chance. I told Grace Landau about the town and recommended the Peace Corps place a Volunteer there.

A few weeks later, Grace sent out Lauren Smith. Lauren had already completed her two years of Peace Corps service and extended for an additional year to be the coordinator for the agriculture group. Part of her job included traveling around the country to identify potential sites for new Volunteers. It seemed like a pretty sweet gig.

Shortly after she arrived, we hiked to *Las Estancias*, gathered as many town members as we could find, and held a meeting to see if they were interested in having a Peace Corps Volunteer. People the world know the line from John F. Kennedy's inauguration speech where he challenged Americans, "ask not what your country can do for you—ask what you can do for your country." Fewer people realize that President Kennedy was talking about the Peace Corps. A year later, in 1961, Congress passed the Peace Corps Act with the following stated goal: "To promote world peace and friendship through a Peace Corps, which shall make available to interested countries and areas men and women of the United States qualified for service abroad and willing to serve, under conditions of hardship if necessary, to help the peoples of such countries and areas in meeting their needs for trained manpower."

But Lauren was wise enough not to bore the people of *Las Estancias* with those details. Instead, she just asked them about their goals. The folks at the meeting agreed that they'd like to get an asphalt road built to their town and improve the quality of their rocky soil. Lauren explained that we could send them a Volunteer who could help the community organize and make presentations to government agencies. After building strong enough relationships between community leaders from *Las Estancias* and local extension agents, the town could continue to work towards accomplishing its goals long after the Volunteer completed her service. Lauren impressed me with her command of both the meeting and the language. She won the town over and promised we'd send them a Volunteer within the next few months.

We hiked back to my house and cooked dinner with the groceries that she'd thoughtfully brought up from *Penonomé*. Then, after dinner, we meandered down the trails of easy conversation. I was happy to have the company. She had soft, healthy skin and unparalleled energy. I assumed she was about my age, but through the course of the evening I learned that she was thirty-one – a grown woman by Peace Corps standards. Before coming to Panama, she'd been a high school history teacher in Atlanta. I let her read a few of my most recent journal entries. She complimented my work and my home and my music collection.

"Would you mind if I take a shower?" she asked.

"No, of course not."

Should I make a pass at her? She looks good. And she seems into you. But she's stuck here with you in your house in the middle of nowhere. If you make a move and she rejects you, she'll think you're creepy, AND she'll be stuck here with you. That'll suck for both of us. Especially her. Don't do it.

But then she returned from the shower smelling like peaches. She wore a tiny pair of denim shorts. Her dark legs looked delicious. I felt very confused. Was this just a way to feel better about myself in the wake of Elena's rejection? I took a cold shower on a windy night and still didn't know what to do.

Lauren, meanwhile, had changed into her pajamas. She wore a little pink tank top with buttons down the front and matching pants. I'd never seen a Peace Corps Volunteer wear real pajamas before. She looked amazing. Maybe it wasn't about Elena's rejection. Maybe I was just horny.

"This bed is big enough for us to share, right?" I asked.

"Yeah, I'm fine with you."

I laughed. "You're *fine* with me?"

I put on Erykah Badu's live album, blew out all of the candles, and climbed into bed. Lauren turned her back to me, allowing me to spoon with her. The cut of her pajama top invited me to nuzzle her bare back. My arms curled around her waist and the tops of my feet pressed against the bottom of hers. The wind began to pick up and bash my roof and shake my shower stall. The violent crashes scared Lauren and made her flinch in the bed.

I had a raging erection that pressed against her bottom. The thought of ignoring it all night struck me as ridiculous. Surely she felt the stupid thing pushing into her. She wasn't moving away from it either.

"I don't think I can do this," Lauren whispered.

"Why not?"

"I keep seeing your girlfriend's face."

"I don't have a girlfriend."

"What about Elena? I met her at AVC. She seems nice."

"She is nice. She also broke up with me."

"Really?"

I squeezed Lauren tight and she murmured something unintelligible. She rolled over and we began to kiss.

She had big lips. They were bigger than mine. I wasn't sure that I liked kissing her, but she seemed to be having a good time.

I pulled off my shirt and kissed her neck and jaw and collar bones. She was all heated up. She unbuttoned her little top and slipped the spaghetti straps off her shoulders and I kissed her stomach and sucked on her hard nipples. Lauren suddenly ripped off her bottoms and panties and threw them clear of the bed.

Holy shit! This woman is going to give me the ride of a lifetime!

"I'm going to take my time with this," I warned her. I worked my mouth slowly down her body. "You've got the body of a 20 year-old. You're spectacular."

"Twenty? Why not eighteen?"

"Alright, eighteen."

She giggled. "Thanks."

I slid my tongue along the crease where her inner thigh met her pelvis and then I licked the same crease on the other side. She quivered with anticipation. She decided she wouldn't wait any longer and shifted her hips and pressed herself against my mouth. "You're delicious," I told her as she squirmed and gasped. I'd never eaten such a wonderful pussy before.

I didn't want her to cum too soon and then get a chance to realize she didn't want me inside her. "Should I get some protection?" I asked her.

"Yes."

I rolled on a condom and tried to slide into her sopping wet pussy, but I just . . . couldn't . . . get it . . . in.

"Owww," she protested. She tried to be stoic, but I was hurting her. The tremor in her moans thrilled me. I felt guilty, but not so much that I'd stop. We struggled together. I worked on her with a couple of fingers, but it didn't seem to do any good. I simply couldn't get inside her.

"I've never done this before," she said sheepishly. Tires squealed to a standstill, leaving smoke and rubber all across the highway. This older, ostensibly more exper-ienced woman, who had been flopping around on my mattress only moments earlier like a landed fish in my house in the hills, was a *virgin*.

"How can that be? You're a beautiful girl. Surely you've had your chances." She was 31 years old with a rock-hard body and a sweet southern sensibility that made her so easy to be around. I couldn't understand how she could get to her thirties without giving herself to *anyone* and then suddenly want to give herself to *me*. It seemed utterly perverse.

"I guess I always thought I'd been waiting for the right reasons, but I'm not so sure anymore."

Whatever the right reasons were, these weren't them, but who was I to deprive her of what she wanted? So we continued the struggle. I held her tight, trying to convey with my arms that everything would be ok, even if my dick was telling her that I was tearing her in half. I finally got the tip inside her, but she screamed out into the night. *If I keep this up, the neighbors might show up on my doorstep thinking I'm trying to kill her.* So I eased up and her screams turned to pathetic whimpers - whimpers that were the most erotic sound I'd ever heard in my life. I felt dark for the pleasure I took in her pain, but I kept at it for an hour.

Finally, I got inside her, but the foreplay had been too intense, for too long. Within a few minutes I shot an uninspired load into the tight rubber wrapped around my prick. We collapsed, exhausted, and just lay next to one another for a while.

"Am I really that small, or are you that big?" she asked.

"The truth is, I'm hung like a bear." I laughed out loud at my own audacious lie.

"Or a bull." She giggled.

I curled up with Lauren and wrapped my arms around her, not because I wanted to, but because she deserved it. Within a couple of minutes I let go and rolled over to the other side of the bed.

"Thank you for being so sweet about all of this," Lauren whispered.

Nothing about the last hour seemed sweet to me, but I was glad she felt otherwise. I missed Elena.

Chapter 31 – Nasty Volcano

Lauren clapped for me as I flipped omelets in the frying pan. She got on the bus and we waved goodbye. I felt ashamed for letting her waste her virginity on me. I also felt like I cheated on Elena. It didn't matter that she had broken up with me.

After Lauren left and I showered, I noticed a sore on my ankle. I didn't give it much thought. I assumed it was just a bug bite that I'd scratched and gotten infected, so I put some medicine on it, covered it with a bandage, laced up my boots, and went to work. I repeated that routine every morning for the next several days, but it didn't do any good.

Within a couple of weeks the sore grew to the size of a dime. The edges were dark and purple and cracked. The center was raw and pink and slimy. It smelled putrid.

By the time I got to the city and showed it to Bernard, my ankle had swollen to twice the size of the other one. I couldn't put any weight on the foot. The wound was the size of a half-dollar. And it was deep. The edges were black and crusty. The center oozed pus that dripped down my ankle when I poked at the surrounding skin. It looked like a nasty volcano.

"I think I have a badly infected bug bite," I told Bernard. "I let it go too long before I came in to see you."

"This isn't an infected bug bite."

"It's not?"

"Have you been using the mosquito net we issued you?"

"Usually, yes. But a couple of weeks ago Lauren Taylor spent the night. I gave her my bed and I slept on

196

the floor." The least of my concerns had been closing my mosquito net behind me, but Bernard didn't need to know the sordid details.

"That could explain it. You have leishmaniasis."

"I have what?"

"Leishmaniasis. It's a disease caused by protozoan parasites. A sand fly carrying the disease must have bit you in the night when you were sleeping on the floor. They're not active during the day."

"So I have a disease?"

"I'm afraid so. What you have is called cutaneous leishmaniasis. There are other forms of leishmaniasis, like visceral leishmaniasis. It attacks your immune system and eats your organs. It can be fatal."

"I'm glad I came to see you when I did."

"You're damn right you are. You should have come weeks ago."

"So now what?"

"Now we treat you. You have to stay in the city for the next three weeks."

"But I thought I'd be here for only a night or two. I barely have any of my stuff here. Can I go get some things and tell my community what's going on?"

"You can use my phone to call if you want to, but we're not letting you out of our sight until you're better. Sorry."

The Peace Corps put me up at the *Hotel Mocambo* and paid for all of my meals. Each morning, I took a taxi over to the Peace Corps office where Bernard administered my medicine through an I.V. drip. I didn't mind the treatments, but after just a week, my wrists grew sore from the needles. Bernard tried to ease the burden by leaving a connecting hub in my arm for a couple of days at a time, but his plan did more harm than good.

During the night, as I rolled around in my sleep, the connecting hub got snagged in the sheets. The bedding jerked at the needle in my wrist. Lightning bolts of pain jolted me awake, and I found myself in a small pool of blood. The housekeepers couldn't wait to get rid of me.

Regardless, each morning's treatment took only a half-hour, so I had the rest of the day to do as I pleased. I spent most of my time eating ice cream and watching matinees in air conditioned movie theatres. The creature comforts were nice. But I missed *Los Altos*.

And I agonized about Bonito. I imagined him returning to his old ways, scurrying down the road, looking for meals with his head held low in perpetual anticipation of a beating. I called the town payphone for days before I finally got a hold of Alejandra. I asked her to explain to Jose and his family what was going on and to please send someone to look after Bonito while I was gone. She told me not to worry, but I did.

Fortunately, when I finally got back to town, Bonito was waiting for me on my porch. His tail thumped happily against the ground as I walked up the path. Finally, when he couldn't contain his composure any longer and the anticipation of our reunion overflowed inside him, he bounded toward me. He hopped up on his back legs and pushed his dirty paws into my stomach. I scratched his head and mussed his hair. He looked a little thinner than I remembered, but no worse for the wear. It was good to be back.

Chapter 32 – Childish Sensibilities

I sat at my desk, reading in the soft glow of my kerosene lamp, when I noticed Nelson standing in my open doorway. I didn't know if he'd been there for ten minutes or ten seconds.

"Hey there," I greeted him.

"Hello."

"Did you go to school today?" The students had just finished their first week back at school after the summer vacation.

"No." He smiled a sheepish smile.

"Really?"

"Really."

It annoyed me that he wasn't using his natural gifts. "Why aren't you going to school?"

"Because I don't have a backpack."

"That sounds like a bad excuse. I know that all of the kids want cool backpacks with cartoon characters on them, but that's no reason not to go to school."

"You have to have a backpack," he answered timidly.

I resented him trying to bullshit me. "You're a smart kid," I barked at him. "You should be going to school."

"But I don't have the clothes."

"First you tell me you can't go to school because you don't have a backpack and now you tell me you can't go because you don't have the clothes. Which is it?"

Every child in town was poor and every child in town seemed to have school clothes, if nothing else. "You need to go to school."

Nelson retreated to the shadows by my door where he escaped the weak light cast by the kerosene lamp. I couldn't see him, but I could hear him. He cried softly. I'd been too hard on him.

He was just a kid. He acted so adult around me that I forgot he had childish sensibilities, but the tears reminded me of his innocence. I pretended not to notice that he cried, for both our sakes. He wouldn't want me to know he was less of a man. I felt like a shit-heel.

"Do you *want* to go to school?"

"Yes," he sniffled.

"Listen, we'll take care of this tomorrow, ok? Everything is going to be fine."

"Ok."

"Good night."

"Good night."

The next morning I went to *La Tranquilidad*. I arrived there late and missed Eduardo and Jose who had gone to work in some corn fields a few miles away. I wasn't in the mood to try and find them on my own and get lost in the forest as I had a few times before. Maria served me weak black coffee with sugar and we sat at the kitchen table.

"A little boy told me that he couldn't go to school because he didn't have a backpack. Can you believe that?"

"But that could be true. The schools require it."

"Really?"

She nodded knowingly.

"That seems silly. Why would the school prevent someone from learning because he doesn't have a backpack?"

"I suppose they want the children to be organized with their books and papers."

"So if a child can't afford a backpack then he can't go to school and get an education?"

Maria only shrugged.

I felt even worse than I had when I pretended not to notice Nelson crying in the corner. "Thanks for the coffee. We'll see each other soon."

I hiked back down the trail to the main road and straight past *Timshel*, headed in the same direction I'd seen Nelson run off towards almost every evening for the last few months. After a half-mile, I found some kids playing on their front lawn.

"Do you know where Nelson lives?" They pointed further up the mountain. "Will you show me?"

I followed the kids until they stopped twenty yards short of the house. They pointed again and I thanked them for their help.

The yard was littered with discarded wire and rusty tools and broken toys. Two small girls appeared from around the side of the house. I recognized them as Nelson's little sisters. Sometimes he brought them to my house and they played on my porch while he cut the grass. The older one motioned for me to follow them.

The family was in the backyard by the fire. All the families in the area still cooked with wood-burning fire hearths on a stone or cement surface. Nelson's house was no different. In all of the other houses I'd visited, however, the families were clean and organized. The area around Nelson's house had junk everywhere.

I tried my standard opener: "It's hot!" A simple comment about the weather usually resulted in at least ten minutes of light conversation, but I got only a nod before Nelson's father disappeared inside the dark house. The easy banter and warm hospitality that I'd encountered all over Panama wasn't forthcoming. If they didn't want to chat, I'd get right down to business.

"As I'm sure you know, Nelson spends a lot of time at my house. I've spent enough time with him to know that he is a very smart boy." His mom tended the fire like a zombie. She showed no hint of joy or even recognition of the compliment. Nelson stood out of the way and poked at the dirt with his bare toes. "He *needs* to go to school," I continued. "If he gets an education, he can get a good job and help support your family. With your permission, I would like to take Nelson to *Penonomé* and get him the things that he needs to go to school."

"That's fine," his mother answered.

That's it? No questions? No reservations? She was going to let me, a virtual stranger, take her 10-year-old child to a town a few hours away just like that.

"But Nelson is going to need your support," I continued. "If I help him get the clothes and other things that he needs, you need to encourage him and support him to make sure he goes to school and does his homework. That's the only way he will succeed. Education can give him a better life."

"That's fine," his mother repeated. She couldn't have been less interested. I thanked her and left with Nelson.

On the ride to *Penonomé*, Nelson sat up on the seat with his legs curled under him so he could look out the window. We didn't talk much, though I impressed upon him, again, the importance of getting an education. I hoped that I hadn't shamed Nelson's parents with my offer, as though it suggested they couldn't provide for their own child and had to rely on some *gringo* to do it. My intentions weren't to show them up, but if their egos got bruised in the process, so be it. Besides, they didn't seem any poorer than anyone else in town, just sloppier and lazier.

All of the large clothing stores in *Penonomé* were owned by Palestinians who emigrated to Panama after the invasion. "You have any idea which store we should go to?" I asked Nelson.

He only shrugged.

"Then let's find the biggest one."

Once we found the right place, I prevailed upon a pretty sales clerk.

"Are you Panamanian?" I asked her.

"*Sí.*"

"And you went to public school?"

"*Sí.*" She seemed a little wary.

"Perfect. My friend here needs clothes for school."

"What does he need?"

"You know better than I do. I trust you. Just get him what he needs."

"At your service."

She took Nelson into the dressing room and brought him his sizes. I could hear them whispering back

203

and forth to one another, but I couldn't make out the words. Whatever they were saying sounded earnest. A few minutes later, Nelson and the sales clerk walked out of the changing room and stood before me to see if her selections met with my approval. Nelson stood next to her, at attention, in a white button down shirt that he'd dutifully tucked into a pair of navy blue slacks.

"You're looking sharp," I told him. He smiled and blushed and looked at the floor. It was the first time he'd smiled all day.

I wondered what the sales clerk thought of us. We obviously weren't family. I hoped she didn't think I was some creepy pedophile. Then I realized I didn't care what she thought. Nelson was happy and proud. Nothing else mattered.

"That looks good," I said to the clerk.

"And the backpack?" Nelson asked.

"And we'll need a backpack too." Nelson's smile turned into an ear-to-ear grin. But then he became all business. He took the backpack selection process very seriously, turning down the first few bags the sales clerk suggested. After some intense, internal deliberations, he found one to his liking.

"Ring it all up," I said to the clerk. I bought Nelson two pairs of pants, two shirts, two pairs of socks, two undershirts, a pair of shoes, and a backpack for only $48.

"Now that we got you all this stuff, you're going to go to school every day and study hard, right?"

"Yes," he promised.

Such a small amount of money had never made me feel so rich.

Chapter 33 – Games

A few days later I went to *La Tranquilidad* just to hang out. Eduardo's wife, Angela, had given birth to a baby girl only three weeks earlier. I was glad to share the joyous time with them. As we sat around the kitchen table and talked, the baby napped in a tiny hammock that served as her crib.

I was admiring the family's blessing when Nelson arrived. He couldn't catch his breath. He grabbed his knees with his hands just to keep from falling over.

"I looked for you everywhere," he panted.

"You found me."

"You have a phone call. . . . I think it's your *señora*."

"OOOOOOHHHHHH." Angela and Maria both erupted in smiles and laughter, teasing me about my lady. "You should go quickly," Angela ribbed.

I hadn't told the Ojo family, or anyone else in *Los Altos*, that Elena had broken up with me. Maria would've been particularly heartbroken. They wanted to see me settled down. They didn't think it was good for a man to be single.

"Excuse me," I said to them.

"Just go!"

A couple of minutes later I arrived at the phone.

"Hello?" I asked.

"I want to change my mind . . . if that's allowed. . . . I guess what I'm saying is I want to be with you." Her words swirled through my ears and down my throat and fluttered around my stomach. "The only way I can think to put it," she continued, "is this analogy I came up with:

It's like being in a soccer game, and being tired, and needing to call a time-out, but instead you panic and have the ref call the game."

"Who *is* this?" I teased.

"*Elena!*"

"I know it's you. Take it easy." Her point made sense, but I wondered if it was lost on her that she compared our relationship to a game. I didn't want to play games with her. But her inability to get a handle on what she wanted had taken its toll. I'd spent weeks waiting for a call that hadn't come . . . and just when I accepted that the phone wasn't going to ring, she dialed my number. It crushed me that she wasn't as sure about me as I was about her. "As far as I'm concerned," I said, "you can call me a friend, or a boyfriend, or whatever you want. I'm sure we'll figure out a way to cross paths soon. We'll see what happens then." I wanted to tell her that I loved her and only her. And that she was always the last thing on my mind before I went to bed and the first thing on my mind when I opened my eyes in the morning and frequently she walked amidst the dreams in between. But I didn't say any of that. I was too proud. And too hurt.

And with that I hung up.

Chapter 34 – Liquid Silk

A week later I was reading a book in my hammock when Elena appeared on my porch. She looked at me with moist, doe eyes.

"I've missed you," she said softly.

"That's kind of you."

"I guess I deserve that. Do you mind that I came?"

"I don't know yet." I spent a lot of lonely nights convincing myself not to walk down to the payphone to call her. But being proud when she was far away was easier than when she was standing in front of me. She looked good and she sounded fragile. I wanted to get up and hug her and hold her, but my trembling legs wouldn't cooperate. My stomach grew vast and nervous. My ears tingled and my cheeks were hot. I wondered if she could see the rush of blood that I felt in my face.

"Can I sit down?" she asked.

I put my hand on the wall so the hammock would stop swinging and she could climb in. We lay head to toe, in silence, just as we had a few months earlier when the silence was comfortable. But this time the silence was thick and awkward. The hammock mashed us against one another. The familiar warmth of her body pressed against mine. And I loved her and felt weak. I hated myself for loving her. I didn't know what to say, so I said nothing. Elena made some efforts at small talk.

"Have you heard about Don?" she asked.

"No. What happened?"

Don was one of the guys in our training group – a good country soul from Hendy Grove, California. Don, however, wasn't short for Donald. It was short for Posei*don*, the Greek god of the sea.

Don's dad, Bobby, was a big-bearded surfer from San Diego, but long before Don was a glimmer in his old man's eye, Bobby decided that southern California had grown too crowded. So Bobby headed north for Mendocino County where Don was born into nature and the slow life. Done was one of my favorite people in Panama.

"He had an accident," Elena said. Don lived in an indigenous community, amongst the Ngobe, in *Bocas del Toro*. The closest hospital was several hours away.

"Really? Is he ok?"

"Sort of. He was walking back to his house after helping a neighbor clear some land. He was making his way down a muddy hillside when he slipped and fell. But the fall itself didn't hurt him."

"What do you mean?"

"He'd been carrying his machete when he fell. I guess the point of the machete hit the ground first."

"Oh no."

"As Don fell, he lost his grip on the machete's handle. His hand slid down the length of the long blade and his palm split open like an overripe grapefruit."

"That's horrible! He could have cut his fingers off!"

"He nearly did. I saw him in the city on my out here."

The cut, Elena described, went from the webbing between his thumb and index finger, straight across his palm, and nearly took off his pinkie and index finger. He needed twelve stitches to close up the wound. The doctors were concerned about permanent damage. They wouldn't know for some time if he'd ever regain full use of the hand.

The Peace Corps required all Volunteers to carry their machetes in leather sheaths – or *vainas* as they were called in Panama – and we'd all bought them when we were trainees. But *vainas* were expensive. I'd paid thirteen dollars for mine. Because they were so expensive, none of the *campesinos* had them. And because none of the *campesinos* used them, we Peace Corps Volunteers felt goofy using them, so we left them at home and carried the machetes around loose like all the locals did.

Don had paid the price for wanting to fit in. There was a valuable lesson to be learned there, and it wasn't to use a *vaina*. If you're walking around with a machete and you start to fall, throw the machete aside. As a result of the incident, Don's neighbors bestowed him with a *Ngobe* name: *Ngotrochi*. It translates roughly as "body of a man, but mind of a child." The thought of Don's swollen hand and crusty wound, peppered with sharp plastic sutures, made me cringe.

"On a brighter note, I'm making some progress in *Quebrada Brava*," Elena offered. "I think I'm really getting them to believe that their culture is special and worth preserving and that they have rights worth standing up for. I've had some success with the women ever since I helped them sell their baskets in the city, but now even the men are starting to listen to me. They treat me differently ever since I tried to help Gloriela's son.

"In a sick way," she continued, "that tragedy may have been just what the community needed. Once the water got contaminated, the town finally realized how desperate their situation is becoming. The men are beginning to hold meetings. They don't invite me, but I get the feeling they have something in the works."

"And you think something will come of it?"

"I hope so. These people have been ignored and marginalized for so long. Their own language isn't even taught in the few schools they have. Their health centers are a joke. It's not hard to understand why they've never felt like they had a voice before. But if they can stand together and make some noise, maybe the government will have to listen and do a better job of protecting their land."

"They're lucky to have you. I'm glad all your hard work is finally paying off."

"Thanks."

The mountains in the distance turned from green to purple to navy blue as the sun went down. Songbirds flew back to their nests for the night and left the evening quiet for a while. Then the frogs hopped out from their holes and replaced the birds' music with that of their own. Without inviting Elena to join me, I got up and moved inside. I sat down at my desk and disinterestedly flipped through a photo album of the life I had before joining the Peace Corps. A few minutes later, Elena came inside and sat down in my lap.

"I'm glad you came," I finally admitted.

"Thank God. I was beginning to wonder if you were going to make me go prostitute myself at the *cantina* for a place to sleep. I've been waiting an hour just for some sort of sign that you don't hate me."

"I don't hate you."

Far from it. Every time I looked at her, ever since the first time I'd seen her, I got the feeling she'd spent her formative years soaking up the California sun just to take it with her and share it with the rest of the world, warming those around her with her easy glow. And her eyes were so soft and understanding. It often seemed like the most important parts of our conversations weren't in the words, but in the eyes. I felt more nervous than I did our first night at XS.

After we looked at the last photo, I shut the album, stood up, and helped her slip out of her tank top while she stayed seated in my desk chair. The light from the kerosene lamp reflected off her smooth, tan skin. I unclipped her bra and cupped a breast in each hand, appreciating their weight as I brushed her nipples with my fingertips.

She folded her arms on the desk and lay her head down and I took the opportunity to unbutton my shorts and step out of them. My erection stood straight up, howling at the moon. I leaned down and kissed her on her sweet spot just below her left ear. She jumped suddenly to her feet.

She wrapped her arms around my neck and slipped her tongue deep into my mouth as she took my cock in her hand, delicately squeezing and tugging at it. I pulled away and sat down in the chair and untied the knot in her sarong so the thin fabric could brush off her hips and fall to the floor. I hooked my thumbs into the waistband of her cotton panties and pushed them down past her knees before she did a little dance to wriggle out of them. Then I turned my hand sideways and slid it between her legs and found her sopping wet. I kept sliding my index back and forth as I kissed her stomach, ever conscious of the blaze just below my chin. She shivered and gasped. She took my shoulders in her hands and climbed over me.

For a few frantic seconds it quivered and jumped at her as she desperately shifted around to find it. Finally, she found the right spot and dropped down on my panicked erection. All of it at once. Liquid silk. A ripe mango.

With both feet flat on the floor she began to rock forward and back, clutching my head in both hands and pulling it sideways to her chest. We kissed deeply as I raised my mouth to meet her. She began to move up and down, using every inch of me to satisfy herself. I reached around her and felt the base of my erection. I liked how it fit perfectly against her tightly stretched skin.

Elena was panting, working hard, up and down, feeling the unrealized orgasm inside her and begging it to show itself. I cupped her ass in both hands and lifted her up a few inches, so I could move in and out of her on my own terms. I couldn't believe how wet she was. The thought of it drove me wild. I knew if I continued to slide around at will I wouldn't last another second.

I let her sink down on me, little by little, until I was as far inside her as I'd ever been. We gasped together. She took control and rode me with rhythm. I wrapped my arms around her and held her tight, telling her telepathically, "I love you, I love you, I love you."

"With me," she panted, letting me know how close she was. She picked up the pace, riding me furiously with short, quick strokes. Her panting grew heavier, her moans closer together. It maddened me. My orgasm took me by surprise. I blew up, shooting into her, groaning like a wounded animal. The sound must have excited her. Three times she rose slowly and thrust herself down on me. Then she froze. Her back went rigid. Every few seconds she lurched, and I could feel the muscles in her vagina spasm, convulsing and squeezing me, milking me of my every drop.

After she finished we sat perfectly still, silent, neither of us moving an inch as my diminishing penis slowly went flaccid and slipped out of her. Elena stood up and looked at me. We were both speechless, dumb-founded. She was straddling my leg and I felt my cum drip out of her onto my knee. It felt odd and I told her so. We both laughed. I went outside to smoke a cigarette and Elena went to pee. The cool breeze felt wonderful on my prick.

Chapter 35 – Fedora

When I came back inside, Elena was already in bed. She lay curled up on her side, facing away from me, with the sheet pulled up to her chin. I stood there for a moment and watched the sheet rise and fall like a buoy floating in a gentle sea. Then I silenced the radio, blew out the candles, and climbed into bed. I wrapped my arm around her middle and gave her a squeeze as I pressed up against her.

"There's something else I need to tell you," she whispered.

"Go for it." I felt spent and calm and full of myself. Any bitterness I'd felt towards her over the past few weeks had flowed out of me just a few minutes earlier.

"This is serious," she warned.

"Alright; I'm listening."

Elena sat up on the bed and pulled her knees underneath her. She had big, scared eyes. I wondered what had been her latest hardship in *Quebrada Brava*. Whatever it was, I told myself, I could hold her and make it ok and be her hero.

"I haven't been to a doctor yet, but I'm pregnant."

"What do you mean?" I asked stupidly, sitting up in bed so our faces were only inches apart.

"I mean I'm pregnant," she answered impatiently. "I mean there's a baby growing inside of me. What do you think I mean?"

"But how can you be sure? You said you haven't been to a doctor."

"I'm sure."

"But how?"

214

"I missed my period a few weeks ago. At first I wasn't too concerned because a lot of Volunteers have messed up periods due to crappy nutrition, but then I went to the city last week and bought a test at the pharmacy. I went back to the *Hotel Mocambo* and peed on the stick and a plus sign showed up. I'm pregnant. It's real."

"Was anyone with you?"

"No. I didn't want anyone to know. You're the first person I've told."

"Why didn't you call me? I would've met you in the city."

"Be glad I didn't. I was a wreck for the first couple of days."

"And now?"

"It's still pretty surreal, but I'm better. I think I'm more at peace with it now than I was a few days ago. Last week I just walked around the city crying and crying. People on the street came up to me to ask me if I was ok. They thought I was a tourist who'd been robbed."

We sat in silence for a few minutes and I tried to digest it all.

"Is it mine?" She didn't dignify my question with a verbal response. The equal parts of scorn and hurt in her eyes were answer enough. "Sorry," was all I said.

"It's ok. . . . I mean it's not ok, but I forgive you. I don't think there's any right way to react to this."

"Thanks. . . . So now what? I mean, what do we do?"

"I don't know."

"Are you going to keep it?"

"I don't know yet. Part of me wants to keep it, but look at our lives. I don't have a real job. I don't have any money. I don't have a house or a car. We're in the Peace Corps for chrissake!" She started to cry. "Sometimes I think I should just get an abortion. What kind of life could I possibly be able to give a child? I can barely take care of myself!"

"You'd figure out a way to make it work. You'd be a great mother. Any kid would be lucky to have you as a mom."

"You're sweet, but I'm not sure I share your confidence."

"I'm not just saying it. I mean it. I'll marry you."

"Gee. Thanks."

"I'm serious. We'll get married," I told her. The words came out suddenly and impulsively and surprised me, but as soon as they crossed my lips I knew that I meant them.

"Slow down," she answered. "No one said anything about getting married. I don't want you to feel like you have to marry me just because I'm pregnant. That's the last thing I want."

"But I love you."

"John." She sighed. "I love you too, but it's not that simple."

"Why not?"

"Love won't feed a baby or pay for diapers. You're as broke as I am. You're also in the Peace Corps, remember?"

"We'd quit. We'd go back to the States. I'd get a job. We'd get an apartment. This isn't impossible."

"You make it all sound so easy."

"Why not? Lots of people have kids and manage to make it work."

"Maybe. I don't know. I don't know if I'm ready for all of that."

I sulked. "It sounds like you've already made up your mind then."

"That's not true."

"Then what's next?"

"I've got at least another few weeks before I have to tell the Peace Corps. That should give me enough time to tie up some loose ends with my community and the projects I'm working on. Then I'll tell Bernard about it and I guess the Peace Corps will medically separate me and send me back to the States."

"You're still thinking about your projects!" I stared at her in disbelief, but she looked back at me as though *I* was the crazy one.

"I came here to make a difference," she insisted. "My town has a come a long way. I don't want to leave them in the lurch. I want to finish the job."

"I think they'd understand," I snorted.

"Maybe they would, but that's not the point. I *want* to finish what I started there."

I wanted to grab her by the shoulders and shake her back and forth and ask her what the hell she was thinking. To yell at her that she had a baby inside her. That she needed to go to a doctor and find a comfortable bed and take care of herself and let me pamper her.

I also knew that if I said any of that, it would go over like a turd in a punchbowl. Elena was way too stubborn to be brow beaten. Instead, I took the soft approach.

"What about the baby?"

"I've thought about that. I'm taking prenatal vitamins. And I'm resting a lot and staying in the shade and making sure to drink even more water than usual. I have to pee like every fifteen minutes." She laughed awkwardly, as though trying to make light of a situation that we both knew was a big, big deal.

"This is crazy!"

"But it's not crazy. This is why I wasn't even sure I should tell you. Lots of women get pregnant in the *campo*. Besides, I haven't even made up my mind about what I'm going to do, remember?"

"I remember. And I still think we could make this work."

"You'd have to quit the Peace Corps."

"I know. I don't care. The Peace Corps doesn't matter."

"How can you say that? You love it here. And you love the Peace Corps."

"But I love you more. I wouldn't regret it."

"You really think we could do this?" she asked, giving the idea a real chance for the very first time.

"I really do."

"You don't have to fuss over me," she said as I bounced around my tiny house, making her tea and breakfast and asking her twenty times if she'd taken her vitamins. "I'm still the same person," she added. "I can take care of myself."

"Sorry," I answered. But I wasn't sorry. I was excited. I wanted her to keep the baby. I wanted her to keep *our* baby.

I imagined a life with her in the United States. I imagined kissing her goodbye in the morning as she sat at the breakfast table and nursed the child before I ran out the door to go to some job in some office somewhere, a newspaper folded under my arm and a fedora on my head as though it was 1955. The last year with Elena in Panama had been make-believe, but a family in the United States: that would be real.

"You don't have to head straight back to *Quebrada Brava* you know. You're welcome to stay here for as long as you want."

"I know. But we went through this last night. I want to get back there and finish as much as I can while I still have some time."

"And you're sure that's a good idea?"

She laughed. "You need to calm down. I'm beginning to think you're more nervous about it than I am." She looked at me with a soothing smile.

"Ok. I'll try. But you'll let me know as soon as you decide anything, right?"

"Of course I will. I'll figure this out soon. I promise."

"I'll be waiting."

Chapter 36 – A Collective Sigh

Consumed with Elena's news, I found myself climbing the walls of my cinder block house as I wondered what she was thinking. I constantly fought the urge to sprint all the way to town to pick up the phone and call her and ask her how she was and what she was going to do. But I'd already made my feelings clear and I didn't want to put any more pressure on her. So I buried myself in my job.

I organized a nationwide farm planning workshop to occur at *La Tranquilidad*. I took several five hour trips to the Triple-C headquarters in *Capira* and filled out the same copious forms half a dozen times, but it wasn't until Victor vouched for me that Triple-C gave me five hundred dollars for my workshop.

Eduardo, Jose, and I built a makeshift dorm for the participants. We used nylon tarps and rope to build two huge tents where we set up cots that the Red Cross lent us. Eduardo and Jose built a couple of latrines and shower stalls too. The accommodations weren't very glamorous, but they'd get the job done.

For five dollars per person, per day, Maria and Angela agreed to prepare breakfast and dinner for all of the participants. Breakfast was simple: coffee, a fried egg, and an *hojaldra*. Dinner was a little more substantive: chicken or fish served with a heap full of rice and beans. The money went far, especially because Maria could use eggs and chickens straight from her own farm. The family was thrilled with the opportunity to share their farm and their knowledge and make some cash in the process.

Nothing much happened on the first day. Guests trickled in throughout the afternoon and began to get to know one another. I invited fifteen Peace Corps Volunteers and asked each Volunteer to bring one or two members from their respective communities, so by the time everyone had arrived, the participants represented all ten of Panama's provinces and four different indigenous groups. Counting the local farmers who I invited, my workshop included over seventy attendees. But Elena wasn't one of them.

I invited her, but she said she didn't think it was a good idea. She wanted to stay in her community and "figure things out." I held out hope that she'd show up anyway at the last minute, but the sun set and there was no sign of her.

During the course of the week, Maria taught the participants about medicinal plants, Jose taught them how to make organic fertilizers, Eduardo taught them about contour planting, and Angela taught them about raising chickens. Other neighbors facilitated workshops on organic insect repellants, rice paddies, seed beds, seed storage, green manures, reforestation, and fish farms. My neighbors hadn't known many of those techniques when I first arrived in *Los Altos*, but here they were, just a short time later, having mastered the details and getting the chance to share that knowledge with others.

I knew that if my work was going to have any lasting impression at all, the Panamanians who I worked alongside, who would always be there, would have to evolve from students into teachers. The workshop gave Jose and his family that opportunity. My role at the workshop wasn't nearly as much fun as theirs, but I tied all the pieces together. I connected the folks, made sure they had a dry place to stay, that the cooks had enough food for everyone, and that all of the lessons happened on time.

At the outset, most of the participants were shy and reserved, but by the end of the week strangers from all over Panama came together and became friends. On the last night a tall gregarious cowboy from the *Azuero* suggested that all of the participants celebrate the completion of the workshop by heading down to the cantina in town for an impromptu dance. His new best friend, a *Kuna* school teacher from *San Blas*, echoed the party cry. Even the *Ngobe* participants from *Chiriqui* and *Bocas del Toro*, known for being isolated and suspect of outsiders, opened up and laughed and danced with the others.

The next morning, we had a closing ceremony at Maria and Jose's house. "I'm very glad you were all able to participate in this small workshop," I told them. "But there is a small cost each of you must pay for your attendance." The crowd looked perplexed. They looked at me as though I just ruined the party. "In exchange for all of the knowledge that we've shared with you this week, we expect you to go back to your communities and share your experiences with your neighbors." The group let out a collective sigh and laughed to one another.

Maria and I called each participant's name and handed out diplomas that I printed off of a Peace Corps computer, signed by both Grace Landau and myself. Eduardo had fashioned miniature *sombreros*, no larger than a silver dollar, and distributed them as mementos from *La Tranquilidad*. The participants gave little speeches as they received their diplomas. All of the speeches were more or less the same, thanking me and Maria and everyone else for the fun, friendship, and knowledge, and promising that they'd take what they learned back to their communities. I drifted off into my thoughts.

I still had almost a year left in Panama, but I couldn't help but feel like I'd peaked as a Volunteer. I taught everything I knew about sustainable agriculture to every neighbor who'd shown even the slightest bit of interest. I taught a few of them how to teach others and how to reach out to government extension agents when they needed a hand. I knew I could do the same sort of workshop over again and reach even more people outside of the community, but it was tough to get excited about it. It was time to embrace new challenges. I wondered how Elena was doing and whether we would have a future together.

Chapter 37 – Shotguns & Chainsaws

Two weeks later I was relaxing in my hammock, listening to *Voice of America* on my short wave radio after a satisfying meal of pasta with homemade tomato sauce. I heard the bus before I saw it. Then its headlights came around the bend and lit up the dirt road. It was odd to see the bus lumbering up the mountain at that late hour, but I didn't give it much thought until the bus came to a halt in front of my house.

Elena? It must be her. She's made up her mind. Is she going to tell me that we'll go to the office together, hand in hand, and explain to them that we're sorry, but things happened that we didn't plan on and we have to say goodbye now and go to the States and build a life together? Or is she going to tell me that she isn't going to keep the baby at all? My heart raced with anticipation.

I could see only the silhouette of the passenger who climbed off the bus in front of my house. It had to be a Volunteer. No Panamanian traveled around with a backpack like that, but my visitor was too big to be Elena.

It was Kyle. Once he reached my porch, I could see he looked wan and tired. The usual sparkle in his eyes was missing. "What's up, man?" he asked.

"It seems like I should be asking you the same thing." Bonito was curious too. He got up from his spot under the worm box to give our visitor a couple of sniffs.

"That dog is uglia than the dogs that came back in <u>Pet Cemetary</u>," he told me.

"He's beautiful on the inside."

"He must be."

"You should have seen him before his hair grew back. Besides . . ."

224

"Yeah?"

". . . nobody asked you."

"I hit a nerve, huh? Sorry. You got a fine dog there. Say, you got anythin' to drink?"

"Nope. Didn't know you were coming."

Kyle slung his backpack into a corner of the porch and sat down in my hammock. The only sounds came from the frogs chirping in the pasture and the rope of the hammock creaking back and forth against the rafter. I waited for Kyle to start talking, but he didn't seem ready yet.

"Elena's gone," he finally said, breaking the silence.

I laughed. "You mean she's lost her mind? I knew that a long time ago."

"No dude. She's *gone*. She flew back to the States. She's done."

"She never said anything to me."

"I know. It was unexpected. It was only random chance that I saw her befaw she left."

"You saw her?"

"Yeah. Just befaw she left. We were both in the office."

"When's she coming back?" I asked, refusing to imagine she'd decided to leave without me.

"Yaw not gettin' it. She's not comin' back. She's finished. She C.O.S.'d."

"You mean she E.T.'d?" I asked him.

E.T. stood for Early Termination and C.O.S. stood for Completion of Service. You didn't get to C.O.S. unless you finished your two years of service. E.T.'s were for quitters. Or in Elena's case, for someone who had to be medically separated. *She's decided to have the abortion and do it before telling me.*

"She didn't E.T. 'cause Grace let her C.O.S." He let out a slow sigh. "There was an *incident*." It was odd to hear Kyle use such a carefully chosen word. After a long pause he continued, "She got hurt John. She has a broken nose and a pretty bad shine'a. She wasn't movin' aroun' so good. I think she might have broken ribs too."

"What are you talking about?" I leapt from my seat, grabbed the rope on the hammock, and jerked it to a stop. "What happened to her? Was she in a *chiva* accident?"

The Inter-American Highway was a nightmare. Huge busses and tractor trailers barreled down pot hole-filled, narrow lanes. Drivers of cars and trucks alike had little concern for their passengers, cargo, fellow drivers, or seemingly even themselves. Just a month earlier two cars had been racing each other down the highway and bumped. One of the cars had gone airborne, crossed the median, and landed right on top of Doug Butler's car. He was killed instantly. He'd survived Korea and Vietnam, only to be done in by the Inter-American Highway on a trip into the city. If Elena had been in an accident on the highway, I was just happy she'd survived. But what about the baby? How could she not call me?

"Did she say anything about her *condition*?" I asked, testing Kyle to see if he knew anything about Elena's pregnancy.

"She didn't have much of anything to say to me. She just told me she was leavin' and said goodbye and turned her back on me. She looked like a ghost of herself. No one in the office wanted to talk about it eetha."

"*So?*" I demanded, pacing back and forth as he stared up at me from the hammock with a blank look on his face.

"I'm getting' there, man . . . shit. Just shut up and listen." He sighed. "I sweet talked Bana'd's secretary a li'l bit. She's a sucker for my chams." He gave a weak smile, but his heart wasn't in it. "She said that Elena got in some trouble with the cowboys near her village. I guess the people in her town had been starting to organize and push back a little bit. It got out of hand one night. Some of the Wounaan from Elena's community got riled up and burned down the cowboys' camp. I guess the cowboys blamed Elena."

"*And?*"

"They broke into her house in the middle of the night. From the look of her, she put up a pretty good fight too. But there were too many of them."

"What!? This is insane. Didn't anybody in her town do anything?"

"I guess some people woke up and came outside when they heard the commotion, but the cowboys had shotguns and chainsaws."

"They *shot* people?"

"I don't know. I don't think so. Maybe they just used the weapons to keep people at bay."

"What do you mean 'keep people at bay'? You mean to make it a fair fight between several men and one woman? This is the craziest thing I've ever heard!" It still wasn't sinking in.

"Would you *please* shut the *fuck* up and let me talk. This isn't easy." Kyle let out another big, slow sigh and summoned the strength to tell me what he'd traveled all the way to *Los Altos* to say:

"The cowboys raped her."

"What?" I stammered, reaching blindly back for the chair and collapsing before I even realized I'd decided to. All of the impatience and frustration and disbelief I'd been feeling throughout Kyle's account washed away as though sucked into some giant vacuum. *Los Altos* disappeared. The rest of the world disappeared. Everything beyond my small porch was gone, white-washed with cold and quiet like an empty street in the early morning after a giant snow storm.

"The cowboys just left her there before disappearin' into the jungle and headin' back to their camp," Kyle continued. "No one from the village could do anything until it was over. I guess she worked with some basket-weaving group?"

"Right," I muttered vacantly.

"Well, some of those women spent the rest of the night with her in her house. Then in the mornin' they used their basket money and took her to the embassy and told them what had happened. The Peace Caw wanted to do somethin' about it . . ."

"I *sure as hell* hope so!" I yelled, filled with anger I had nowhere to direct.

". . . but Elena just wanted to leave. She didn't want to stick aroun' long enough to identify anyone or press cha'ges, so Grace said there was nothing the police or the embassy could do."

"But . . ." I started to say before stumbling to the edge of the porch and puking on my tomato plants.

"Are you ok?"

"No."

"I'm sorry. I didn't want to be the one to tell you, but I couldn't imagine *not* being there when you foun' out. I think it's probably best you didn't see her. I'm really sorry man."

"What about the baby?" I pleaded.

"What baby?"

Chapter 38 – Abruption

I spent three unreal days holed up in my house, unable to concentrate on anything, eating badly and sleeping worse, staggering back and forth between bouts of insane rage and bottomless sorrow. The brutal sun cooked my corrugated steel roof and baked the concrete block walls, but I afforded myself not a moment of daylight to think in. I endured the stifling heat without any breeze or natural light as my stomach cramped and twisted and screamed, as though my self-induced suffering was some sort of homage.

My lips curled with blood-lust directed at the faceless men who had done deeds I couldn't bear to imagine. Other times I found myself furious with Elena. Why was she so stubborn? How could she have gone back to her site when she had our baby inside her? Most of all, how could she think to leave Panama without sending me so much as a word? I knew she'd been through hell, but that was my baby too.

On the third day, I shuffled down the road to the center of town, looking at the ground all the way, careful to avoid the possibility of eye contact and the pain of human interaction. With an unsteady hand I picked up the phone and called the Peace Corps office.

"Bernard?" I asked.

"Yes?"

"It's John Dillon."

"Hi John. What can I do for you?"

"I heard . . . I heard about Elena," I stammered, surprised at how hard it was to get the words out.

"Yes?"

"I know about her *situation*," I huffed, choking back tears.

"I'm afraid the news seems to have traveled. It's very upsetting."

"That's not . . . what I mean . . ." I gasped between sniffles. "I'm not talking about what happened in her site. . . . I'm talking about her pregnancy."

"Oh." We both remained silent for a moment. "I didn't realize anyone knew about *that*. She said she hadn't told anyone. Does that mean you're . . . responsible?"

"Yes."

"I see. Even so, there are confidentiality issues. I can't talk to you about it. I'm sorry."

"*Bernard!*"

"This is the government John. There are rules. I could get in a lot of trouble."

"But is she ok? Are *they* ok? Just, just tell me that."

"John . . . ."

"Come on Bernard. I won't say anything to anyone! Please. I'm begging you. Tell me if they're alright."

"I don't know. I'm sorry."

"What do you mean you don't know? Don't do this to me."

"It's not that, John. Honestly, it's not. When I say I don't know, I mean I really don't know."

"What?"

"It's complicated. A pregnant woman who has suffered that sort of trauma could have a host of issues."

"What does *that* mean?" I asked in a panic.

"Well, speaking strictly *generally*, you follow me John?"

"Yes. Of course. Thank you Bernard."

"Speaking strictly generally, a woman in that situation could have a placental abruption."

"What is that?"

"That occurs when the placental lining separates from the uterus. It can cause very serious problems if it's not identified quickly enough."

"But what does that *mean*? Are you saying she's in danger? Or are you saying she could lose the baby?"

"Theoretically, those are both possibilities. But there's also the possibility that everything will be fine. We just don't know. The classic symptom of a low grade placental abruption is moderate vaginal bleeding. But those symptoms are also typical of a savage sexual assault. So, in this case, a mere physical examination doesn't give us a very clear picture of what's going on.

"Unfortunately, she wanted to leave the country before getting all the necessary tests. I expect she just wanted to get away from all of this. I'm sure she'll get an ultrasound back in the States. After she gets the results, I'm certain she'll let you know."

I didn't share his confidence. I knew Elena. The way things had been going between us for the last few months, if the baby wasn't ok, I'd probably never hear from her again. I imagined Elena would deal with what happened by not dealing with it, by putting everything that happened to her in a locked chest and never opening the latch. And I'd be on the inside of that chest along with all the other bad memories. Otherwise, I'd be a constant reminder of Panama and everything she hoped to forget. Even if the baby was ok, I knew she still might want me locked away.

John? Are you still there?"

"Yeah," I answered, though the most important part of me wasn't still there.

"Maybe you should come to the office. We have people you can talk to."

"Yeah. Thanks."

And then I found myself hanging up the phone and sobbing with shame for thinking badly of her. Of course she didn't say anything to me before she left. What would she have said? That she didn't know anything? That *maybe* she would have a healthy baby? That even if the baby was healthy it would force her into a life – with me – that she wasn't sure she wanted *before* she'd been beaten and raped? Only now the baby and I would be ever-present symbols of another horrible chapter in an already sour family history?

And then I wondered if she was feeling guilty for going back to her site. Too guilty even to face me? And I knew all the while that I couldn't possibly imagine what she was feeling and thinking. Surely she was swimming at sea inside her own mind. The thought of her desperate pain devastated me.

I sat down that night and reached for the pen she gave me. With a trembling hand, I wrote her a letter. I told her that everything would be ok. I told her that if she wanted to keep the baby I would support her. And I told her that if she couldn't go through with it, I'd support that too. I just wanted her to know that I missed her and cared for her and wanted her to feel good. I told her that I would be whoever she needed me to be, even if it meant my reluctant withdrawal from her life. It was only then that I realized I cared more about her than I cared about myself. It was only then that I realized what it meant to truly love someone.

And then I realized I had nowhere to send the letter. I considered sending it to her parents' house in Feather Falls . . . for all of a minute. After everything she'd been through, perhaps *especially* after everything she'd been through, I knew she wouldn't go back to her father. She wouldn't let him think, let alone say, "I told you so."

Elena.

Chapter 39 – Birdshot

I paced back and forth on my small porch. Five steps one way. Five steps back. Bonito sat on his haunches in the corner, perplexed. He watched me with his head cocked at an angle, as though waiting for me to share my thoughts with him. We both turned when the rumble of the bus started coming up the mountain. "C'mon Bonito. Let's go."

I shouldered my pack and walked down to the road. Bonito trotted after me. After my leishmaniasis episode, I wouldn't leave Bonito again if I could help it.

"You can't bring that dog on the bus," the driver snapped at me.

"He's a good dog. He won't be a problem."

The driver started to shut the door on me, but I blocked him with my arm.

"He'll pay for his seat." I held up a ten dollar bill, twice the fare for an adult to travel from my site to the city.

He opened the door back up and snatched the money out of my hand. Bonito stuck close to my heels and followed me warily to the back of the bus as we both received dirty looks from the other passengers.

"That dog is *feo*," an old woman scowled at me.

"You think you're so beautiful?"

She tried to look appalled, but I pretended not to notice. I motioned for Bonito to take the seat in the back corner and he obediently hopped up. I worried he might get anxious cooped up on the bus, but he was happy just to stare out the window.

"Your first car ride, huh?"

235

He gave me a brief, sloppy kiss on the neck before quickly returning his gaze to the blurry landscape.

A few hours later, Bonito and I found ourselves in *Cacique*. Kyle and I shared a smoke at the end of the rickety pier in the center of town. The full moon reflected off the water. Bonito hung his head off the edge of the pier and stared between his paws into his reflection below.

"You loved her," Kyle said, finally breaking the silence. "She knew. She loved you too." I couldn't tell if he was just humoring me or if he really believed what he was saying. "It's hard for me to think you've seen the last of her." Those last words gave it away. He was just humoring me.

"I'm going to visit her village."

"Why?"

"I'm not sure. It just feels like something I should do. I never once visited while she was there. I always promised I'd see the place before we were through, but I never got around to it."

"You going to do anything stupid?"

I hadn't figured it out yet. I wanted to change the subject. "Can Bonito stay with you until I get back?"

"I guess so."

"Thanks. You know, I never asked you what happened when you took that double dose of Aralen the first week of training."

"Ha. Nothin' good. I had a bad headache in the morning and . . . you can't tell anyone ok?"

"I can't tell anyone what?"

"I shah'ted on the way to *Cerro Verde*."

236

"You sharted?"

"You know what a shaht is. You can't tell me it's nevah happened to you."

"What's never happened to me?"

"I fahted and a little bit of shit came out."

"On the bus? That's *awful*!" I howled with delight.

"It *was* awful, you basta'd, so wipe that grin off yuh face. I had to sit in the bus like that for an ow'wa. And then I had to show up on my host mom's dawstep with shit in my pants. Talk about embarrassin'. I had to excuse myself to go to the bathroom the second I got there. My first memory of *Cerro Verde* is throwin' my soiled boxers down into the da'k abyss of the family latrine."

"Brother, you know I love you, but you're a dumbass. I needed a night like this. Thank you."

"I love you too man. And yaw welcome."

In the morning, we ate fried fish for breakfast and I said goodbye. I made my way to the city, ran an errand, and found the bus to *Chepo*. From there, I found my way to *Puerto Coquira* and caught a boat to Elena's village.

The captain, a Latino man who looked to be in his forties, guided his double-wide, wooden canoe slowly down the *Rio Chepo*, letting the current do much of the work. Then, when he hit the Pacific Ocean, he fired up the boat's small outboard motor. We skipped along the clear blue water, about a quarter mile from the coast. Sea spray popped from the sides of the boat and peppered our faces.

The hum of the motor and the rhythmic bouncing of the boat hypnotized me. I stared into the wake and remembered the boat ride from *Barro Colorado* when my head rested contentedly in Elena's comforting lap. I lost myself in my thoughts, reminiscing about the past year before turning my attention to the place I was going and what I would do once I arrived there. I worked through each and every detail in my mind, imagining all of the eventualities and how I'd react.

The captain brought me back to the present when, after nearly an hour of traveling across the open ocean, he suddenly swung the boat around towards forested coastline. Whatever he saw, I couldn't. To me, it looked like we were headed straight into the rocks where our boat would smash to splinters.

But the captain had made the trip countless times and knew the route well. He slowed the motor down and steered the boat towards murkier, brackish waters. I quickly realized that the seemingly endless forest disguised the mouth of a river.

"This is *Quebrada Brava*," he shouted over the buzz of the motor. He obviously spoke for my benefit, for the few other passengers all lived there. Otherwise, they'd have no reason to go. Except for government extension agents and the rare graduate student, outsiders never made the trip. "The village is up this way."

"How far is it?" I asked.

"It's not far. We'll be there in a few hours."

I sat hunched at the front of the boat on a wooden slat seat. My knees nearly touched my chest. I was already getting sore, so I sat up and rubbed my lower back and stretched out as best I could in the cramped conditions. The men and women around me seemed indifferent to the discomfort, or at least they seemed resigned to it, but I wondered how I'd endure several hours sitting like that.

Within moments, however, we entered the river and I lost myself in the magical scenery.

Dense, primary forest stretched out beyond the shore. Howler monkeys groaned in the distance. Bamboo plants crowded one another along the river's edge where they sprung high into the air before curving back towards the water under their own weight.

"Look," an old man in the boat called to me. I followed his pointing finger and saw a lone toucan fly out of the jungle and across the river in front of us. I marveled at its bright, multicolored beak before it disappeared into the forest. It was the first time I'd ever seen a toucan in the wild. "*Un tucan*," the captain's helper explained. "They're pretty, no?"

I smiled and nodded. "This is a beautiful place," I added. He looked satisfied with my answer as he lounged proudly in the boat's bow.

"I grew up here," he boasted. "I'm Candido." Unlike our Latino captain, Candido had the distinctive broad nose and big, round cheeks of the Wounaan. Though he looked to be in his late teens or early twenties, his hands were already rough and calloused from a life of hard work. "This is your first time here?" he asked, already knowing the answer.

"Yes."

"Welcome."

It wasn't hard to understand how this place captivated Elena.

I looked at the man who pointed out the bird with an expression of wonderment, as though to share my appreciation and awe, as well as my gratitude. If he hadn't pointed out the moment, it surely would have passed me by. The man just smiled and nodded. Then he turned to the others and said something in Wounaan. Whatever he said must have been pretty funny, for they all laughed, presumably at my expense. But there was no meanness to their laughter and I laughed with them to share in their joke. The Wounaan had no money, but they were far from poor.

We made our way slowly, steadily upstream before we came upon a large tree that blocked the entire width of the river. "There was a big storm last night," the captain said before guiding the boat to the river's edge. He turned off the motor to conserve gas while Candido used an axe to chop the fallen tree.

Candido made short work of the tree and we were on our way again. An hour later the boat pulled up to a small dock. There was only one house in sight. A thick palm thatch roof covered the house like a shaggy head of hair that protected its inhabitants from the near-constant downpours. A young woman stood in front of the house. She carried a baby in the crook of her arm and tended to a cast iron pot that simmered over a wood-burning fire.

The captain hurriedly collected the fare from all of the passengers and made his way quickly to the house, leaving Candido to tend to the boat and its cargo. The captain gave the young mother, who couldn't have been more than half the captain's age, a big kiss on the mouth. The woman blushed, clearly embarrassed by the public display of affection, but the captain either didn't notice or didn't care. The woman, still blushing, turned and waved to Candido.

Candido waved back as he bent down and tossed a scoop of river water into his face. He rubbed it around with his hand, under his chin, and around the back of his neck. Then he turned to the unenviable task of unloading the boat. I dropped my pack on the river bank and lent him a hand.

"Is this *Quebrada Brava*?" I asked, confused by the obvious dearth of people or houses.

"No. But it's not too far. I'll show you."

"I thought *Quebrada Brava* was on the river."

"It is, but the river is too dry right now. We can't go any further without having to push the boat half way there. It's much easier to walk from here."

The river might have been dry, but the hike wasn't. At some points I found myself in mud up to my knees and I had to cross a couple of streams that rushed around my waist. My bag was heavy on my back. If I took a wrong step or the rushing water knocked me off balance, I'd almost certainly drown, so I made sure to unbuckle the waist clips on my pack just in case. I couldn't imagine what it was like during the rainy season. I couldn't imagine Elena's horrific hike through the forest with Leo cradled in her arms.

Candido, meanwhile, deftly crossed the stream and waited patiently for me on the other side. And he carried a fifty pound bag of rice on his shoulder. Rather than laugh at my incompetence, he offered his hand when I got to the side of the stream.

"Thank you friend," I panted, out of breath from the physical exertion.

"It's good," he answered. "Are you Peace Corps?"

"Did you know Elena?" I asked, ignoring the question.

"The *gringa*? Of course. She helped us much."

"What happened to her?"

"Was a shame."

Candido told me all the awful details. Kyle's account, it turned out, was largely accurate. Candido added that some of the men had tried to intervene, but the cowboys fired birdshot at them. He lifted up his shirt and showed me torn skin around his side and the small of his back.

"Why didn't you go to the police? Why haven't there been any arrests?"

"A small group of us went to the police, but they said they didn't believe us. They said we were just making up stories to get the cowboys out of the area. Without Elena, they said, we had no proof." He looked down and closed his eyes and shook his head, as though ashamed of the failure.

"But what about your back?" I asked, pointing with my lips towards the wound he'd just showed me. "Isn't that proof?"

"I thought so too, but they said I could have gotten that wound from trespassing where I didn't belong. They said that if anything had happened to the *gringa* they would have known about it. 'Where is she?' they asked us." After a long pause he added, "but they knew in their hearts that we were telling the truth. They just don't care."

The shame was gone from his face and anger flashed in his eyes. "The cowboys pay the police to protect them. The cowboys can do anything they want. Some of the people here are still walking around with pellets in them because they're too old or weak to make the walk and they can't afford to take the boat ride to the nearest medical center. One man lost an eye. The police respect their dogs more than they respect Wounaan."

We walked along in silence, each contemplating the sad reality of the tale he told. Before too long, the path we walked along opened up into a clearing. We reached *Quebrada Brava.*

Chapter 40 – A Dry Cough

Quebrada Brava buzzed with activity as men came home from a day of fishing and their wives prepared dinner in cast iron pots over open fires. Bright colored *parumas* hung on clothes lines all over the village. I admired the scene as the sun dropped behind the trees and dusk settled in.

The village was smaller than I'd expected. There were only two dozen dwellings scattered about. I imagined they had been built wherever the owner grew weary and dumped the heavy load of lumber that he carried on his shoulder.

All of the houses were built on stilts, several feet above the ground, to get away from insects, forest critters, and the occasional flood. And every home had a large deck where the families went about their daily activities. Only the family bedroom had walls. To enclose more would have been a waste of wood. The large, open decks allowed neighbors to wave to you as you relaxed in your hammock or worked on a rosewood carving.

The forest seemed to go forever in every direction, save for the river that bordered one side of the village, but the last house couldn't have been more than a quarter-mile from the first. Some houses were as close as twenty feet away from the next one. The people of *Quebrada Brava* seemed to have all the space in the world, but had no interest in claiming more room than they needed. Privacy wasn't precious. They didn't live amongst one another. They lived with one another.

A few children ran up to us, but said nothing. They just walked along, staring up at me, whispering to one another and giggling. Candido said something to them in their language and mussed one boy's hair. They reminded me of my neighbors in *Las Cascadas*. I tried to offer the children a friendly smile, but it felt forced and fake.

"Can you show me which house was Elena's?" I asked Candido.

He gestured towards a house at the far end of town. Elena's house was the only house that wasn't overflowing with life. No children played there. No one washed dishes in a big bucket. No clothes dried on the line.

I climbed up the ladder, dropped my pack on the floor of the porch, and massaged my shoulders. The kids that greeted us when we first arrived scurried up the ladder after me. I imagined they were Elena's closest friends in town, playing on her porch all afternoon as she went about her business. She'd prepare her dinner as they swung from her rafters. When the sun went down she'd tell them it was time to go and they'd reluctantly run off to their own homes.

I imagined the excitement the little boys, and the grown men too, must have felt as Elena walked from her house to her shower stall just a few feet away, knowing all that white skin was getting wet and clean under the open air. I wondered if the boys tried to spy on her as she changed in her house. I sure as hell would have.

"You speak Spanish?" I asked the kids.

They looked at each other and giggled. The oldest one answered, "*Sí*," and they all giggled again.

"I'm tired from my trip. With all respect, I want to be alone for a while." The older one translated for the others. They looked disappointed, but obediently climbed back down the ladder, one after another.

The door of Elena's bedroom was open and I mustered the courage to walk inside. Part of me hoped that she'd be inside waiting for me, as though nothing had ever happened. But something *had* happened. There wasn't so much as a cooking pot or even a hook on the wall. The only sign that Elena had ever been there was the date she completed the house. It was carved into the door frame. I knew Elena had carved it herself; only Americans write the month before the day.

The wood plank walls were unsanded and unpainted, hardly removed from the generous forest that provided them, so the house had the warm, honest smell of sawdust and rain. From the outside, the palm-thatch roof looked round, but on the inside, the roof had four distinct sides that came together in a point, like a pyramid. I lay down on the floor, cradled my head in my hands, and admired the workmanship for a while. I spaced out into the interlaid palm leaves and imagined the life Elena had breathed into the house and the community. I wanted to hear her voice.

I woke up in the middle of the night. The town was perfectly still, but for the sound of a small child coughing. His cough sounded dry and painful. I could feel the burn in his chest. I heard his mother whisper something soothing to him. I fell back asleep.

"*Buenos dias!*" someone called out. I walked out to the deck and saw Candido at the bottom of Elena's ladder.

"*Buenos dias*," I answered without much enthusiasm. I'd been wearing the same clothes for thirty hours. I felt dirty. My back hurt from sleeping on the wood floor.

"I brought you some breakfast. You must be hungry." He raised his arms over his head to pass me two bananas and a piece of fish.

"*Gracias.* Please, come in."

Candido climbed up the ladder and we both sat cross-legged on the deck. I tore into the bananas and the fish. I was hungrier than I'd realized.

"You're *Juan*, aren't you?" he ventured.

"Yes."

He nodded solemnly. He didn't say anything. I didn't either. We sat there quietly for a while.

"The fish was good," I said after several long minutes, finally breaking the heavy silence. "Thank you."

"You're welcome."

"Did you cook it?" I asked, just to make conversation.

"No," he laughed. "My wife made it. Would you like to meet her?"

"Sure."

Candido climbed deftly down the ladder and I followed clumsily after him. His house, like all the houses, was close by. A woman picked through a large, hand-made fishing net spread out on the ground before her. As I got closer I saw the net was filled with freshly caught river shrimp.

"This is my wife," Candido said proudly. She looked strong and able, though she had smooth skin and a young face.

"Thank you for breakfast."

She nodded, wiped her palm across her hip, and delicately shook my hand with a bashful look on her face.

"This is *Juan*," he told her knowingly, emphasizing my name. It seemed to make her even more uncomfortable. I felt awkward standing there in front of her and shuffled my feet a bit.

"It's very pretty here," I said to no one in particular.

"How is Elena?" Candido's wife asked me. She made eye contact with me for a fleeting second before looking back down at the shrimp.

"I don't know." I let out a breath that I felt like I'd been holding in for a long time.

She nodded again without looking up.

"How long are you going to be in our village?" Candido asked. "Are you going to live in Elena's house now?"

"No. I don't think I'll be here long at all."

"Why not? You should stay a while."

"Thank you. I appreciate that. But I came to find the cowboys. Do you know where they are?"

Candido looked taken aback. "No. . . . Not exactly. They move their camp every few weeks, but they are never far. Why do you want to find them?"

"I just do. Will you show me where to go?"

He nodded. Then, after a long minute, he asked only, "when?"

248

"Soon. But I need to make a call first. Does this town have a phone?"

"Yes," he answered, pointing off in the distance, "but I don't know if it's working these days."

Candido led me to a solar powered payphone. I didn't imagine the repair man made many trips out to *Quebrada Brava*, so I took a deep breath and hoped for the best when I lifted the receiver. To my relief, there was a dial tone. I quickly punched in a familiar number.

"*Buenas?*" the voice at the other end answered.

"Antonio?"

"Yes. How are you Juan? It's good to hear you."

"You too. Forgive me, but I need a favor."

"Anything."

"Do you still have that car of yours?"

"Of course."

"Good. I need you to meet me at *Puerto Coquira* near *Chepo* in two days."

"*Chepo?* You're a long way from *Coclé*. Are you ok? Is everything alright?"

"Everything is fine. I'll explain myself when I see you. I'll be at the dock. Do you think you can be there?"

"I'll have to juggle my schedule at the restaurant, but I'll be there. Don't worry."

I hung up the phone and went back to Elena's house. I strapped on my pack before Candido led me out of the small village. We walked along the river's edge for some time.

Chapter 41 – The Soft Sell

After a couple of hours we came upon the devastation. Giant trees lay strewn about like discarded matchsticks, as though a hurricane had chewed up the jungle and spit it back out.

"What is this?"

"This is what they do. They clear the forest with chainsaws and then build fences so they can bring in their cows to graze. This looks like it was done recently. They haven't burned the fallen trees to clear the land yet."

"So they're close?"

"Probably. I don't even see any fences yet, but they will surely build them soon. I'll come back in a week and cut the wires."

"I think I can find them from here."

"Are you sure?"

"Yes." I didn't want to get Candido involved any deeper in my foolishness. I didn't care if anything happened to me, but Candido had people to take care of. My people were gone.

"Ok. If you find a fence, you've found them. If you get lost, you can follow the river back. Here, take this." He pulled a couple of corn meal cakes wrapped in banana leaves out of his pocket and handed them to me. "You know you can't drink this water?" He pointed to the river.

"I know. I've got some water in my pack. Don't worry."

"Be careful." He looked reluctant to leave me alone out there.

"I will. Thank you."

"Good luck."

I continued along for another hour or two, but my progress was slow. I was beginning to lose hope when I came across a two-string, barbed wire fence. The dirt around the fence posts was loose and soft. My heart began to race.

But I'd have to wait. The sun was almost all the way down. Hiking with rubbery legs and a bulky pack was hard enough in broad daylight. I wasn't eager to try it in the dark, so I resigned myself to camping for the night. I cleared off the brush the best I could, pulled my small tent out of my pack, and set it up.

My camp was meager. I had no lantern and no stove. But it was only one night. I could make it through one night. Worst case scenario, I'd just hike back along the river to *Quebrada Brava* in the morning.

With that tiny sliver of comfort, I climbed into the tent and zipped it up tight to make sure I didn't wake up with any snakes. Once inside the tent, I opened up a can of tuna fish with my pocket knife and ate it with the corn meal cakes Candido had given me. It was a sad dinner, even by camping standards.

The apex of the tent had sheer netting that let me stare at the sky as I lay on my back. With no light for miles around, the sky revealed more stars than I'd ever seen. I started counting the shooting stars. Eventually, I drifted off to sleep.

I woke up with a jolt. The whole tent shook. I opened my eyes and saw it was already light out. The tent shook again.

"*Oye!*" a gruff voice shouted, "who's in there? What are you doing here?"

"*Ya voy,*" I called back.

Holy shit. shit. shit. shit. What do I do?

Whenever I'd played out the harebrained scheme in my mind, I'd always found the *colonos.* I'd always had the element of surprise. But it was clear I wouldn't have to find them; they'd found me. I rolled over and sat up on my knees, took a deep breath to gather my courage, and unzipped the tent door.

I found myself staring at the tip of a machete. A man squatted in front of me, balanced on the balls of his feet as though ready to spring. He held the machete straight out in front of him and pointed the tip right at my nose. I recoiled into the tent and fell on my back.

"Who are you?" he demanded.

He had a creepy, sparse mustache that would never grow in no matter how long he tried and shoulder-length, black hair that he combed straight back.

"*Buenas,*" I said as meekly as I could.

"Who are you?" he repeated.

"No one."

"*No one?* I've never met anyone named no one," he snarled.

"I mean, *Arturo.* My name is *Arturo.*"

"*Arturo?*"

"Yes, *Arturo.*"

"You don't look like an *Arturo.* You look like a *gringo.*"

"I am a *gringo.* My name is Art. But in Spanish it's *Arturo.*" I pointed at the machete. "May I get out?"

252

The man stood up and backed off a few feet. When I climbed out of the tent I could see there were three of them. A tall, lanky man held a shotgun. He had one hand on the stock and the other hand on the fore-end, pointing the barrel at the sky, like a corrections officer watching a chain gain. When he saw me looking at the gun, he moved his finger to the trigger.

Am I going to die today?

Only Kyle knew where I was. Surely he'd tell the Peace Corps if no one heard from me for a while, but how long would he wait? Would these men even bother burying me? Or would they just burn my corpse? Or toss me in the river? Or just leave me to rot in the forest?

I'd made a terrible mistake. I wanted to be back in *Quebrada Brava*, or *Las Cascadas*, or better yet, in Philadelphia. *But you wanted this. You went looking for this.*

"So what are you doing here?" the man with the machete asked. "What do you want?"

That's a little embarrassing." I stared at the ground to look as sheepish as possible. "I tried to find you yesterday, but I got lost."

"Now you found us. But what do you *want?*"

"I don't really *want* anything. I am a volunteer here. And I have heard that some of the volunteers in this area work only with the Wounaan. That doesn't seem fair to me. I think our job is to help all Panamanians."

"So you're saying you're here to help us?" He thought it over as he combed through his mustache with his filthy fingernails.

"That's right. I'm here to help, but only if you want my help."

"Why should we trust you? The *gringo* volunteers have been nothing but trouble for us."

"Why shouldn't you trust me? Look around. I'm all alone out here. And there are three of you. If you want me to leave, all you have to do is say so." I shrugged. "But, if you want, you could let me work with you today and then decide if you think I can help. After all, it's free labor." I looked at the other two men to lobby for their approval.

The third man hadn't said a word. But he didn't need to. He looked like a *Latino* Paul Bunyan. I had little doubt he could have lifted me clear over his head if he were so inclined.

"If he works with us, we can finish faster," the lanky one suggested.

"He's right," I agreed. "And if you decide I don't do good work or you just don't want me around, just say so at the end of the day. I'll go on my way and find others to work with." I'd practiced the soft sell in my head a hundred times during the boat ride to *Quebrada Brava*. "What are you all working on today?" I asked.

"Why do you want to know?" the boss asked.

"It's hard for me to help if I don't know what to do." I laughed exaggeratedly.

"Don't be so suspicious," the lanky one interrupted. "We could use the extra set of hands. I can't wait to get out of here."

"We're building fences," the boss explained with a measure of reluctance. "We have some cattle nearby, but they'll need a new area to graze soon. Can you dig holes?"

Chapter 42 – Mending Fences

I spent the rest of the day cutting fence posts and digging holes for them. It was brutal work in the stifling humidity. My hands were sore and my back throbbed. But the physical aches and pains weren't the worst part. I felt like a traitor helping these men build fences. But I had to gain their trust.

We worked straight through the day, talking little and resting even less. No matter how vile these men were, I couldn't deny they worked hard. I struggled to keep up with them, just as I'd struggled to keep up with the men in *Las Altos* when I'd first arrived there. By the time the sun started to set, I was wearing a thick layer of dirt and sweat. My hands were covered in small nicks and cuts from working all day with spools of barbed wire.

"We did good work today," I said. "We accomplished a lot."

"It's true," the boss conceded. "Thank you for your help."

"Do you want me to camp with you all tonight so that I can work with you for a few more days?"

"You're not gay, are you?" the lanky one teased.

"*Solo me gusta la chucha*," I answered. All three men started laughing.

Paul Bunyan grinned at me. "The *gringo* knows a lot."

With free labor and vulgarity, I was winning them over.

"That's fine," the boss answered. "Our camp isn't far from here."

Once we settled in around the campfire, I knew I was in their good graces.

"So what do you all do out here when you're not working?" I asked.

"Nothing. This is it. We work and we sleep."

"We can do better than that." I pulled two bottles of Seco out of my pack. All three men were visibly stunned. It was a better reaction than I'd hoped for.

"I thought that if we have a drink together and talk for a while, we can figure out how I might be able to help you . . . besides just building fences."

Paul Bunyan nodded eagerly. "That sounds pretty good to me."

"I wouldn't mind having a drink," the lanky one agreed.

"Fine . . . . But we still have to wake up early and work all day tomorrow," the boss warned them.

They passed the bottles back and forth in a flurry of grabby arms. I expected I'd be able to bribe their trust with the liquor, but the extent of their ravenousness still surprised me. They barely came up for air as they took shot after shot. Meanwhile, I waited patiently for the booze to lubricate their tongues.

"But she's a beautiful mare," the lanky one said.

"If you say so," Paul Bunyan answered.

"I'm telling you! The way the pussy of a mare feels wrapped around your cock! You'll never be satisfied by a woman again."

"*Que cochina!*" the boss squealed.

"I'll take my mare over your wife any day," the lanky man added.

256

"Who wouldn't take a mare over his wife?" The bearded one howled and all three men erupted into laughter.

I just shook my head in disbelief.

"You've never been with a mare?" the lanky one inquired.

"No, never," I assured him.

"You don't know what you're missing, *gringo*."

"I'll take your word for it."

"So you're really here to help us?" the boss asked. He poured himself another drink. They'd put half the bottle away in less than ten minutes.

"That's right. I'm here to help anyone I can," I said. "You'd be surprised how hard it is to find people to work with."

"Good. It's about time you people learned. The last volunteer here wanted to help only the indians. Because of her, the indians forgot their place. They've made life difficult for us."

"They've made life *difficult* for you?" The Wounaan had lived in the Darien long before the cowboys ever showed up, but the Wounaan had made almost no mark on the forest. Practically overnight, however, the cowboys destroyed their own land, crossed the isthmus of Panama, and clear-cut half the Darien. They ravaged the Wounaan's food supply, contaminated the drinking water, and threatened their entire way of life. They even killed little Leo. Yet, with total sincerity, they had the stones to complain that the Wounaan had made life difficult for *them*. "What do you mean they've made life 'difficult' for you?"

The boss took another long drink. "For one thing, they've started complaining to the police. That costs us a lot of money. The local police don't care about the indians, but every time they find out about us cutting down trees, they come to us with their hands out. And we have to pay them or they'll stop us from harvesting lumber or grazing our cattle. We're barely making enough money to get by as it is."

"How is that the *gringa*'s fault?" I asked.

It felt strange to call Elena "the *gringa*." It felt more than strange. It felt like a betrayal. She wasn't "the *gringa*." She was the only thing that mattered. And she was gone.

They would soon understand that the *gringa* had a name. That she radiated light and goodness. That she was the woman I wanted to grow old with and the mother of my unborn child. They would pay for what they had done.

I imagined gagging them and binding them and dropping boots and fists on them until my hands were swollen bags of broken bones. Then I'd turn to a dull, rusty machete to slowly flay the skin from their rancid bodies before dropping it strip by strip into the fire, watching it shrivel and char and disappear into the nothingness that was still too good for them.

But such revenge was too far-fetched to exist anywhere but in my mind. True revenge would have to wait. I was alone and outnumbered and I would have to be smart. I would have to be patient. I clenched my jaw and waited for an answer to my question. What could they possibly have as an explanation? "Seriously, how was it the *gringa*'s fault?"

The boss sneered. "Of course it was the *gringa*'s fault. Before she came here, it never occurred to the indians that they had any rights. They feared us. They never would have dared to complain to the police. Now the indians realize they can make a difference with the politicians too. The Wounaan have more votes than anyone else in this area, so the politicians have to pay attention to them. Now the politicians stand up and tell the indians that they're going to protect the forest. The newspaper writes articles about it and it attracts even more attention. If *she* hadn't come here, none of that would have happened. The indians would still be living in the dirt and staying out of our way."

Paul Bunyan interrupted his boss. "And the indians burned one of our camps too. That only happened because the *gringa* stuck herself in our country and convinced the indians that they should stand up for themselves."

"It's true," the boss continued. "Now we have to stay out here for weeks at a time to protect our camps and our cows when we should be home with our families. Our wives miss us. Our kids miss us. But we can't spend time with them like we used to. If we try to leave for even a couple of days the indians will burn the camps and cut our fences. Then we'll have to spend days tracking down our animals and building new camps in this horrible heat."

"That does sound like a lot of work," I admitted.

They'd already finished off the first bottle.

"So we taught that *gringa* a lesson." The boss grinned from ear to ear. "Now she knows just how *hot* it can get out here in the rainforest."

"What's that supposed to mean?" I asked, knowing full well what it meant, but I had to hear him say it.

"It means," he explained, rising to his feet and then rocking his hips back and forth as though to show off his technique, "I have a way with the ladies."

I felt like a rabid tiger on acid that had been locked in a cage at the zoo, surrounded by spoiled, pimply-faced kids who were teasing me and poking me with sticks. I wanted nothing more than to leap across the fire, grab a fistful of that long, greasy hair and bash his smug face into the edge of the fire pit. I'd smash his teeth into the rocks over and over again, laughing maniacally as blood spurted out of his mouth and across the others' stunned faces.

But I kept my hands at my sides. Even as my fingernails dug into my thighs, I stayed glued to my seat and maintained steady eye contact with my hosts.

Be patient. You can do this.

Meanwhile, the blaze dropped from the fire. The sphere of light grew smaller and the curling branches of the fallen trees disappeared. A faint glimmer lit only the closest tree trunks.

"After all," the boss added, "not all of us are horse fuckers, you know?" With that, they couldn't contain their sniggering and erupted into laughter. I forced my teeth into a gritty smile and shook my head.

"What are you saying?" I asked him. "You did something to her?"

"Are you kidding me? We did *everything* to her! You should have seen the look on her face when *this* one got a hold of her!" he bellowed, pointing at the big, bearded one with his thumb. "This guy is bigger than the horses!" He made a fist with his one hand and grabbed his arm just above the elbow with his other hand, as though to show me the size of the man's prick. The big man flashed me a self-assured smile that sent shivers through my core.

"Oh, how that *gringa* screamed when he stuck it in her. I thought he was going to tear her in two!"

The lanky one started laughing so hard that he fell off the side of the tree trunk where he sat. He landed with a thud in the dirt and looked up at the rest of us with bleary eyes, as though to check if he'd been pushed. Then he dusted himself off and perched himself back on his seat as though nothing had happened.

The others laughed at him. "You see him?" the boss asked me, slurring his words and swaying back and forth where he sat. "Javier is an embarrassment to the *Santeños*. He drinks like a child."

"Hey." The big one turned to me. "Aren't you going to have a drink?"

The greedy bastards were already into the second bottle before any of them thought to offer me a drop of my own liquor. "Why not?"

The boss started to stand up to pass me the second bottle, but he started to wobble and lose his balance, so he steadied himself with his seat and sat back down again. "Here," he stammered, offering me the bottle with his outstretched arm.

"Don't worry. I brought my own." I'd prepared for that moment. I knew ahead of time that I couldn't get into the Seco with them, so I brought a flask full of Jack Daniels along for the trip. I pulled the flask out of my pack.

For all they knew, I could have been drinking water out of that flask, but they were too self-absorbed, and too drunk, to think about it. Regardless, I was glad I had the whiskey. I needed the liquid courage. I raised my flask high in the air and the men raised their cups. "May the worst of your past be the best of your future," I toasted them.

"*Gracias. Salud!*" the lanky *yeguero* toasted me.

"*Salud!*" the boss echoed.

"*Salud!*" the giant agreed.

Chapter 43 – Brown Blur

"It sounds like you solved your problem with the *gringa*," I said, "but, if you want, I can help you in other ways. Besides just digging holes, that is."

"How can *you* help us?" the big one asked with obvious disdain.

"Well, I could teach you about better pasture grasses. You could plant them right here where you've already cleared land. Then you wouldn't have to move around so much and cut down so much forest."

"You believe this *gringo*?" the big one said. "We are *Santeños* and he thinks that he can teach *us* about raising cattle."

"I don't feel so good," the *yeguero* complained.

"That's because you can't handle your Seco," the boss told him.

"No. It's my stomach," he whined, clutching at his belly with both hands. "I think I'm going to be sick."

He stumbled out towards the edge of the camp, doubled over, and began to vomit violently on the ground. White gruel splashed off the earth and splattered his pants. Then he fell to his knees and curled up into a fetal position. "Oh no," he cried, struggling to his feet.

"Look!" the big one shrieked with delight, "he shit himself!"

Sure enough, green diarrhea dripped from the *yeguero*'s pants' leg and ran down his boot.

His boss sneered. "You're a pig. Go to the river and clean yourself up." Then he turned to me and apologized for his man.

"It's fine," I said. "I've seen few Panamanians who can really hold their liquor."

The big one scowled at me. "We can drink."

"But not like *gringos* can," I said.

"Of course we can. We can drink more than the *gringos*!" he shouted indignantly.

He was taking the bait. "Yeah?" I asked.

"Yeah!"

"Let's see then." I raised my flask to my mouth and took a long drink, perhaps longer than I should have, deliberately looking him in the eye all the while. The whiskey warmed my belly too much and I thought I might throw up, but I managed to keep it down. Within a few seconds the nausea passed and the well-being settled in. I felt good. The whiskey calmed my nerves just enough. "You think you can drink like *that*?"

He snatched up what was left of the second bottle and held it to his lips, raising the bottom of the bottle high into the air. He gulped defiantly at the fire water. I thought that he'd stop after a drink or two, but he kept going. Five seconds, six seconds, seven seconds. He drained it all. Then he stood up, panting for air. He glared at me as he wiped his mouth with the back of his hand and then smashed the empty bottle into the fire.

"I guess the Panamanians can drink," I said. He nodded and took a seat on the tree trunk where the *yeguero* had been.

"Javier has been gone a long time," the boss said.

I quickly rose to my feet. "I'll go check on him," I said before either of them thought to question the idea.

"*Está bien*," the boss answered indifferently.

Neither man seemed to notice when I picked up the shotgun on my way towards the river. When I reached the river's edge, I found the *yeguero* shin-deep in the black water. His pants were down around his ankles as he splashed water up onto himself.

"Are you alright?" I asked. The question caught him off guard and he quickly tried to cover himself with his hands.

"I'm fine."

"You don't look fine."

"I still feel pretty nauseous," he admitted, "and I have an awful headache. It must've been something I ate."

"It must've been."

He began to shuffle towards the river's edge where he'd left his boots, still covering himself with his hands as he approached me. When he was back on shore and struggling to lace up his boots I asked him, "You remember that *gringa* you were talking about?"

"*Sí.* What about her?"

"Her name was Elena. She was pregnant with my baby."

Still bent over his shoes, in a position of utter vulnerability, he looked up at me with wide eyes as his mind registered the alarm. I had the smooth metal barrel of the shotgun gripped in both hands like a baseball bat. He tried clumsily to get out of the way, but it was too late. The heavy wooden stock came around like a brown blur and caught him squarely across the face. He reeled around and collapsed on the river bank as though his bones were made of jelly. His nose split across the bridge and spurt blood into the air, but he was out cold.

I wondered if he was dead. And then I wondered if I would care. I tossed the shotgun into the bushes and made my way back to camp to finish what I started.

"Did you find him?" the boss asked.

"I found him alright. He's passed out by the river with his pants around his ankles. He's a filthy mess. I tried to wake him up, but he was out cold. I imagine he'll find his way back when he wakes up." My legs trembled from the adrenaline, so I sat down quickly and tried to steady myself.

"He better be able to work tomorrow. I don't care how hungover he is."

"Speaking of work, we still need to figure out if I can help you in any way. I don't have to teach you anything about grasses or raising cattle. Maybe I can teach you how to take care of yourselves out here in the Darien. It's very different than the *Azuero*."

"Different how?"

"For starters, this rainforest is full of malaria."

"So?"

"Aren't you afraid of getting malaria out here? There are mosquitoes everywhere."

"None of us have ever contracted malaria," the boss answered. "We already told you: we are *Santeños*. We are strong."

"You never know." I shrugged. "Don't you ever get bit by mosquitoes?"

The boss waved a hand dismissively. "That's why we build a campfire."

"But your fire can't possibly last all night. It must burn out before dawn. You must get bit sometimes."

We sat around the fire in silence for a minute as the boss contemplated what I said. The big one struggled just to keep his red, bleary eyes open. Polishing off that bottle may have been *macho*, but it was also the dumbest thing he'd ever done.

"And what about leishmaniasis?" I asked.

"What thing?"

"Leishmaniasis. It's a flesh eating disease. If you don't get it treated, it starts to eat up all of your skin and leaves terrible scars. It can kill you."

"How do you get this thing?" the boss asked.

"The sand flies carry it."

"But there is no sand here." He laughed at me. "We have nothing to worry about."

"They're called sand flies because they are the color of sand. I used to live in the mountains and I got bit by one." I rolled up the leg of my jeans and showed them the scar on my ankle. It looked like someone had maimed me with a blow torch. It got their attention.

"How many of those things do you have?" the big one asked.

"Just this one."

"What? That can't be," he blathered, pointing at my leg with a wavy finger.

"You're drunk," the boss told him. "He has only one scar there."

"But . . ." the giant protested, rising wobbly from his seat, still reaching out with his long, thick arm. He stared bewilderedly at my leg. His mouth hung open as though he had something to say, but no words came out. I couldn't tell if he meant to point out the scars or if he intended to reach out and touch my leg to see for himself.

267

And I'd never know, for once he took a few awkward steps towards me, he staggered clumsily, his eyes rolled up into his head, and he fell face-first into the ground at my feet.

He began to writhe and convulse, flopping about like a shark on the deck of a ship lost at sea until his body went rigid and he lay still on the ground, save for his heaving chest. Saliva ran from the corner of his mouth. Mixed with soil from the forest floor, it formed a filthy cake on his face.

"Ha!" the boss laughed. "You should see the look on your face!" he said to me.

"You think that's *funny*?" I asked, shocked that he could be so indifferent to his man's obvious distress.

"He can't handle his liquor either."

"You think he's *drunk*?" I asked in disbelief.

"Look at him!"

I walked over to the giant and poked him with my boot. "He doesn't look drunk to me."

"He doesn't?"

"Well, maybe he's drunk, but didn't you see him flopping on the ground like that? I don't know about you, but I've never seen a drunk do that before. To me, it looked more like he just had a seizure. He might even go into cardiac arrest."

He laughed nervously. "A seizure? No. You don't know what you're talking about. He's just drunk."

"But how can you be so sure?" I circled around the fire towards him. "Maybe it's something else."

"Like what?" he asked uneasily.

"Well, I'm not an expert, but it looks like he's having a drug overdose."

"You're crazy. We don't use *drugs*."

"Maybe you took some drugs and didn't even know it." I raised my eyebrows. "Maybe you feel short of breath? Maybe your vision is blurry? How's your hearing? Any ringing in the ears?"

"What are you talking about?" he asked. He stared at me through narrow, squinty eyes. It was beginning to dawn on him. "What have you done?"

"I'm helping you, remember? And speaking of malaria, you should know there's a drug called Aralen that protects you against the disease. The Peace Corps gives it to all the Volunteers."

"So?" he asked angrily.

"So it's got a lot of bad side effects. It can even cause you to go into cardiac arrest if you take too much of it. Imagine if someone took a lot of it and put it in a couple bottles of Seco."

"What?"

"You and your friends just drank a six-month supply of Aralen. I'm surprised your big friend didn't drop dead when he drank that bottle."

"But why?"

I took out the pen that Elena gave me, and I clicked the top.

"*Are you kidding?*" the man's voice played back, "*we did everything to her!*"

"Who . . . who *are* you?"

"I'm the man who loved her," I told him. "And you are going to jail for taking her away from me." I waved the pen back and forth in front of his face.

"Give me that!" he growled, flailing for the pen.

"You'll have to take it."

He balled up his hands and lumbered towards me, but he lead with his drugged, drunken face and I was able to side-step him with ease, like a *matador* evading a badly wounded bull. And as he passed clumsily by me, I landed a hard right cross just above the corner of his dirty mustache. He let out a howl as he went sprawling into the dirt. And despite the unrelenting pain and rage I'd carried for the last several days, I admit feeling extraordinary delight and satisfaction when he rolled over and looked up at me with fear in his eyes.

"If I were you," I warned him, "I'd concentrate on relaxing. With all that Aralen pumping through your veins, I'm surprised you haven't had a heart attack by now. Do you want to end up like him?" I pointed with my lips at the motionless giant who lay face down in the dirt.

He started to get up again, but I cocked back my fist and he shrunk down before crab-walking several steps away from me. "Give me that," he whined.

"Enjoy the forest tonight. You won't be seeing it again for a long time." I left him sitting there, broken, in the dirt, and I started the hike back to *Quebrada Brava*.

Chapter 44 – The Toughest Job I Ever Loved

I arrived in *Puerto Coquira* in the early afternoon. Antonio wasn't there yet, but I knew he wouldn't let me down. I sat down on the curb in front of the public market, took out the pen that Elena had given me for my birthday, and wrote a short letter.

"Grace,

It has been my privilege to serve our country as a Peace Corps Volunteer. I will always cherish the time I had with the people of *Los Altos de las Cascadas*. Nonetheless, as the enclosed recording demonstrates, my service has run its course.

I apologize in advance for any inconvenience my conduct may cause you or the Peace Corps, but I trust you will use the information in a manner that attains justice for Elena Alexander and honors the work she performed on behalf of *Quebrada Brava*.

Very truly yours,

John Dillon"

I was tempted to write more, but I knew that each additional word would make only more trouble for Grace. I'd put her in a bad position. If she used the recording intact, the Panamanian government would raise hell about Peace Corps Volunteers running wild, unchecked, assaulting Panamanians. The ambassador would come down on the Peace Corps and the Peace Corps would come down on Grace, wanting to know why she couldn't control her Volunteers. But Grace could weather that storm. She'd argue that her Volunteers did too much good work around the country to be derailed by one selfish individual. And she'd be right and ultimately she'd prevail. I was sorry I'd put her in such a position, but not so sorry I'd have done it any differently.

I wondered what the penalty for assault was in Panama. Or attempted murder. Would the Peace Corps try to intervene on my behalf? Or would they cut me loose and leave me to fend for myself? It didn't matter. I'd never know.

Once Antonio picked me up in *Puerto Coquira*, I explained everything. I showed him the pen and how to use it. As we drove along the Inter-American Highway, we listened to the entire recording. Then we listened to it again.

Antonio's mouth hung open in disbelief, but his eyes only smiled. My voice sounded funny and far away. It was like the whole thing happened to someone else.

"Have you seen *Rambo*?" he asked me. "You're like his little brother!"

"I just want to sleep."

I made Antonio promise that he would give the letter and the recording directly to Grace. Antonio also promised he'd go back to *Los Altos* to pack up my belongings and send them to me, but I told him not to bother. Instead, I gave him the combination to the lock on my front door and asked him to give all my stuff to Alejandra and Eduardo.

I was sorry I wouldn't get to say goodbye to Jose or Nelson or any of the others. But I took solace in the thought that I'd convinced Jose and Eduardo that they had a lot to offer, that their community needed them, that their government worked for *them*, and that they should have the confidence to stand up for themselves when they don't get the attention they deserve.

I hoped I'd been a good neighbor during my time in Panama and shown some folks that not all Americans are rich and beautiful and indifferent.

Antonio pulled up to the airport and dropped me off at the curb. He helped me get my pack out of the trunk. We hugged goodbye. I turned and walked on down the road and back to this world.

CHARLES THOMPSON

Acknowledgments

I'm grateful to everyone who helped make Aralen Dreams a reality. In particular, I'd like to thank Group 44 for helping me live it; Michelle Aielli, Eli Glasser, Abigail Fay, Naomi Dathan, Rodney Jones, Steven Pemberton, Brian Todd, KA Smith, Julie Shaw, Stef Mcdaid, Iva Polansky, Margaret Woodward, and countless other members of the Authonomy community for helping me edit it; and my wife, Olguita, for putting up with it. And, of course, I'd like to thank the Peace Corps for giving me the toughest job I ever loved.